THERE IS A PLAN FOR THE DAY AFTER.
IT'S CALLED THE BLUEPRINT.
AND THESE ARE THE MEN WHO
WILL MAKE IT HAPPEN . . .

Wilson—Expert pilot, sniper and mechanic. Flunked out of combat school for being too aggressive.

Sloan—Electronics and computer genius. Quick with gallows humor. Deadly with a grenade launcher.

Rogers—The group's medic and utility outfielder. He doesn't take prisoners.

McKay—The leader. His maximum experience in land warfare, urban combat and antiterrorism made him a natural.

THE GUARDIANS
AMERICA'S FUTURE IS IN THEIR HANDS

THE GUARDIANS

FREEDOM FIGHT

JOVE BOOKS, NEW YORK

THE GUARDIANS: FREEDOM FIGHT

A Jove Book / published by arrangement with
the author

PRINTING HISTORY
Jove edition / March 1988

ISBN: 0-515-09484-6

Jove Books are published by The Berkley Publishing Group,
200 Madison Avenue, New York, New York 10016.
The name ''JOVE'' and the ''J'' logo
are trademarks belonging to Jove Publications, Inc.

PRINTED IN THE UNITED STATES OF AMERICA

10 9 8 7 6 5 4 3 2 1

PROLOGUE

"Shit," the lanky sonofabitch yelped, grabbing protectively at his cowboy hat as the wind tried to jerk it away. The little feather doodad stuck in the band of the hat wavered frantically. His Adam's apple rode up and down like a hamster in a boa constrictor. "Damn this old blue norther, anyway. Oughtn't to be so damn cold this far south. Man might as well be in Kansas."

Inside the plasterboard guardhouse set next to the road a boom box was moaning out an old song about guitars and Cadillacs, in doomed competition with the wind's white-noise howl. The tape kept slipping.

"It's that nucular winter, Jimmy Earl," his partner said glumly. He was a stocky man in cammie trousers and an old army-issue parka with the hood down, allowing long Silver Fox hair to whip around his bearded face. He had an M-16 slung over his shoulder. "Like they wrote about before the War."

"Bull*shit*, Bob Ed," Jimmy Earl said emphatically, jogging from one pointy-toed, hand-tooled boot to the other. He grimaced and clutched at the butt of his own slung rifle, where it was banging his kidneys through his wool-lined denim jacket. The tape made Dwight Yoakam sound like he was being goosed at intervals with a cattle prod. If he hadn't been preoccupied, Jimmy Earl might have said he liked him better that way. He preferred your more modern brand of country music. "That's when they don't have no summer, ever. We had us a summer since the War, we surely did. Don't you remember how you spent three months bitching about how it was too damn hot to sit out here staring across the Rio Grand'?"

"That's different. The reason we got this weather up here is the War messed up the climatic patterns. That's the nucular winter. Read all about it before the War, when I was stationed up to Bliss."

"Hooey."

"You got no understandin' of science, Jimmy Earl."

"Hooey. Yi—! Went and did it again. Damned wind goes straight up my leg like a snake climbing a fence post."

"You bloused your pants into your boots proper, that wouldn't happen," Bob Ed said smugly.

Jimmy Earl looked shocked. "Man don't blouse no cowboy boots, unless he wants to look like some old accountant from New York who saw *Urban Cowboy* and got all het up."

"And where the hell'd you ever see a snake climbing a fence post?" Bob Ed demanded, realizing he'd been outflanked.

"Didn't never. My granddaddy used to say that."

"Ain't he the one got put away?"

"What of it?"

"Shit. I bet he's the one they made that chainsaw movie about."

"Bull. That was some guy in Michigan."

"Why'd they put it in Texas, then?"

"Shit. I can't talk to you. I'm gonna go back in the shack and drink some coffee, 'less you let it all boil over."

He started into the shack. The song ended and a more recent one fired up, about what a bitch it was to be fighting in Nicaragua.

"Wait up, boy," Bob Ed called. "We got us some company."

Jimmy Earl stopped, winced as the M-16's butt caught him in the kidneys again, stood blinking through swirls of fat-flake snow. A ragged caravan was crawling across the Jimmy Carter–Luis Echeverria International Friendship Bridge—a half-dozen trucks and cars, riding low on their springs beneath high-piled loads of furniture, wide-eyed kids, and huddled oldsters.

"Git on the horn to Carrizo Springs," Bob Ed ordered. "I'll go meet the new arrivals."

Gratefully, Jimmy Earl vanished into the guard shack. His partner sauntered down a khaki slope that was almost covered by snow, except for little dry tussocks of grass that stood up like hairy warts. The lead vehicle, a staked-bed truck, grunted past the burned-out U.S. Customs complex at the American end of the eight-lane span, and halted with steam curling out from under its slightly sprung hood.

The huge highway bridge was a road to nowhere, built as part of a Federal make-work program during the bone-hard recession of the Eighties, largely as a sop to a Mexican government outraged by increasingly arbitrary American immigration laws. Only dirt tracks trailed away into the chaparral on either side of the brown cold river.

People began spilling off the heap of worldly goods on the truck, putting Bod Ed in mind of a momma possum with her babies clinging on her back. They clustered around grabbing at the sleeve of his parka and pointing back off across the bridge, where the slow khaki rise of the normally arid valley was obscured by falling snow.

"Shee-*it*," Jimmy Earl said, sticking his head out. "Radio's out. What're these here people carrying on about?"

Bob Ed was frowning and scratching behind one ear. He'd grown up with the twangy *norteño* Spanish they were speaking, but they were rattling on so fast he had trouble making sense of what they were saying.

"Something about *cristeros*," he said.

Jimmy Earl squeezed his eyebrows together, which made his prominent ears slide up. "What's that mean?"

" 'Christers,' " Bob Ed said. "Don't make no sense to me neither."

He trotted out some Tex-Mex Spanish on them, trying to get them to go slow and explain. They talked faster and pointed more urgently.

A mustached man in his thirties came walking up. Despite the chill, he was in shirtsleeves and jeans. He had a white straw cowboy hat and a Mexican army-issue M-1 Garand slung over his shoulder.

"I'm Eulogio Vasquez," he said. "We've come to ask for sanctuary in your country."

"Well, now, the Republic's got itself an open-door policy.

But just for my own information I'd kinda like to know what y'all got your bowels in such an uproar over.''

"The cristeros. They've driven us from our homes." A couple more lean and well-armed young men had come up, and they excitedly pushed into the conversation.

"Slow down, here, boys. That don't mean nothing to me."

"*Soldados de Cristo Rey y la Guadalupana,*" Vasquez said. "Soldiers of Christ the King and the Virgin of Guadalupe."

Bob Ed frowned some more. "Well, now, I thought y'all were all good Catholics."

"We're Catholics, señor," Vasquez said urgently. "These are fanatics."

"They ain't no Catholics like I know of," one of the young bucks said, a rawboned kid with mesa cheekbones and Apache eyes.

"They're crazy," said his partner, who was smaller and rounder and possessed of a great Zapata mustache.

"Bob Ed," Jimmy Earl called down the slope. The wind took most of the juice out of his voice. "Here come somebody else."

The older man turned to look. Just rolling onto the bridge was a tan Toyota four-wheeler mounting an incredibly ancient Browning .30-caliber machinegun—not as old as the one with the fat water-cooling jacket, but the sort with the perforated sleeve around the barrel, like the jackets on the upright exhaust pipes of 1950's diesel pickup trucks.

"Who-ee," Bob Ed said. "*Now* what?"

The refugees were visibly agitated. Vasquez shouted some orders, and they began piling back on their vehicles. "Now, those ain't the cristeros, are they?"

"*Policía,*" the plump Zapatoid spat.

"What do they want?" Bob Ed asked.

By way of an answer a loudspeaker mounted on the four-by Toy crackled and said, "—return to your homes at once. There is no cause for panic. Return to your homes."

Some of Vasquez's armed cadre shook fists and hooted. The refugee-laden vehicles were now grinding and lurching their way up the grade.

The four tan-uniformed men in the jeep were all fat. Bob Ed was unsurprised. All the Mexican cops he'd ever seen were fat, except the odd congenitally skinny one. You became a cop in Mexico in order to get fat. Except for the *montañeros,* tough

Indians recruited by the Federal Police as hunter-killer squads, who didn't speak much Spanish and hated everybody who did. *They* became cops in order to kill people.

Vasquez stood waiting for them with his fists on his hips. The Toyota came on until Bob Ed thought the driver might try to run the rancher down. It stopped with its bumper a few centimeters shy of his shins.

The man next to the driver adjusted his mirror shades and his peaked cap and rolled out. "You, Eulogio," he said. "I expected better from you. Running away to North America as though you'd forgotten you were a Mexican."

Vasquez spat into snow-dusted gravel. "We held as long as we could. We were fighting for our homes. But there are just too many of them."

The boss cop slapped himself on the chest. "We're the police. We're here to help you. Now, get your people turned around and headed back onto their proper soil."

"Help us?" the tall kid asked incredulously. "Where were you when they swarmed over the Redondo *estancia*? Not once have we seen the police since the cristeros crossed the Sierra Madre Oriental, nor the army either."

"The government's very busy, boy. Our country has been threatened with anarchy since our president was murdered."

"Yeah," said a cop sitting in back keeping the Browning company. "Your country needs all her sons to help her. So you better get those people turned around real quick, if you know what's good for you."

"Easy, now," Bob Ed said. "Easy, everybody."

"Here, here," the first cop said. "We're all sons of common soil. You must return, Eulogio, and help defend that soil."

Vasquez's hardened face worked, seemed to lose some of its tempering. "You don't know what it's like." His voice rang hollow beneath the wind. "Nothing can stand against them. They destroy everything before them."

The boss cop puffed his chest till it almost reached the extent of his belly. "*We* shall stand," he proclaimed, "you and us, shoulder to shoulder—"

"The day I see both cristeros and police at the same time," the plump ranchero said, "will be the first."

"This looks like your big day, then," called Jimmy Earl, crunching down the slope to join the parley. He stopped and pointed over the heads of the group.

Heads turned. For a moment all they saw was a blank, roiling curtain. Then the wind blew the snow aside, revealing a column of people marching down the road, spilling out across the slope to either side.

"Holy shit," Bob Ed breathed. "Must be a thousand of 'em."

"Ten thousand," Vasquez said grimly.

The main cop had lost quite a few shades of complexion from his face. He clutched Bob Ed's arm. "You must get out your heavy weapons. Hurry."

Glumly the Texan shook his head. "Got none. We're just down here to keep tabs on people comin' across, not to keep out no army." He patted the black butt of his M-16. "All's we got're these here little mouse guns."

"Oh, lordy," Jimmy Earl said, his Adam's apple bobbing up and down. He'd missed the bulk of the conversation, but from everybody's reactions he was getting the strong sense that all those people across the river were not out for a stroll in the lovely weather. "Jesus shit howdy."

On they came in their hundreds, thousands—maybe even ten thousand, just like the man said. Calmly, not hurrying, not marching in ordered ranks, but cohesive, clumped around high-held banners bearing the famous image of the Virgin of Guadalupe as it had miraculously appeared—so the story went—on the cloak of the Indian Juan Diego, back in colonial times. They were mostly men, but women marched in that throng, and children too. And even across the river the two Texans could see that all were armed; some with rifles and some with clubs and hoes and axes, but each and every one.

The wind veered, and the men standing on the American side could hear a song—not loud, but powerful, like the rumble of distant thunder:

Yo soy un cristiano
Y soy un mejicano—

The boss cop turned and scrambled back to the jeep, his mirror-polished boots throwing up little plumes of gravel and powder snow.

"Where y'all goin'?" Jimmy Earl demanded. Then he had to jump back to avoid being run down as the Toyota peeled out and lit out after the last of the refugees' trucks, just disappearing over a rise. The tough-talking cop held onto the machinegun by its barrel shroud, to keep it from swinging around and bashing somebody in the head.

"*Maricones!* Queers!" the plump rancher with the mustache shrieked after them, shaking his fist.

Bob Ed jerked his head at a battered Ford pickup still parked next to the abutment. "Reckon you boys better get a move on."

Vasquez and the others shared looks. "They move too quickly," the tall kid said. "The devil aids them. Our people's trucks are too slow."

"We have to hold them," Vasquez said.

Bob Ed gazed out across the bridge.

"*Que viva mi Cristo,*" the multitude sang, "*que viva mi Rey.*"

"Looks like you boys got a job of work cut out for you." He unslung his rifle.

"Wh-what we gonna do, Bob Ed?" Jimmy Earl asked.

"Son, stand and fight," the older man said. "This here ain't no peaceful immigration. This is an invasion."

The rancheros—six of them, including Vasquez and the other two who'd been talking to Bob Ed—scattered, unlimbering weapons and looking for cover. It wasn't in plentiful supply. Vegetation down here on the lower Rio Grande ran to scrub cedar and mesquite chaparral, usually good for snooping and pooping. But this particular stretch, around the American end of the Carter–Echeverria Bridge, was pretty barren. Nor was digging in much of an option: though it was a long way from cold enough to freeze the ground, the earth here was hard-packed Southwestern *caliche,* tough as cement. There weren't even any decent rocks to hide behind.

Jimmy Earl gaped as Bob Ed ran past him to the guard shack. He could carry both his gut and his years with surprising speed when he had to. "Where you goin'?" the kid asked. He never would have figured his partner for the type to bug out.

The older man ducked into the shack. A moment later he emerged, holding a bullhorn in one hand and a knapsack stuffed with loaded magazines in the other.

"What the heck do you think you're doing, Bob Ed?"

"Got to observe the formalities, son." He tossed the sack to his partner.

The ranchers watched him from the pitifully exposed firing positions they'd found. They were too keyed up to shiver from the snow layering onto their thin shirts and jackets and Levis. To their amazement he walked right down to the foot of the bridge, next to the derelict Customs compound.

The cristero mob hadn't quite reached the far side, four hundred meters away. Bob Ed planted himself, boots wide, legs braced, head thrown back so that the wind whipped his silver hair. He raised the bullhorn.

"I'm asking you people to hold it right there," he said in Spanish. "We can't permit you into the country until we know what your intentions are."

The crowd rolled on. No surprise. Bob Ed heard wind-raveled wisps of—what was it? *Laughter.* Like the sound of kids on a playground far away. For a moment he thought of his own children, Emily Ann and Buddy, and baby granddaughter Rosemary, who'd survived the bombing but not the plague that had followed.

He could hear them singing. Louder now:

> *Qué viva mi Cristo*
> *Qué viva Cristo Rey!*

"In the name of the Republic of Texas and President La-Rousse, I order you to stop!" he shouted.

Bullets gouged snow and bits of blacktop from the pavement around his boots and whined off into the snow. "Well," he remarked, "hell's out for noon now."

A ragged volley cracked out from the ranchers behind him. He hoped they had sense enough to aim high, though he knew that it wasn't going to matter much what they did, not for very much longer. He ran over behind the end of the cement guard-rail and sat down, taking a turn of the M-16's sling around his left forearm and settling into a steady firing position.

The cristeros were on the bridge now, singing and laughing and firing random shots. Bob Ed lined up his sights on the foremost banner-bearer. It was a woman, a dowdy, middle-aged woman in a cheap, thin dress that must have been cold as hell. She was laughing and bobbing her banner around like a kid with a kite on the first day of spring.

Hell of a note, making war on women, he thought. But it had to be done—anything to give the women and children of the refugee caravan a fighting chance to get clear. *Hell of a note.* He took a breath, half-released it, held, and fired. The front of the dress went dark between capacious breasts. The woman fell.

A growl of outrage rose from the crowd, a scarcely human sound. Eager hands caught up the sacred banner before it hit the blacktop, and the mob surged forward. Bob Ed picked another futile target and fired.

Fifty meters upslope of him, Jimmy Earl fired a burst into the crowd. He felt a strange turbulence of fevered excitement and nausea. He'd shot at people before, and hit them, too; there'd been some mighty hairy times gone down since the balloon went up. But he'd never had the chance to fire full-auto at a mob of people before, packed so close you couldn't even miss, making not the slightest effort to get out of the way of the bullets. There was something of the predator's rush in his blood, the taking of helpless prey, the flush-cheeked pleasure of hitting those who can't fight back. But there was guilt, too, and horror.

And fear. Because Jimmy Earl knew this tidal wave of living flesh was far from helpless.

Maybe he hoped to turn them. The M-16 didn't sound all that impressive, even firing flat-out, and it didn't have much recoil to let you feel how much power you were putting out. But there was a nasty crack in the supersonic harmonics of the reports, and Jimmy Earl could see how the needle-slim bullets went through two or three people before stopping. There were a lot of people falling on that bridge. But there were a lot more coming behind.

The seemingly endless torrent of cristeros had washed out to either side of the far end of the bridge, spreading out along the bank. Some even plunged down into the water, holding rifles high, trying to swim across, though with very few farmers remaining between here and the San Luis valley in Colorado to divert the river for irrigation it ran high and fast and mighty cold. Few of the swimmers made more than thirty meters before they cramped and sank. There were always more behind them.

The plump young Mexican with the sweeping mustache was the first defender to die. A blunt, slow-moving .30-30 bullet from across the river knocked a wedge-shaped chunk out of his skull, like a watermelon being plugged at Safeway. He rolled over on his back, kicked twice at the uncaring ground, and was gone.

The forefront of the mob was nearing the American side of

the bridge. Bob Ed slammed home a fresh magazine. He'd been working with a strange calm detachment, firing shot after shot, hitting every time—who could miss, under these circumstances? And it did not one damned bit of good.

One of the norteño ranchers panicked. He jumped up from behind a *huajillo* incongruously flocked with snow, like a low-rent Christmas tree. Instantly shots kicked up dirt around him. One took him in the leg. He fell.

Bob Ed squeezed off two more shots, taking his time. A cristero bullet shrieked off the cement guard barrier, gouging his ribs. He fired again, barely noticing. Another bullet struck him in the chest. He wavered, fired. The cristeros were almost on him now. He let go the rest of the magazine in a burst. A half-dozen cristeros fell, thrashing and screaming. Others closed in, firing their weapons from the hip.

For a moment bullets struck Bob Ed almost as rapidly as the fast-falling snow. He lurched to his feet, fumbling to change the magazine. A full charge from an ancient single-barrel shotgun went into his chest with a soft-hard sound of impact. He went over backwards and lay on the caliche moaning softly while the life oozed out of him.

A hailstorm of bullets walked up the slope in advance of the cristeros. The two nameless ranchers were shot to bits. Vasquez came up on one knee with a thumb-thick stream of blood pumping from a hole in his neck, firing his Garand, and went down beneath a wave of bodies. The tall kid with the Indian eyes grabbed his jammed rifle by the barrel and charged full tilt into the mob, clubbing left and right. An axe caught him in the back. He went to his knees. Hard brown hands wrested his weapon away from him. The faithful gathered around him, raising implements of work, and they brought them all down together.

Jimmy Earl dragged himself to the guard shack. The right leg of his jeans was drenched with blood from the bullet in his thigh. All he felt was a heavy numbness, as if a horse had kicked him hard on the muscle.

He propped himself against the doorframe and picked up the microphone with fingers that felt as thick and cold and unresponsive as frozen hot dogs. Shots hit the guard shack, knocking out little speckled jigsaw pieces of plasterboard. The cristeros were singing again, louder than before.

"*Que viva mi Cristo—*"

"Top Dog," Jimmy Earl shouted into the microphone. "Top Dog, this is Bluetick. Come in, Top Dog. Oh, lord God, Mayday, Mayday!"

"*Que viva mi Rey.*"

"Bluetick, this is Top Dog. What is y'all's situation, over?"

Jimmy Earl almost dropped the mike. The radio gods had decided to smile on him, make the radio work after all.

"*Que viva mi Cristo—*"

"They're coming across." Peripheral vision showed him flickers of movement; they were surrounding the shack. "There's thousands of them. They—" The words and Jimmy Earl died in a scream as a score of bullets ripped through the shack.

"*Que viva Cristo Rey!*"

Orange flame spread out from the windows of the guard shack like a flower unfolding petals to the falling snow. The plump man on the far bank of the river shifted excitedly from one foot to another. "You see? No one can stand against them."

The man beside him was taller, though not by much, and lean as a whip. He was holding a pair of binoculars with both hands, letting his cane lean against his thigh. He carried it for support in the spells of weakness that still recurred, not because there was anything wrong with his legs.

"Yes, Manuel," he said ironically, "and it only took them odds of about four hundred to one to accomplish it." He spoke Spanish, American-accented, with a tinge of something his companion couldn't identify. In any event it was better than the round man's English.

The shorter man's round little shoulders slumped. "But did you see the way they kept moving in the face of that gunfire? It was awesome. Truly, their faith in the Virgin is great."

The other lowered his glasses. The wind whipped strands of blond hair that stuck out from under his watch cap. His companion might be idiot enough to venture out in this weather bareheaded; not him. You lost more heat through your head than any other part of your body, and in his weakened condition he could afford to take no chances.

"Religious fanaticism's a marvelous thing," he said, trying to keep back a wince. Every breath of this frigid air was lancing agony, like the bullet entering his chest again—worse, actually, since all he'd felt when it hit was a hammerblow and then numbness. What the cold truly recalled was the hours after he regained consciousness in a hospital bed.

"Still," he admitted, "it was an impressive performance." *Every dog must be thrown a biscuit now and again*. "Though if those *federales* had hung around, their machinegun could have proven troublesome."

"Ha," the fat man said, and spat. "*Federales. Canalla.* The followers of *Hermana Luz* don't fear them."

The blond man allowed himself a thin smile. "You mean your followers, don't you, Manuel?"

The other turned his eyes sideways for a moment, then grinned. The wind carried scraps of triumphant song to them. "The followers of *la Hermana* are mine, my friend. That much is true."

"I wonder what they'd do if they found out?"

He didn't even bother to look for the smaller man's reaction. The round, mustached face was pale, he knew. The cristeros would be unhappy indeed if they knew how their teenaged prophet was being manipulated.

The guard shack exploded. The flames must have found a propane tank or something similar. "Poor bastards," the blond man said. "I hope they were decently dead before the fire started."

He shook his head. For a professional assassin, Colonel Ivan Vesensky, late of the KGB, had a fairly broad compassionate streak.

Across the river, the cristeros danced around the bonfire and sang.

CHAPTER
ONE

"No preservatives," Billy McKay grumbled. His voice rose: "No *preservatives!*"

He upended the brown bottle. A stream of yellow fluid cascaded onto the frozen Montana ground. "What a thing to advertise. No preservatives. So after it sits on a shelf awhile, it winds up tasting like rancid camel piss."

"How can you tell the difference?" asked Sam Sloan, who was sitting on the front glacis of the Cadillac Gage armored car the Guardians called Mobile One—and home, for the most part. The vehicle was pulled onto the shoulder of a divided highway dotted at wide random intervals with the rusted-out hulks of cars. "American beer always tastes like that."

"Beer snobs," McKay sneered, stuffing a cigar into his face. "Spare me. Wine snobs are one damn thing. Wine's designed for you hoity-toity starched collar types who went to fucking Annapolis and learned not to say ain't. Beer's something else. God intended beer to be drunk by sweaty blue-collar assholes."

He pumped up his chest and arm muscles. Inside his baggy coveralls they didn't make much of a show. "Like *me*. *I* know what beer's supposed to be, and it's not no damned Limey syrup. And one more thing: It ain't nothing that turns to slop

13

because a buncha goddamned health food freaks made 'em take the *preservatives* out.''

He cocked his arm and hurled the bottle as far into the tan waste as he could. It might have been snowing on the lower Rio Grande, but up here in the north the ground was dry and the sun was shining. Sort of.

''And fuck the lecture on littering you're about to give me, too!'' McKay bellowed at Sloan. He stalked a few meters down the blacktop band that connected the eastern horizon with the west.

Across the road a semi lay on its side. The weather had faded past legibility the colorful legend painted on the corrugated slab sides of the trailer. The tractor's engine compartment was gaping open, gutted long since by scavengers, road gypsies perhaps, or maybe just prudent passersby. With America's own industrial capacity smashed flat, and the trade arteries with manufacturing centers in Japan and Brazil and mainland China long cut, replacement parts were a precious commodity, worth dying—or killing—for. It was the Guardians' main mission brief to change that situation. Or, rather, get the Blueprint for Renewal put together so it could.

''My, my,'' Peter Lynch said. He had on a mauve jogging suit and white turtleneck that fit him impeccably and had come from God knew where. He looked comfortable and collected despite the nylon restraints that shackled his wrists behind him. ''Testy today, isn't he?''

''And fuck you too, Lynch!'' McKay roared. ''Who ever heard of a preppie terrorist?''

''There's only me,'' Lynch said, unruffled. The wind tousled his hair. ''I'm sui generis, you might say.''

''McKay wouldn't,'' Sloan said under his breath.

''You know, it turns out a lot of preservatives are maybe good for you,'' Casey said from the driver's seat. His three buddies heard him over the bone-conduction phones taped behind their ears, Lynch through the car's open side door. ''It's like Grace Slick said: Maybe they're, like, preserving us.''

Peter Lynch looked sidelong at Sloan and cocked an eyebrow. The rangy ex–naval officer shrugged. Casey was frequently not on the same planet as everybody else in the world. Sometimes he made Sloan wonder if he were half bright, or just too literal-minded. Or maybe just having a huge joke at the expense of the rest of the world. His prejudices as an old line officer in the surface navy notwithstanding, he realized you didn't get to be a fighter jock—and ace—if you were dim.

"Just what's eating your esteemed commander, if I may be so bold?" Lynch asked.

"Billy's always like that," Casey offered nonchalantly.

"He's not always this bad," Sloan corrected. "I mean, uh, testy, as you said. But his nose still hurts after his close encounter with that outsized pal of yours. And then there's the little matter of the misunderstanding with Washington that's led to our continuing to enjoy one another's company longer than anticipated."

Peter Lynch was the last survivor of an elite counter-Guardian team called the Liberators, which had been handpicked by Chairman Yevgeny Maximov himself—lord and master of the Federated States of Europe—to hunt down and destroy the American unit that had caused him so much grief since the One-Day War a year and a half before. It hadn't worked out quite as planned. The Guardians had hunted the Liberators down and destroyed *them,* in an abandoned Blueprint for Renewal facility out here in the middle of nowhere, i.e. Montana. The last one dealt with was the American renegade known only as Cowboy, a giant combination of Jason and Buddy Holly. He had battered Billy McKay considerably before pitching over the cliffs and into Little Dry Creek, which hadn't been either little or dry at the time. McKay was still nursing a broken nose, though the bruises had mostly faded.

As a high school football player and long-time barroom brawler, having his beak busted was not a new experience for McKay. What mostly had him torqued was the runaround they'd been getting from Washington. The C-130 that brought a fresh team of specialists from the capital—the first planeload having been bushwhacked on landing by the Liberators and lost with all hands, including Tide Camp war chief Steve Tyler—was supposed to pick up the prisoners the Guardians had caught.

Instead, the plane came to stay awhile. The pilot had new orders no one had bothered to tell the Guardians about: He was to stay on the ground while the Blueprint heavyweights evaluated the plant, in case they wanted to send anything back to Washington for further analysis. The FSE Blueprint specialists the Guardians had caught would be debriefed by their American opposite numbers on-site. The three Soviet paratroopers, remnants of a security team that had been inserted to help the Liberators, were to be given a kick in the ass and sent packing, to survive as best they could amid the shambles two sets of their former masters, the Soviet government and the FSE, had made of America. Only Lynch was to go to the nation's capital, and a second, smaller aircraft was to be sent for him.

It didn't make a lot of sense to the Guardians. Oh, bits of it did: For example, there was every reason in the world for American Blueprint personnel to want to grill the captive Europeans, since Maximov had a better database on the Blueprint for Renewal than the U.S. did, thanks to the treachery of William Lowell, last elected president of the United States, who had delivered Heartland Complex into the hands of the FSE Expeditionary Force almost a year before. And there was no point in hauling three sadsack Soviet paratroopers all the way back to D.C.; somehow, they didn't strike even Billy McKay as constituting a serious threat to American security. Even the shit about Lynch, that made a sort of sense: The heavy-hauler Herkie might be needed in Montana, and there was no point in using a humongous cargo plane to ferry a single prisoner, no matter how important.

But put it all together and it didn't quite add up. Especially the way it was popped on the Guardians: surprise. The Guardians had had a lot of surprises the last few weeks, none of them good. And they had other reasons for being leery of Washington.

"Somehow we never thought we'd be messin' with bureaucratic snafus *after* the Third World War," Tom Rogers remarked from his post behind the big Browning .50-caliber and the Mk-19 automatic grenade launcher mounted in Mobile One's turret.

"The great stone face speaks," Lynch said with exaggerated surprise. In the past week he'd spent enough time around the Guardians to learn that Rogers was a man who spaced his words pretty far apart.

"Target incoming, azimuth ninety-five degrees," Casey reported. The baby radar set, extruded from the top of the turret, had just spotted something. "ID confirmed; she's ours, Billy."

Given all that had gone down recently, a mere IFF—for Identification, Friend or Foe—beacon wasn't enough; the computer onboard the incoming packet aircraft and the one in Mobile

One had just exchanged a whole slew of passwords and secret handshakes before each decided the other was what it claimed to be.

McKay turned back from the edge of the blacktop. "I hope to Christ we ain't bein' hosed again."

"We're not, man," Casey said. "Trust me." The ex–fighter pilot's voice carried a note of amusement.

"I'm sure the pilot's hoping the same thing," Sam said.

The first time Washington tried to send a team to Montana it had been a trap laid by the FSE, which had somehow gotten its hands on the Guardians' codes and recognition sequences, the whole nine yards. The second Hercules had brought new codes to cut the bad guys back out of Guardians commo, but nobody felt like taking much for granted. They'd been compromised once, and nobody knew how that had happened . . . .

"I see it," Sam said, pointing off to the east. Everybody looked to see the flat silhouette dropping out of the eastern sky, black against the high haze of overcast. With a squeak of rubber on asphalt it touched down a klick away.

It was one of those new courier jobs, privately developed and procured in limited numbers right before the One-Day War; McKay didn't even know the official designation. He didn't especially care to. When he was growing up and going into the Marines, an airplane looked like an *airplane,* with the tail in the back and the props in the front—if the plane was humble enough to have props at all.

What was rolling toward them was not an airplane, by Billy McKay's lights. The wedge-shaped snout of the gleaming white aircraft was normal enough, but not the canard foreplane jutting to either side like a bone through its nose. Riding high on the fuselage, the wing didn't alarm him, but those little upturned fin thingies on the ends—winglets, that's what they were called, God knew why—looked alien and unnecessary. Worst of all, the propellors of the twin engines faced the rear, and as the craft taxied close and they cycled down into visibility he could see they had just too damn many blades altogether, and curved like a Gurkha's *kukri,* not straight, as God intended.

Sometimes, secretly, Billy McKay was glad the One-Day War had called time-out on progress.

The weird contraption angled sideways across the road and halted thirty meters from Mobile One. The side hatch opened and a metal tongue of ramp licked down to the pavement. Three men in suits got out. One of them carried a slim briefcase. The other two carried Uzis.

Billy and Sam looked at each other and their eyebrows did a little semaphore dance.

"Good afternoon, gentlemen," said the one with the brief-case, as soon as he was near enough that his voice had a chance against the dying whine of engines. "I'm Ronald FitzSim-mons."

McKay tilted his weight back on his heels and stuck a cigar in his face. "That's nice. Who's that?"

A flicker crossed the man's face. It was a smooth, profes-sional face, long-jawed, with bunches of muscles at the hinges of the jaw. They eyes were gray, the skin was tanned, though where in hell this dude found a working sunlamp in the Washington ruins McKay couldn't even guess—you could find anything at the Rubble Mart, of course, but FitzSimmons didn't look the type to know the way to a place like that.

Instantly the tremor of emotion vanished and a smile stretched in its place, and McKay realized where all the jaw muscles came from. "Right. You don't know me. I'm a special advisor to President MacGregor. National security. Used to be with the Company."

Sam Sloan, trying as usual to keep from looking appalled at his leader's rudeness, had been sticking out his hand to the newcomer in welcome. Now the fingers wilted back, like the petals of an orchid hit with a blast of gamma rays. "The CIA?" he asked in a tone of brittle neutrality.

Again that flicker; the gray eyes ticked from McKay to Sloan and back. "Right. That's right; I understand. You had a little trouble with some of the boys before."

"A little trouble's one way of putting it, yep," Sloan said. During their initial run across an America devastated by ther-monuclear warfare, the Guardians, with newly sworn-in Pres-ident Jeff MacGregor in tow, had been hunted every inch of the route from Washington to Heartland by renegade CIA agents in everything from fast cars to Spectre gunships.

"Well, you don't need to worry yourselves, gentlemen. I was never one of the Romans."

" 'Romans'?" McKay repeated.

"Trajan's crew. The ones you had your little run-in with.

They all had code names from Roman history: Hadrian, Cicero, Lucullus. Like that.''

Sam looked down at his hand, willed the fingers straight, and shook with FitzSimmons. With his cigar crammed way down in a corner of his mouth, which made him look more like the Marine Corps mascot than usual, McKay followed suit.

''And what have we here?'' FitzSimmons said, eyes tracking past the Guardians even as he gave McKay's hand a perfunctory pump. McKay thought about crunching his well-manicured fingers for him. ''The guest of honor, right?''

''Actually, I'm a reporter with *Soldier of Fortune* magazine,'' said Lynch with half-closed eyes.

FitzSimmons cranked an automatic smile into place. Then he frowned. ''What schools did you go to?''

''Andover and Yale.'' The captive tipped his head to the side. ''You?''

''Philips Exeter and Princeton. Say, weren't you—?''

''The racquetball invitational! The Ivy Classic— I remember you now.''

''Hell, yes.'' FitzSimmons shook Lynch's hand and clapped him on the shoulder with a warmth well removed from anything he'd shown the Guardians. ''You remember that little redhead who worked in that pizza joint near the Old Campus?''

''With the prodigious secondary sexual characteristics? Old man, one doesn't forget such wonders of nature. I seem to recall now that you had your eye on her attributes.''

''Right. Well, the night the tournament ended, I went over there—''

The two drifted out of hearing, with FitzSimmons's two Uzi boys floating along behind like heavy clouds. Sam stared thoughtfully after them, rubbing his jaw.

''Reassuring, ain't it?'' McKay growled around his cigar. ''I can tell it's gonna help me sleep sound at night, knowing our man from Washington is in tight with all the right sorts of terrorists.''

''*Eh, bien,*'' a voice boomed out over the dying engine whine. ''So where's the greeting for an old friend? No dancing girl, no champagne—what hospitality is this, *hein*?''

CHAPTER
TWO ——————————————

"*Loup Garou!*" Sam Sloan exclaimed. "Well, I'll be dipped in shit and fried for a hush puppy."

"I hope not, my friend." The tall, strut-lean figure in army cammies stuck a thin black cigarillo under his Zapata mustache with the hand that wasn't a hook—the left one—and strolled down the ladder.

McKay was giving Sloan a sidewise fish-eye. "You country bumpkins sure got some colorful expressions, there, Sloan."

"Sorry, sir. Surprise got the better of me. It won't happen again, sir; didn't know it was possible to gross out an ex-DI."

"Yeah, well even we got standards. 'Fried for a hush puppy.' Sheesh."

By now the dark-haired stranger was close enough for Sloan and McKay to read the LANDRY stenciled on the breast pocket of his camouflage blouse. The two Guardians shook hands with him, left to left.

"My sister sends regards, Commander Sloan."

"Uh, thanks. How is she?" Sloan was trying hard not to blush. He didn't *know* Luc Landry would kill him if he knew he'd slept with his younger sister. He wasn't too sure Landry didn't know he had.

Landry grinned his wolf's grin. "Jeune-Marie is doing fine.

21

Still down on Wolf Bayou, riding herd on the scientists at Starshine and keeping her eye on what's left of the Cubans and Effsees. Oh, Sergeant Gates sends his regards as well. He says if you ever need a backup, you know where to find him.''

McKay's pale malamute eyes flicked to FitzSimmons and Peter Lynch, who were engrossed in arm-slapping reminiscence on the far side of the car. "That's good to know."

The driver's-side door of Mobile One opened and Casey's head popped into view above the frontal armor slope. "Were-wolf One! Um, um, permission to leave my post, Billy—?''

"Yeah. Come ahead. I don't want you peeing your pants on me."

Casey came bounding over like a happy hound pup and caught Landry in a backbreak hug. Captain Luc "Werewolf" Landry was an old comrade in arms from the three-way fight in the Louisiana bayou country against an FSE battalion and a renegade Cuban frigate, for possession of Project Starshine and the unlimited fusion energy it offered. But there was an even greater natural bond between the top fighter ace and the champion tank-buster chopper jock of modern times.

McKay gestured with his cigar stub. "That crate there's damn near as funky-looking as your last one."

Landry hung his Bowie-blade nose over Casey's shoulder and grinned. "She's pretty, no? *Quelle chouette.*''

He disengaged himself from Casey. "Still, she cannot compare to a genuine flying saucer, equipped with a real live death ray."

He wasn't kidding. The technical wizards working on Project Starshine had rigged a prototype of a verti—a craft that was a cross between a helicopter and a light plane—into a passable imitation of a flying saucer, using mirrorized Mylar, bright lights, and some very interesting black boxes. They had also mounted it with one of the super-powerful lasers they were using in their fusion experiments, providing a crude but *very* deadly death ray.

A shadow briefly darkened Landry's black-tanned face by several shades. "I'm just a bus driver today. Though they tell me this mission is vital to the national interest, and all that shit.''

Casey clapped him on the shoulder. "I know where you're coming from, man."

A corner of Landry's mouth quirked up. "Ah, you do, don't you? You've been away from where you belong far longer than

I, my friend, so I can't complain too loudly. So now, are we going to stand out here until we freeze solid?''

"Not if I can pry our frat rats loose from Old Home Week," McKay said. "If they haven't gotten to the Atomic Balm-in-the-jockstrap stories yet, we might get outta here before our balls turn blue."

"First things first," Ronald FitzSimmons said, seating himself on the edge of a long dining table with an institutional-drab Formica top, and crossing his arms over his tie, his short-sleeved white shirt and his plastic pen-holder. It was an unexpected touch of the nerd to go with his Ivy-League jock veneer, Sam thought.

McKay planted a fresh cigar in his face. It was relatively fresh, too—a trader had given it to them as they crossed the mountains into California not too many weeks ago, on their way to give the FSE Expeditionary Force a nudge in the direction of withdrawing back to Europe, which had been invaded by an army of Turks hungry for *jihad*. Bill Bukowski claimed it had been made in Indonesia after the War and smuggled into occupied California under the Effsees' sharp noses. As far as McKay could judge, he'd been telling them straight. He was no connoisseur, but the cigar had a weird taste—and you didn't have to be a connoisseur to know the root hadn't been sitting on some shelf turning to shredded cardboard the last two years.

"So let's hear it, McDonald," he said, scratching a match alight with his thumbnail. He made sure to have a supply of wood matches on hand—they were a primo item of post-holocaust barter—with just that little stunt in mind. Hell of a lot more impressive than flicking your Bic.

The hooded eyes snapped toward him as if mounted on gimbals. He puffed blue smoke. His face stayed wooden. He didn't have the poker face Rogers did, but he could get by in a pinch.

"Wrong name, McKay. It's FitzSimmons."

McKay took out his cigar and studied it. "Sorry. I have trouble keeping all these mick names straight."

Casey snickered. Sam chewed hard on the inside of his cheek and stared around at the little squares of milky sunlight that were the windows of the commissary to the robotized factory he and his buddies had liberated from the Liberators.

FitzSimmons switched his smile on and off. Not that he got

the joke. He wasn't the sort to get jokes, though in the proper circumstances he was probably quick enough to laugh at them.

"Well. Anyway. To get back to the big issue: You boys've been cleared."

The laughter evaporated right out of the air. The commissary was chilly; the generator was down, and the Blueprint techies didn't want to waste fuel or juice from the solar accumulators on keeping the dining hall warmed up during daylight. The temperature dropped a few degrees.

"Just what do you mean by that, FitzSimmons?" McKay said in a flat voice.

The man from Washington frowned around at the Guardians' faces, honestly puzzled by the blankness—or hostility—he read there. "What's eating you gents? It's good news. You've been cleared of any wrongdoing. In that little mess we had, you know."

McKay ground his cigar to trash in his big scarred fist, ground the ember into the linoleum with the heel of a combat boot. "I thought we cleared ourselves ten days ago. When we wiped this joint with the Liberators."

"Oh. Yeah, sure, sure." FitzSimmons tried a little laugh on for size. It didn't fit. "But, well, there were still some sticky questions. You know—how the FSE got hold of your access codes, how they got into our communications."

"The one answers the other," Sam said in a slightly strained drawl. "With the right codes, they could climb right into our net. Same's we did to them."

"Of course, of course. But that leaves the problem of where they got the codes to begin with. We did a little checking—"

"'We'?" Rogers asked. He stood next to the wall beneath a framed aerial photo of the plant, his arms folded, his square face impassive.

"Counterintelligence, Lieutenant. Some boys from the Company, some from FBI— Everybody has to set aside petty rivalries in these tough times, right? We—they—investigated our end."

"And you solved everything, just like Sherlock Holmes?" McKay asked sarcastically.

FitzSimmons grinned. "Hey, I appreciate the vote of confidence, McKay. But I have to tell the truth. When we started bearing down, our man cracked up. One of the Tide Camp commo boys. Wrote a confession, laid it all on the line. Seems some of our friend Maximov's people had touched him back before the War, when he was teaching at Ranger school in Germany.''

The Guardians passed a look around. ''What happened to him?'' Sam asked.

''Shot himself. We never got close to him. He went off duty one night, went back to his quarters, wrote his piece, and ate one from his Beretta. Just like that.''

'' 'Just like that,' '' McKay echoed.

FitzSimmons rubbed his hands together. ''So. We've got that business behind us. Water under the dam. And I should mention that we're instituting security procedures to make sure we don't get a repeat on this. Background checks, that sort of thing.''

''I hope to hell we pass,'' McKay said.

''Oh, I'm sure you will,'' FitzSimmons said with a shrug.

''Surely that wasn't the only thing that brought you all the way out here in the boondocks from the fleshpots of D.C.,'' Sam said with enforced heartiness, keeping a sidelong eye out in case McKay went for the spy and he had to interpose himself. He hoped he wouldn't have to; for all the killer karate and hand-to-hand combat training he'd got in Guardians training McKay could steamroll him in no seconds flat, and he knew it. But McKay was merely standing with his head hunched down on his treetrunk neck, staring at FitzSimmons as if he were afraid he might step on him if he didn't watch where he walked.

''Ha-ha. Not that the fleshpots are all that fleshy. Not with Maggie Connoly keeping an eye on things. Not much fooling around, if you know what I mean.''

''I thought Dr. Connoly was a liberal,'' Casey said.

''Well, economically. But she thinks traditional sexual morality's good for public policy—her words. Helps condition the population to the sort of discipline we're going to need to rebuild.''

''So, like, what *does* bring you out this way?'' Casey asked, sounding as close to exasperated as his laid-back SoCal ways would permit.

''We got a new objective for you. Down Texas way. A nuclear-powered water desalinization plant outside Houston.''

''Houston got nuked, man,'' Casey objected.

''Twice,'' FitzSimmons said smugly. ''Once a two-megaton

ICBM, once a sub-launched six-hundred KT. Air bursts, both cases—maximum damage, minimal fallout. In neither case was the hypocenter close enough to cause substantial blast damage, and thermal effects should have been distance-attenuated enough so they did no real harm. Place wasn't really flammable to begin with.''

''How do you know all this shit?'' McKay demanded.

FitzSimmons smirked at him. ''Data from satellites and seismic stations, some of it recorded as it was happening,'' Sam said.

''They got all that in Washington?''

''They got it in *Heartland,* Billy. And the Effsees got it from there, and our friends—erstwhile friends, maybe—at Freehold stole it from them.''

''Or those poor kids in Pineholm,'' Casey said glumly. He was truly sorry for the youthful geniuses of Vista Systems in California, massacred by the Liberators as part of their counter-Guardian campaign. But what really got him down was thinking about Colorado's Freehold. The closest thing to a leader that band of high-tech anarchists acknowledged was Angie Connoly, daughter to Dr. Maggie—and what McKay, in one of his less crude moods, would have termed Casey's main squeeze. She'd been one of the targets for another slaughter the Liberators had pulled off—and that time they'd left plenty of evidence behind to implicate the Guardians. The Effsee death squad had missed their main goal, but so far had accomplished their secondary aim, that of driving a wedge between the Guardians and some of their most useful surviving allies. And, incidentally, Casey and a woman he was close to being in love with.

''It's all surmise,'' Sam said, with a shrug. ''Wind and moonshine—how far off was I, Mr. FitzSimmons?''

The Company man had been staring at him like a cobra eyeing a gerbil. The tension in his face broke. ''You mean you figured it all out by yourself? I'm impressed. I thought there was another security leak.''

''Sloan's an expert,'' McKay said. He looked as if the words pained him. ''He knows all that computer shit like you know your mama's tits.''

''I was a bottle baby,'' FitzSimmons said primly.

''Ronald *McDonald?*'' Werewolf One repeated, incredulous. ''You called him that? And he didn't get it?'' He tipped his head back and laughed a hearty Cajun laugh.

Billy McKay didn't join in. He hunkered down with a new bottle of beer propped against one powerful thigh, staring into the tiny fire of dried grass and oil-soaked rags. Yellow light from the wind-whipped flames made his pale eyebrows vanish against his heavy, frowning face.

"What's the matter, McKay?" Sloan asked. Unconsciously he pulled his parka closer around him. It was cold out here in the Montana winter night, even in the lee of Mobile One and the brick buildings of the factory. But the commissary had been taken over by the boys from Washington, and somehow the Guardians felt more comfortable taking chances on the chill.

"Is that beer rancid too?"

"Huh?" McKay cocked an all-but-invisible eyebrow in incomprehension, then glanced down at the bottle. "Naw. It's just all this, this stuff with Washington. There's some funky shit going down."

"That's real articulate, McKay," Sloan sneered.

"Shove it up your ass, navy boy!" In a flash that belied his bulk McKay was on his feet. Foaming beer gurgled from the mouth of the fallen bottle and sank slowly into the cementlike earth. Luc Landry and Casey shoved themselves between Sloan and the hulking McKay.

"Hey, now," Casey said. "Mellow out, guys."

But the ex-Marine made no move toward his comrade. He stood with head lowered and nostrils flared, like a bull looking to get a piece of a picador.

"There is something wrong," Rogers said.

Everybody turned to look up at the former Green Beret. He was sitting up atop the car with his legs hanging down into the turret, a black silhouette against a star-smeared sky.

"Like, what do you mean, Tommy?" Casey asked.

Rogers sat for a moment, silent and immobile as a Mount Rushmore head. Speech didn't come easy to him. But on the occasions when he found something to say, his buddies had learned to listen up.

"We all sense it. Things are happening in Washington and we ain't being told what. That's eating on us. Making us jump on each other."

A pause, a shrug. "Not that we got any business questioning our orders, I guess."

"Tom," Billy McKay said, in a voice so calm that Sloan

did a double-take, "we ain't thinking of questioning our orders. We're gonna saddle up and ride out for Texas, just like Ronald McDonald said—*after* we make a call to Washington to confirm.

"But we ain't just grunts, Tom. We're *Guardians*. That's special. We got a responsibility for what goes down in this country until things are back to normal."

"You sound like you think you've turned into a cross between Rambo and JFK," Sloan said.

Casey looked nervously from him to McKay, but the chief Guardian just shook his head. "Sloan, if you'd just listen to what I'm *sayin'*—and not just look for a chance to make shitass comments."

For a moment the two men's eyes locked onto each other across the fire. Then Sloan dropped his gaze. "All right, McKay. I was out of line. Say your piece."

"It's not much different from what Tommy said. First there's all this backin' and fillin' about us hauling Peter Lynch back to D.C. Then there's this bullshit about some dude from Tide Camp blowing us up to Maximov's boys."

"Wait a minute, McKay," Sloan interjected. "Are you saying you don't believe what FitzSimmons told us?"

"Fuckin'-A straight."

"But it sounded plausible to me."

"That's why I'm boss of this chickenshit outfit and you ain't. It's too neat. Shit don't turn out that neat in real life."

"Are you saying somebody, like, put one over on the counterintelligence people?" Casey wanted to know.

"Maybe. Maybe not. The point is we're getting cut out of what's going on. And we *belong* there, dammit. We take our orders from the president himself—or from Doctor Jake, as the senior survivor of the Project Blueprint brass. Not from some civilian errand boy who used to play racquetball with a terrorist."

He hunkered back down, picked up the fallen bottle, examined it woefully. Fragrant beer mud caked one side of it; it was mostly empty. Or just a teensy bit full, if you were an optimist. Billy McKay wasn't.

"It's Maggie Connoly," he said, and killed the beer. "That bimbo in Coke-bottle glasses is trying to turn America into a tinhorn dictatorship. Jesus Christ, Sloan, *you're* the bleeding-heart liberal. I'm the redneck blue-collar reactionary asshole, just like you used to get such a big yuk out of, watching reruns of *All in the Family* on the boob tube when you were a brat. So why are you sticking up for this police state crap? I tell you what, navy boy. I'm used to putting my ass on the line to keep this country free. I don't do it so that Maggie Connoly can take over and run America any way she damn well wants, and that lady is trying to cut us out of the picture.''

''We don't know that that's what's happening, McKay,'' Sloan said.

''No. I guess we don't. But something's happening, and I don't think I like it.''

''So what will you do, McKay?'' Landry asked across heavy silence the wind's whisper did nothing to lighten.

McKay sighed. ''Call a man,'' he said. ''Then go to Texas.''

CHAPTER
THREE ——————————

Three days later the Guardians were tooling across the
Texas panhandle, and McKay and Rogers still didn't feel a
whole hell of a lot better about the deal.

McKay was sitting back with one hand on the wheel, a pair
of shades perched upstream of the break in his nose, and a
cigar in his teeth—unlit, to save him from being lynched by
his fellow Guardians, leader or no leader—and glowering a bit.

Outside, the western Texas panhandle's share of the high
plains scrolled past like the map on the navigation-computer
screen, and showing about as much relief beyond the occasional
limestone bluff shouldering up from the flat. The land's flatness
was illusion; it pitched up here and tucked in there, and you
were never more than a hundred meters from dead ground that
could start sprouting bad guys with RPGs—of which fact the
Guardians were acutely aware. Still, you could push your eyes
on out to the horizon any which way you cared to look across
terrain streaked with swatches of snow like whitewash too
sparsely applied.

As McKay had promised, he'd called Washington first thing
on the morning after FitzSimmons's arrival to confirm the Guardians' new orders. Somewhat to his surprise, commo was still
being handled by Tide Camp personnel. The operator McKay

31

talked to was sullen and subdued, but passed him along readily
enough.

McKay had picked up some static from flunkies, but he'd bellowed and blustered until he got a direct line to President Jeffrey
MacGregor. President Jeff confirmed the assignment amiably
enough, but with an exasperated edge to his voice. He had a
country to run, after all.

Next on the agenda was a call to Dr. Jacob Morgenstern in
California. One of the original architects of the Blueprint for
Renewal, Morgenstern had to some extent replaced the shadowy
Major Crenna—the man who'd come up with the idea for both
Blueprint and Guardians—as guiding light for the elite four-man
team. Not that anyone could *really* replace the one-eyed major,
who had given his life to cover the escape of the Guardians
with President MacGregor and a pack of Blueprint scientists
from occupied Heartland, denying the invading FSE Expeditionary Force the use of the super-sophisticated facility. But
Dr. Jake came close.

Even before the Guardians found him, a few weeks after the
War, the Israeli-born economist had been working on a private
scheme to rebuild at least California—in tandem with the Blueprint if possible, independently if not. Now he was engaged
in trying to clean up the mess the Expeditionary Force had left
behind.

At the moment they called he was at the Vista Systems house
outside Pineholm—or, rather, what the Liberators had left of
it. Chairman Maximov's death squad had done a pretty sloppy
job. Two of the whiz kids who'd been at the big cedar house
the night they hit it had survived—an injured boy who pulled
through by feigning death and a girl who slipped out and made
it to safety in the woods while the FSE killers were mopping
up. At least half a dozen other Vista kids had been away that
night, which was no fault of the Liberators.

But their worst oversight had been their failure to destroy
the computers and communications equipment comprehensively. The hardware was designed for easy repair and replacement, and spare boards, drives and other gear could be scarfed
—scavenged—with little trouble. Even the antenna for the satellite uplink/downlink, which the Liberators blew up, had been
replaced, drive, dish and all, simply by a quick trip to a derelict
TV and video store. What was truly irreplaceable, aside from
the dozen lives lost, was the incredible software, the design of

which had made Vista a going concern before and after the Holocaust. And every bit of that was backed up on storage media buried in a waterproof and fireproof vault near the pump house; the Liberators never came close to it.

But there remained a lot of work to do, not least on the psyches of the survivors. Dr. Jake had clearly been impatient to get back to it.

"Shut up and soldier," was his response when McKay explained the situation to him. In just about that many words. Morgenstern had seen combat with the Israeli Defense Forces as both a paratrooper and a tank commander, and while he never used profanity, he wasn't a whole hell of a lot less blunt than Billy McKay.

All the same, the concern in his Negev-dry voice came through clearly. He wasn't any happier about the mysterious machinations in Washington than the Guardians were. But reclaiming the Blueprint was the number-one priority for all of them.

"I have access to certain assets of my own in Texas," he'd told them. "It may be they can be of some use to you."

"You wouldn't wanta pass along a situation report on the old Lone Star state, now would you, Doc?"

"If our superiors in Washington didn't see fit to brief you, then it's hardly my place to do so," Morgenstern responded. "But I'm sure you'll be well able to cope with what you find there. Gentlemen, I have work to do." And he broke the connection.

"I wonder why he said that?" Sloan mused as he shut down the console spread before the Electronic Systems Operator's seat in Mobile One, which he currently occupied. "The good doctor isn't exactly famed for his slavish regard for authority."

"Because he didn't think our commo link was secure, schmuck," McKay said, and shook his head. "Jeez, how naive can you get?"

"Billy," Tom said from the ESO seat. McKay glanced sideways at him. "Think I got something."

Following usual procedure, Tom—as the Guardian whose turn it was in the electronics barrel—had been playing with the computerized freek scan, monitoring the radio traffic in the area, checking it out over his headphones when the computer noticed a particularly strong or otherwise interesting channel.

"Probably catching a sideband of KFSU in Okie City," Sloan remarked. "At this range it practically comes over the fillings in your teeth anyway."

"Or maybe Del Rio, man," Casey offered.

"Why couldn't them damn Bible-beaters have been blitzed off the air by EMP like everybody else?" McKay said.

"Oh, no, man. The gospel stations were rolling in the bread. They could afford all that neat gallium arsenide stuff to beat electromagnetic pulse."

"Don't be too hard on Del Rio," Sloan said. "They always have nasty things to say about Reverend Forrie."

Way down there at the southern tip of Texas, the evangelical station in Del Rio felt secure enough by reason of distance to hurl abuse at its longtime rival, KFSU—now the most powerful radio station in America by any meaning of the word, owned and operated by Nathan Bedford Forrest Smith, the former boy-wonder TV evangelist who had succeeded the madcap Josiah Coffin as Chief Prophet of the Church of the New Dispensation, and who was by way of being emperor of a goodly chunk of the central U.S.

As a matter of fact, Reverend Forrie owed his accession to the top spot in Coffin's new religion directly to the Guardians, who had been responsible for the radiation-resistant messiah's transfer to an even higher office—or a much, much lower one, depending on your theology and opinion of the departed. For some reason Forrie Smith failed to feel gratitude for this. Which fact accounted for the very wary path the Guardians had picked from Montana, down along the front range of the Rockies, with a wide detour around Denver and its former Federal Center, now doing business as the New Dispensation's studliest strong-hold outside of Oklahoma City itself (and with Casey suffering in silence as they passed within a hundred klicks of Freehold, which was just across the mountains in the San Luis Valley). From there they'd driven straight south into New Mexico, gassed up from a cache laid down before the War near Clayton, and cut east into Texas on U.S. 54, avoiding Route 66, which these days ran mostly to a jillion rusted-out cars, but brushing the southern skirts of Reverend Forrie's ecclesiastical robes a little closely for comfort.

"Billy," Rogers repeated. The word had the slightest tempering of impatience. For Tom, that was the equivalent of a normal person's shouting and grabbing at the mottled white and tan sleeve of McKay's winter-camouflage coveralls.

"All right, Tommy. Put it on the horn."

A static crackle, then: "—closin' in on them now. A dozen trucks and a nice juicy hog. Fuckers're just waiting for it."

"Watch your language, young man! We'll have no backsliding while we're about the Lord's good work."

"Son of—I mean, sorry, Proctor Len."

"You're forgiven, son. Stress of the moment. How are they armed?"

"They, uh, they got a few men up top some of the trucks, carrying rifles." The unseen speaker laughed.

McKay squinted at the console speaker. "What the hell?"

"Road gypsies," Rogers said.

"They're using radios now?" Sloan asked.

"Science marches on," McKay said, while various voices chattered excitedly from the speaker, electronic hunting cries of a pack of high-tech wolves. "What's a Proctor Len?"

"Near as I can figure, he's command control for a bunch of road gypsies. One of Smith's people." Rogers was a deeply if unobtrusively religious man, and he disliked to give Forrie Smith his title.

"It still freaks me out, how the gypsies and Jesus freaks can work together," Casey said, shaking his head.

"Holocausts make strange bedfellows," Sam Sloan observed.

"Jesus, Sloan," McKay said. "Tom, can we RDF the fucks?"

Rogers's stubby fingers flickered over the keyboard, relaying instructions to the computer-driven radio direction finding gear. "Ten point seven clicks, azimuth seventy-four. They're right in our road, Billy."

"Do we take 'em, man?" Casey asked. The mellow mask had slipped ever so slightly, and his voice was edged with eagerness. It wasn't exactly a mask—he really was the laid-back kid he seemed to be . . . most of the time. But he was also a fighter pilot, a combat ace. That meant he had the instincts of a killer under all that mellow.

McKay thought about it hard. For about eight seconds. Their brief was to concentrate on their mission to the exclusion of all else, and avoid involvement in local affairs except as required to fulfill their assignment. Bashing road gypsies on some cracked-asphalt Texan highway was definitely extracurricular to laying hands on a water-purification plant near the Houston rubble.

But the former Marie Kosciusko, better known to Billy McKay as Mom, hadn't raised any dummies. The Guardians' overarching assignment was the rebuilding of America—and what better way to rebuild the stricken country than by taking advantage of a chance opportunity to clear some of the human termites out of the framework? Father Bennie Palermo, SJ, who'd whaled on the young William McKay so frequently and well back at Immaculate Heart Elementary, would've been proud; the boy had picked up something from the Jesuits besides welts after all.

"We go for it," McKay said with a taut grin, and put the pedal to the metal. The big car's diesel roared and the vehicle surged ahead with the relentless force of an avalanche.

Soon Mobile One was up past anything that had been legal since the early Seventies. Nobody was liable to give them a ticket, after all. And if anything got in the way of the hurtling V-450, he figured that was its tough luck—and since the armored car weighed in at a hair over ten metric tons, he had a point.

As the fat, cleated tires ate the klicks, the Guardians cleared for action. Sam Sloan checked the twin ammo bins for the grenade launcher and the fifty-cal, ran a self-test on the electric firing mechanism. Tom Rogers unclipped the single-shot M-79, which fired smaller cousins of the forty mike-mike grenades the turret gun cranked out, from beneath the console between his seat and McKay's, broke it open to check the round up the spout. Aft, Casey Wilson opened a compartment in the hull and broke out his bull-barreled sniper's rifle and switched on its state-of-the-art computerized sight.

McKay just drove. He'd have preferred to have Casey, the team's designated driver, at the wheel when they went into action. But what the hell—they needed to be checked out in all the jobs; he'd been through driving courses during Guardians training until hell wouldn't have it, and he liked to drive fast almost as much as he liked to shoot things. *Maybe I shoulda been a cop.*

As he drove they listened to the road gypsies closing in on their unsuspecting quarry.

"Whoever this Proctor Len is, he's doin' a professional job here," McKay admitted grudgingly.

"It'll almost be a shame to waste him," Sloan said sarcastically, audibly trying to restrain his guilty excitement at the prospect of battle. The stress of going from the white heat of the final fight with the Liberators to days of tedium and frustrating dealings with Washington had been more wearing than any physical exertion. Even Sloan, the team intellectual, was hungering for the catharsis of action.

"Naw," McKay said. "It's gonna be a pleasure. Smart assholes are the worst."

"Targets, McKay," Sloan rapped out. "Ten o'clock, range five-fifty. Two men on bikes."

McKay thrust his head forward and scrunched his head down on his neck, squinting through the laminated glass and plastic armor of the viewport. Though the morning sunlight was filtered through a high gauze of cirrus clouds, it struck a glare off the patchy snow, making it hard to get detail.

Then he caught them, a pair on scramblers, raising a roil of snow as they tore up the deceptively gentle flank of a ridge. Distance and bulky winter clothes hid the distinctively gaudy road gypsy trappings, if any.

"Scouts," Tom said. "We been spotted."

"Fire them up?" Sloan asked.

"Negative," McKay said. "We want this to be a surprise party. Those turret guns'd wake the dead. Case, you handle 'em. Hang on, everybody."

He swerved around a derelict pickup with snow and trash drifted around what looked suspiciously like a skeleton in the bed, hit the brakes, cranked the wheel to the left and skidded sideways for fifty meters along a clear stretch of highway. Before Mobile One had rocked back to portside on its massive suspension, Casey had the side door open and was kneeling down with his rifle at his shoulder. He drew a bead on one of the motorcyclists, not consciously reading the numbers dancing at vision's periphery as the minimicrocomputer in his scope digested data from the low-power laser rangefinder built in. He drew a deep breath, let some out, held it, squeezed.

It's virtually impossible to actually silence a firearm. It *is* impossible to silence a high-powered rifle that punches out a projectile at greater than the speed of sound. The thing that looked like a piece of pipe screwed onto the front of Casey's bolt-action Remington was a sound suppressor; it did a fine job of eating the noise made by the propellant charge going off. There was nothing in the world to do about the *crack* made by the 7.62-mm jacketed round rocketing downrange at several times the speed of sound. On the other hand, road gypsies were your motorized class of scum. Odds were better than half past even that they'd never hear the small firecracker sound against the Great Plains wind and their own engines' roar.

Flight time for the bullet was under half a second. Before it struck, Casey had started to work the bolt, preparatory to lining up the second rider in his Star Wars sight. He was in full combat mode now, precise and unemotional as a machine, evaluating distance, vector, and probability with speed to shame a supercomputer. As his finger tightened he had no conscious memory of his first shot. If it hit, fine; if it didn't, he would try again. For now there was nothing but now—

He fired.

"Two for two!" McKay crowed. "Shut the door and let's boogie."

Casey watched the second rider toppling backwards over the rear wheel of his bike, as if in slo-mo. The other cycle was careering riderless across a last futile few meters of prairie. He felt nothing. He dared permit himself to feel nothing—no triumph, no satisfaction. This wasn't the war he had cut his teeth on, the combat of man against another man cased in a machine, where you could best your foe without killing him and never, *never* see a bullet strike flesh. For a year and a half this war had been his, where you sometimes had to kill a man so close his blood ran across your knuckles, but he had never gotten used to it. Probably he never would. But he was a Guardian. He fought the war he had to.

He shut the hatch on the wind's chilling breath. Only his leopard reflexes and Mobile One's inertia kept him from taking a fall as McKay fed the car full power again. He held the rifle across his body and duckwalked forward to peer between McKay and Rogers as the V-450 charged up the last swell of land between them and the road gypsies.

It opened up like a diorama before them: the doomed convoy strung out along the road where it ran through a broad, shallow valley, the cycles and bizarrely customized vehicles of what looked to be at least a hundred road gypsies pacing it with the menacing purpose of killer whales making their move on a pod of humpbacks. A thousand meters to the northeast an armored

HMMV—a "hummer," a sort of outsized jeep—sat on a hill, clearly Proctor Len's command car overseeing the slaughter to be.

"Strike now, O children of righteousness!" the commander's voice rang from the speakers. Tiny pale blades stabbed from road gypsy weapons. Defenders slumped from view into sandbag nests crudely fixed to the tops of lumbering heavy-laden trucks.

"We're too late," Sloan moaned, as a dozen bikes converged on the lead truck, which once had belonged to U-Haul. "I can't even shoot without hitting—"

The former U-Haul truck exploded.

CHAPTER
FOUR

The thin-gauge metal sides of the truck's box bulged outwards. For a microsecond McKay flashed on a childhood memory of pre-microwave popcorn, the kind that came in a sort of pie pan with a tinfoil cover, how the cover expanded lumpily as the kernels popped, and finally burst open. Before the thought was done the panels had vanished, shredded by blastwaves.

Fifteen bikers went down to either side of the truck as if the Angel of Death had taken a pass at them with his scythe. Momentary flame boiled inside the ruined box of the truck. The vehicle veered, straightened itself and continued straight up the road.

"What the heck?" Sloan breathed.

"Claymores," Tom Rogers said. "It's—"

A "dead" defender suddenly popped into view on the back of the next truck in line. He dropped an M-249 Squad Automatic Weapon onto a sandbag and sprayed a burst into the painted faces peering at him in astonishment from an open Brazilian four-wheel drive.

"—a trap," Rogers finished up.

Tarps came off a stake-bed truck just behind the bright-bodied

41

semi that occupied the center of the column and tangled a biker,
who laid his bike down right in the path of an Econoline van.
The van ran over him without slowing down, and the winter-
cammied figures in the truck bed opened fire with regulated
three-round bursts from long black M-16A2s. A grenade
launcher coughed; frozen dirt and a starfish of white smoke
unfolded in front of a trio of bikes. One went down at once.
The other two drove through the cloud and emerged with riders
beating frantically and futilely at the blue white-phosphorus
flames that whipped from their bodies like pennons.

Along its entire length the helpless convoy was sprouting
guns. The big semi locked its brakes, threatened to jackknife.
The driver brought it expertly under control, stopped it
smoothly. Before its motion ceased, the whole rear plate of the
semi banged down onto the asphalt. A single white-clad figure
roared down the makeshift ramp on a chopped Harley, and
then a whole squad of uniformed troopies came pouring out,
deploying to either side of the semi's trailer with practiced
assurance.

McKay had stopped Mobile One near the top of the rise. He
took his cigar out of his mouth. "Fuck me blind," he said.

The gypsies had long since abandoned all thought of fighting
and were now trying their damnedest to run. They weren't
having much luck. At least six machineguns lashed them as
they fled. An 82-mm mortar chugged from the back of a pickup
whose defenders had tipped its camouflaging camper shell onto
the shoulder beside it.

Proctor Len was a pretty strak field commander, at least
when it came to ratpacking a defenseless convoy. But now he
was proving pretty slow on the uptake. Or maybe he was
reluctant to admit to himself that the Lord would do something
like this to him. In any event, half his raiders were cold or
well done before he belatedly came to life and ordered his
driver to get the heaven out of there. As the Harley beelined
toward it the hummer rolled forward about a meter and a half
and a 90-mm recoilless rifle round hit just above its left front
tire and scattered its engine across half a hectare.

The driver was hard-core; he came out the door with his
K-Mart cammies blazing and an Uzi in his hands doing likewise.
The biker laid a shotgun across his handlebars like a Comanche
firing across his horse's neck, and blew him back into the car.

Then he slewed the bike around and brought it skidding to a halt in a cloud of snow with the aplomb of an Olympic downhill racer.

Fleeing road gypsies were parting to give Mobile One a wide berth to either side.

"Fire those bastards up," McKay ordered Sloan. "Make sure the guns bear well clear of the good guys, so they don't get paranoid."

"How do we know they're good guys, Billy?" Casey asked.

"They're offing road gypsies, ain't they? What's the hangup, Sloan?"

Sam was hesitating. "McKay, they're running—"

"No kidding? I thought they were advancing backwards. He who gets to run away lives to fight another day, navy boy."

Sloan didn't think that was exactly the quote, but now wasn't the time to split hairs. His humanitarian feelings weren't very strong where road gypsies were concerned anyway, so he choked them down, traversed right, and blasted a fleeing Luv pickup with two High Explosive, Dual Purpose grenades.

The lone biker in white had his kickstand down, and he swung a leg over his machine to dismount. The top hatch of the hummer popped, and a figure appeared behind the pintle-mounted M-249. Almost casually the motorcyclist swung up his shotgun and shot the would-be machinegunner. Then he dropped the shotgun beside his bike and walked in a wide arc around toward the hummer's rear.

"Tommy, get a shotgun mike on him," McKay directed. "I want to hear this."

The V-450 rocked to the recoil of a burst from the .50-caliber.

"Jesus Christ, Sloan, belay that shit, will you?" McKay bellowed. "You want to blow our ears out?"

Sloan started to protest that McKay had been the one who told him to open fire in the first place. With his usual perfect timing Rogers channeled the directional microphone's output to the cabin speakers just at that moment.

"—on out," the figure in white called to the vehicle, which was silent except for the crackle of a few feeble flames around the cab. He brought his hands to his mouth, and the distant Guardians saw a puff of smoke whipped away by the wind.

"That's pretty cool," Casey said approvingly. "He's just lighting up as if he didn't have a care in the world."

The man puffed on his smoke, blew some out, dropped his hands to his gunbelt. "We know it's you, Moreland. You could no more resist a target like this than you could fuck a girl without torturing her for a good half-hour first. Come on out, Lennie; we caught you."

"The righteous shall suffer the calumnies of the wicked," a voice came, muffled by the thin armor of the HMMV.

"Calumnies, my dick. What about the people from that convoy last month—the one with the red cross painted on the side of every vehicle? The men you stretched out on the road and ran over their legs with an asphalt roller. The women—well, I guess I can't mention what you did to the women without affronting your virgin ears, can I?"

Silence, with wind. Then: "What do you want from me, you Satan-lover?"

The biker sighed. "What I want has nothing to do with it. I'm under orders to take you prisoner and treat you in accordance with the rules of war."

"So you can put me to death before a jeering mob of devil worshippers! My martyrdom will be avenged, blasphemer."

"No such luck. You bugfuckers still have some good people prisoner. We're looking to trade you for those your pals haven't yet pulled the parts off."

"I—I won't be harmed?"

"You have my word on it."

"The word of a sinner."

"Shit. If I wanted to fuck you over, man, it would be done now. Come out or I'll torch the car."

"Should we take a hand, McKay?" Sloan asked.

"Shut up. I want to hear this." One of the voices coming out of the speaker sounded awfully familiar. But with all the enhancing and filtering the onboard computer was doing to make the distant conversation intelligible, the voices were too distorted for certainty. *Besides, it couldn't be. . . .*

The Guardians heard the sound of a latch working. "Rear door opening," Rogers guessed. A moment later the guess was confirmed as a figure in an unfamiliar uniform emerged from the car, limping and holding its right hip.

"Hands up," the white-clad figure ordered.

Keener-eyed than his companions, Casey spotted something the others hadn't seen. "Billy," he blurted, "we gotta do something—"

"As you wish, unbeliever," the uniformed man said.

"*—he's got a gun!*"

Sure enough, the man in the strange uniform whipped his right hand around his body and up, and even at this range McKay could see he held something dark in his hand. But the other man was already in motion, moving with the swift sureness of a mongoose taking a cobra.

The uniformed man stiffened, staggered back. His weapon dropped to the snowy ground; he followed it as Rogers quickly cranked down the gain on the shotgun mike. An instant after he did so the hammer-rap of a pistol shot cracked from the speaker.

"That concludes our scheduled programming," McKay said. He put the V-450 back in gear. The lanky man in white stood for a moment, smoking placidly and staring down at the figure sprawled unmoving on the ground. Then he holstered his sidearm and turned toward the distant hill where Mobile One sat. "Time to go meet the sponsor."

Down in the valley the troopies who had bushwhacked the bushwhackers had finished off all open resistance. They were now starting to move out in clumps from the perimeter established around the stalled convoy, securing the wounded road gypsies and checking to be sure the dead stayed that way.

At least some of them had been aware of Mobile One's presence up on its hill since the engagement began, and had been giving the big car wary looks. But a rough-and-ready protocol for situations like this had evolved in the turbulent days since the One-Day War: Armed strangers, even heavily armed and armored ones, were no novelty. The usual plan was live-and-let-live; the alternative was *guaranteeing* you had to deal with two sets of enemies as opposed to just risking it.

But now that the fight was over everybody's eyes were on the newcomer at least half of the time, and while the 90-mm and antitank rocket launchers in view were very carefully not pointed in Mobile One's direction, it was clear the hands that held them were ready to turn them that way at an eyeblink's notice. It was not unheard of for third parties happening on disputes in progress to wait for the outcome and then knock over the weakened winner.

Not that these winners looked weak. So total had the road gypsies' surprise been that they'd managed to inflict few if any casualties after the first seconds of the onslaught—and at least some of them had been phony, as witness the "dead" defender on the U-Haul who'd come back to life with a machinegun in his hands.

McKay drove down toward them with deliberate slowness. Away beside the hulk of the man in the white jumpsuit stood by his bike speaking into a handheld microphone. He hung the mike on the handlebars, mounted the motorcycle and rode down to meet the Guardians, long, black hair streaming behind him.

McKay picked his way past a road gypsy buggy that had taken a hit and had rolled over repeatedly along the road—the rollbar up top hadn't done its occupants much good, unless they'd started out that morning looking like fresh hamburger. Gravel squeaked and crunched beneath the tires as he pulled the car back off the shoulder onto pavement and stopped. The biker swung his machine onto the highway and rode straight up to them without an instant's hesitation.

"Here's a brash one," Sloan remarked.

Casey drew in his breath. "Say, isn't that—"

Without waiting for the rest McKay popped the hatch above his seat and poked the upper half of him out into a brisk breeze. The rider was slowing his bike now. He was close enough for McKay to make out a lean, long-jawed face, flamboyantly mustachioed, half-obscured by aviator's goggles and framed by shoulder-length dreadlocks. The face clearly belonged to somebody who would be called black, though its shade evidently owed more to exposure to sun than to genetics. A handsome sort of face, self-assured, more than a touch ruthless. And quite familiar.

McKay rested his thick forearms on the cold front slope of Mobile One's armor. "That High Noon bit was pretty ballsy," he called out to the approaching rider. "You haven't gone and let the fact that you're named Callahan convince you you are really Clint Eastwood, now, have you?"

The man in the jumpsuit halted the bike with its front tire practically touching the tip of Mobile One's wedge-shaped snout and dropped the kickstand.

"Nope," Dreadlock Callahan said, shaking back the long, tightly-coiled strands of hair that gave him his name. "I'm not the right color; I stayed in the oven just a little too long. And that's *Major* Callahan now, by the way. Welcome to the Republic of Texas, McKay."

CHAPTER
FIVE ―――――――――――――――――――

The reunion went quickly, with lots of back-slapping and Texas-style *abrazos*. That out of the way, the first order of business was to police the area of salvageable weapons, vehicles, and reasonably undamaged road gypsies.

The Guardians watched in admiration as Callahan's soldiers quickly and methodically stripped the wrecks of radios, tires, even engines when they were intact enough to be worth pulling, using breakdown pulleys the Texican troops had thoughtfully brought along. In the post-Holocaust world very little was allowed to go to waste. While what the Texican troopies were scavenging from their fallen foes ran mostly to the pretty imperishable, and could be had in heaps from cities long bereft of more fragile items such as human inhabitants, scarfing from the ruins carried its own dangers: radiation pockets, cave-ins, disease, rival scavengers. And the months since the War had brought the message home pretty clearly to anybody with the brain cells to survive them that it would be a good many more months before any more items that called for large-scale manufacture came into existence.

The job of the Blueprint—and the Guardians—was, among other things, to bring American manufacturing back on line ASAP. Until then, the survivors had to rely on scarfing, conservation, and a healthy dose of ingenuity if they wanted to get by at a better-than-Dark-Age level.

"These Texans of yours are pretty damned efficient," McKay remarked, standing with Callahan next to Mobile One, as smoke-flavored wind whipped the cloth of their coveralls around their shins, and troopies piled what salvage couldn't move under its own power—which was most of it, since only a couple of the vehicles the marauders left behind still ran—into the trucks, along with ten more or less able-bodied captives.

Work parties had gathered the booty that was adjudged not worth saving into heaps as best they could in a hurry and were sprinkling them with judicious amounts of scarfed gas and planting small chunks of Composition C-4 explosive. It was an imperative even older than the survival lessons taught by the days since the War: *Don't leave nothing for Charlie.*

Callahan gestured with a cigarillo clamped between fingers the color and consistency of polished hardwood. "Not Texans, McKay. *Texicans.* Helps keep things straight."

McKay gave him a sidelong eye, one eyebrow hiked well up. Callahan smoked and ignored the look. McKay decided not to press. Callahan loved to be mysterious. And while he could crank out a story better than most men McKay had known, if he didn't volunteer information you couldn't get it from him shy of torture. Deep down, McKay doubted even that would work.

The road gypsies who were injured too badly to move were simply killed. Sam Sloan winced and busied himself inside the car, but he didn't object, even though he was the Guardian most freighted with humanitarian concerns. Like a lot of other idealists he'd learned the hard way that people busting their guts just to pull through couldn't spare medicines and treatment facilities for their enemies, if indeed they had them for themselves. Besides, Sloan had seen what the gypsies did to *their* captives.

It all took less than half an hour. Then the column hauled ass for its camp on the outskirts of bombed-out Amarillo, in which the Guardians and their erstwhile captors, India Three, had taken refuge from the Effsees a year before. The Panhandle north of Forty was no-man's-land, and the Republicans—"Texicans," as they apparently called themselves—didn't want to risk running afoul of a relief force of road gypsies or Reverend Forrie's FSE-trained and -equipped regulars.

That night in the lounge of the combination HoJo's and truckstop Callahan's command was using for a base the Guardians explained their mission to their host by the light of kerosene lamps and progressive-country fiddling sawing tinnily out of a solar-pack Sony sitting on the bar. The room's air was cold and thick with the smells of mildew and ash and spilled stale beer and piss and things dead long ago. All the normal post-Holocaust smells. The Guardians hardly noticed them anymore.

Sam was nervous. "*Should we be telling him all this stuff?*" he subvocalized when McKay mentioned the desalinization plant.

No sound was audible over the music; Sloan's lips didn't even move. But the tiny mike held against Sloan's larynx with flesh-toned tape picked up the sound and transmitted it via the calculator-sized communicators buttoned into the breast pockets of the other Guardians' coveralls to bone-conduction phones fixed to the mastoid processes behind their ears.

"*He's good people, Sam,*" offered Casey, who was braving the chill outside on watch atop Mobile One.

"*He's an outlaw biker and a renegade son of a bitch,*" McKay subvocalized, "*but he's our renegade son of a bitch. We go back a long way, Sloan. Besides, we need information, and for that we need to level with him—and anyway, Doc Morgenstern said we'd find some assets here on the ground. Looks to me like we just found one.*"

"*He's right, Sam,*" Tom Rogers said, sipping salvaged Lone Star beer from the bottle. "*We need to level with him.*"

Sam's mouth briefly tightened, but the issue was settled. Tom knew handling "indiges"—indigenous forces—the way he knew handling explosives, which was to say he knew everything.

"*So when the hell did you become a stickler for security, Navy boy?*" McKay jibed. Sloan didn't respond.

Throughout all this Dreadlock Callahan was sitting with legs crossed and hands folded across one knee, gazing at the long dead Pearl Beer neon sign hung over the bar, without focusing his eyes. As one the Guardians became aware of his studied inattention; he knew about their nifty-drifty communicators, and knew perfectly well what they were doing.

When the three were all looking at him he glanced around. "Don't mind me, boys. I'm just here listening to the bunkhouse blaster."

McKay looked down at the tabletop. The wood had been inletted and pre-War coins sunk into it and lacquered down. It said a lot about the state of the nation's economy that no one had bothered to pry them loose.

"Uh, yeah," McKay said. "So, there's this plant. . . ."

Callahan listened, nodding and frowning judiciously and playing with the ends of his Fu Manchu. "Could be we could be of help to each other," he acknowledged. "Sherri, fetch me a beer, will you, honey?"

A tall woman in camouflage battledress tailored in a non-regulation way to tuck in here and stretch real tight there eyed him from the bar, where she leaned next to the Sony deck. She had eyebrows that looked as if they'd been drawn with a chisel point pen and hair the color of the devalued coinage sunk into the tables.

"Wha'd you say?" she drawled. Her tone was honey mixed with Red Devil lye.

"Allow me to translate. Shay-uh-*ree,* fetch me a *bee*-yah, will yuh-all, *huhhh*ney?" Callahan elucidated.

"Yankee asshole." She sashayed around behind the bar.

Callahan watched her with approval. "She's Regular Army, believe it or not," he remarked. "If I'd known there were fringe bennies like her I never would've dodged the draft."

McKay had his suspicions that Callahan had not exactly avoided military service, but that was one of those questions the former biker would never answer. "Where'd you find her? Typing pool?"

"Her MOS was combat infantryman—infantry*person,* excuse me. She's got a marksman's badge and fifteen confirmed kills—post-War, of course."

McKay shook his head. He was still scandalized that they'd started letting women into line units before the War, even if none had gotten into action when the balloon went up in Europe. "Sometimes I wonder what the world's coming to," he grumbled.

"It's already gotten there," Callahan said cheerfully, as Sherri plunked a tray with a frothy glass of beer down by her CO's elbow. "She gives great head, too, by the way."

"How would you know what to compare it to? Only kind

of head you know about's what's on that beer. That one's so full 'cause Ah sprinkled a little ground glass into it,'' she retorted.

''That's why she's my second in command,'' Callahan said with a grin. ''She's resourceful, not to mention subordinate.''

''Motherfucker,'' she said, and sauntered back to the bar.

Callahan sipped his beer and smacked his lips. ''Ah, this is what I call real beer. Tuborg—none of that American cat piss.''

McKay stared at him, thunderstruck. ''Not you, too!''

Callahan stared at him, shook his head, tossed back the glassful. ''Not that I have time to savor it properly,'' he said, rising. ''Got to make a little phone call, talk to a man about what you told me.''

The sky was white, but the day actually threatened warmth. The unlikely-looking convoy ran south across rolling land that was beginning to peek in larger patches through its threadbare snow coat.

Billy McKay, holding down the turret gunner's seat, had gotten sick of the smell of his own sweat and decided some fresh air and cigar smoke were just what he needed. So here he was riding along with the wind freezing his eyebrows, playing Rommel while Dreadlock Callahan's boys—and girls— shouted and waved. A platoon of them were escorting the Guardians down through the Staked Plains west of the ruins of Lubbock in a weird assortment of vehicles both civilian and military.

Yesterday in action Company A of the Second Battalion, 1st Free Texas Motorized Volunteers, had looked strak as could be, like a line outfit with more than a little seasoning. In today's wan light they looked as motley as their transport.

Looking around from the turret hatch, McKay could see that most of them had uniforms of one sort or another, and some would probably even have been entitled to them back before the War. Others wore bits and pieces, whether from army stores or a discount store, and here and there he noted a party in Levis jacket and jeans and cowboy hat, not even making a gesture at military appearance.

Weaponry hewed somewhat closer to regulation—the heavy weaponry was all issue, of course, though the two 90-mm recoilless rifles had to have come from some National Guard armory, and the bulk of the troopies sported M-16s, both the old model and the A2. But he also saw chunky H&Ks; FNs, which as always reminded him of crutches with their outlandishly long barrels; bolt action hunting guns; various members of the Soviet-bloc AK clan; and even one dude riding in the back of a pickup with a helluva belly, a bright red flannel shirt and an octagonal-barreled Winchester.

The hatch over the ESO's seat came open and Callahan stuck his head out. He was riding in state in Mobile One today, while his Harley rode in the back of a truck and his platinum-blond second in command got the command car, a hummer like the late lamented Proctor Len's, but mounting a TOW-II antitank missile launcher.

"So what do you think of my boys?" Callahan asked.

"Pretty raggedy-assed." By a former Parris Island drill instructor's standards, they were a nightmare. But McKay's standards had changed some since the One-Day War. "I guess they'll do the job, though," he admitted, grudgingly.

"That they do. The Texicans got some good cadre to build their units around. Put that together with a year of mixing it up regularly with Effsees, Reverend Forrie's crazies and some of our other not-so-friendly neighbors, you get a pretty tough outfit."

"I'm surprised a man like you isn't with the cavalry, Dreadlock," Sam Sloan remarked. He was off duty, following the conversation from inside by way of his communicator. A spare set had been lent to Callahan as a courtesy and to facilitate coordination between his troops and the Guardians if the hammer fell. Nothing that hadn't happened before. "If the Republic has any cavalry, that is."

"Bite your tongue, my man. Of course we have cavalry. How could the Republic of Texas be without cavalry?" He took a drag. "Only trouble is, they use real horses. Horses and me don't exactly get along. Motorcycles are one thing, but I don't get astride anything flesh and blood unless it's human and female."

"Notice how he don't specify *breathing*," his second in command drawled. She had a loaner comm unit too.

"So what I want to know," McKay said, "is why'd these, uh, Texicans stick a desperado like you in command of their troopies?"

Callahan laughed. "I know where the skeletons are buried, McKay."

"Must be some pretty high-powered skeletons," Sam Sloan said. "At least, that's what I reckon based on that call you made last night."

"You mean to old Lamar? Shit, Sam, that was nothing. Everybody calls the president whenever he feels like it." Callahan produced one of his own slim, black cigarillos and lit it, deftly shielding his lighter flame from the slipstream. "Or she. Prez likes it better that way."

McKay scratched the close-cropped hair behind one ear. At first he'd been sure Callahan was shitting them about the man he had to talk to. But when the former outlaw biker had come back to tell them he was under orders to escort the Guardians to meet with President Lamar Louis Napoleon LaRousse in San Antonio, capital of the Republic of Texas, he hadn't been so certain anymore. At least, he was willing to suspend his disbelief.

"If you're hosing us about this, Callahan," he rumbled, "I'll fuck you up good."

Callahan showed him teeth that could advertise Crest. "Have I ever lied to you, McKay?"

"Always."

The dreadlocked biker was putting on a dumbshow about how hurt he was when a Volunteer riding in the back of the open Isuzu four-wheeler ahead of Mobile One yelled out something and pointed to the eastern sky. McKay snapped his head that way. He caught a hint of a tiny cruciform shape, gray against the gouache of the clouds, before it wheeled upwards and was gone.

Callahan had gone pale beneath his outdoor tan. "Shit," he said, half to himself.

"Effsees," McKay exclaimed. "Callahan, shag your ass outta the ESO seat and let Casey get to his instruments—"

"No Effsees, McKay," Sloan reminded him. "They all went home to help fight Iskander Bey."

"What? Well, hell, so they did. So what's biting your ass, Callahan?"

Callahan was scrambling up out of the hatch, perching with one boot propped against the bar cage protecting the right headlight. "You think the Effsees are the only bad guys left, McKay? If we've been spotted, the shit could hit the fan in a hell of a hurry." He gestured for an M-60–mounted jeep to close in on the armored car.

"Who is it? Forrie's people?"

"Nope." With the monkey ease of a Hollywood stuntman Callahan leapt the meter-and-a-half gap between Mobile One and the jeep, heedless of the pavement sweeping below at sixty clicks an hour.

"*What is going on, Callahan?*"

"Maybe nothing," Callahan said, as his vehicle pulled away. "But like the man said, keep watching the skies."

McKay heard him giving orders to his own team to spread way, way out, along the highway and to either side. He cursed the ex-biker's love of mystery. On the other hand, it probably didn't matter too much just who might be fucking with them.

"Angel, Billy," Casey's voice said with the unwonted crispness that said he had shifted to combat mode. "Fourteen clicks on radial ninety-three. Seems to be heading away."

The search and tracking microradar hunched near McKay's right elbow in its white plastic radome was a marvel of high-temperature superconductor technology, one of the cutting-edge gimmicks Crenna had obtained for the Guardians. Unlike most Star Wars–type toys McKay had encountered in the field it actually worked.

"What's the speed? What's it look like?" At least it was heading in the right direction.

"Slow, Billy. I think it's just a light plane, probably civilian, Cessna or something." His tone was faintly contemptuous in an absent-minded way. If it wasn't supersonic and armed to the teeth, it was barely an airplane to Casey Wilson.

"Whew. I was afraid it might be an A-10 or some shit like that, the way Callahan was freaking out."

"Billy," Casey said in the tone of exaggerated gentleness usually reserved for the senile, "that could be a spotter vectoring in attack craft on us. I'm getting some traffic from that direction, but it's in a code I can't make out."

"Holy shit." McKay dropped down the hatch like a prairie dog who'd spotted a diving hawk. Not that the foamed titanium-alloy armor of Mobile One would do much good against a thirty-millimeter Gatling-style cannon that could chew a T-80 tank to bits with a short burst. Or even against aircraft far less potent than the A-10. But suddenly he had felt real exposed, riding up there in the breeze.

"Sam," he said, "break out a Stinger. We may have company. Casey, get Callahan on the horn; fucker left without saying good-bye.''

In a moment Callahan's voice crackled into McKay's ear. "I'm busy. What?''

"If we have flying friends come to visit, what are they gonna be? Fixed wing? Choppers? Jets? Some little dink prop job with a COIN tray?''

"We don't have much to fear from choppers; we're far enough from Indian country. If we get hassled, it'll be jets.'' He paused. "Up to A-10s.''

McKay winced. The ungainly looking twin-engine jet attack craft—Thunderbolt II to its manufacturers, which had been dubbed "the Devil's Cross" by Tom Clancy's fictional Soviet troops in *Red Storm Rising*, though Americans generally referred to it as Wart Hog—had been in the process of being phased out of the American forces for almost a decade. Not enough mission flexibility, the rap ran; the design relied more on armor than speed for protection, and that didn't cut it in the modern combat environment. As a matter of fact, the Wart Hogs had done just fine in the war on the ground in Europe, as far as that went, which was to say before the Russians pushed the Button. McKay had seen the things on firing passes in training, and they scared hell out of him. Whether or not the boys in the Pentagon were impressed, *he* sure as hell was.

The bottom line was that McKay was no armored trooper anyway; he had no great ambition to get burned to a Krispy Kritter in a titanium-alloy oven fired by exploding fuel and ammo. A tiny ball of sweat rolled down the right side of his forehead to tickle an eyebrow. If the unknown bad guys sent over an A-10 he figured they were fucked.

"Stinger's ready,'' Sloan reported. "Hope the Mark II works better than the old ones.'' The original shoulder-fired Stinger surface-to-air AA missile had gotten a bad reputation—largely in the press, which had trouble grasping that purchasing requirements and performance standards for weapons systems were usually just so much smoke, not intended to be taken literally. Still, there had been problems with the things. Supposedly they were All Better now.

"So do I,'' McKay said.

"Even the new model can't carry enough of a warhead to knock down an A-10, unless you get, like, a real lucky shot,''

Casey offered. His voice was full of enthusiasm; though the Wart Hogs were slow and ungainly, especially by the standards of his beloved F-16s, they were still impressive machines. "Anyway, even the new heat-seeker heads'd probably have trouble tracking, what with the IR suppression kits those babies are fitted with."

McKay counted ten. "Thanks, Case," he said.

"Oh, sure, Billy."

"You don't have any other good news for us, Casey?"

"Well, back before the War I heard they were working on a new tank-buster missile, with an active optic-homing system controlled by an onboard computer, it could, like, identify its target and chase it down—"

"*At ease!*" McKay bellowed.

"Uh, sure, Billy. Anything you say." He sounded as if he wanted to cry.

So I'm an asshole, McKay thought, hunching down into the seat, which wasn't entirely adequate to his giant frame. *Well, I'm a doomed asshole. That's my excuse.*

He stuck his head back into the icy wind and started looking around to see from which quadrant of the sky death would arrive.

CHAPTER
SIX ———————————————

An hour later McKay shifted his aching rump on the turret-gunner's seat and said, "Looks like a false alarm."

The sky split in two over his head.

McKay swiveled his head clockwise as a squat shape, black against the low cloud screen, hurtled across the highway at an altitude that looked lower than it could possibly be. It passed the convoy a third of the way back from the head, then vanished beyond a stand of tall, skinny trees at the top of a swell of ground to the west, trailing a thin scum of black smoke and a whole lot of noise.

"Fucked again," McKay said bitterly. "Tommy, get us the hell off the road."

Vehicles were splitting into the fallow milo fields to either side of the highway. A couple of hundred meters ahead Callahan straddled his bike by the roadside, holding his CB mike with one hand and waving the other over his head. He had forsaken the dubious shelter of Mobile One for his motorcycle after the spotter plane had put in its appearance, and was hurrying his troops toward cover.

The problem was there was no cover shy of the windbreak trees better than half a click to the west, except occasional scraggly clumps of the mesquite and juniper that were busy reclaiming the land above the Caprock Escarpment, from which they had been so painstakingly driven by generations of human inhabitants. The only signs of those inhabitants were the trees and twenty or so bony black whitefaced cows racing off to the southeast with tails held high, and for all McKay knew they might have been wild. It was a desolate, dismal scene, and had just gotten a great deal worse.

As the big car waddled through the ditch to the left of the highway Sam Sloan bailed out carrying two Stinger launchers, one prepped in his hands, one slung across his back. The beasts were supposed to be field-reloadable, but that was one of the glitches that hadn't been caught in the redesign. You could reload the launcher, but it took several minutes—minutes more than you were going to get in the middle of the shitstorm.

McKay ducked as Mobile One ran through a barbed-wire fence with a musical twang. "Jesus shit." He could just imagine a raw end of wire clawing his eye out. He was having that kind of day.

"It's cool, Billy," Casey caroled from the ESO chair.

McKay stuck his head cautiously up and peered aft. Sloan was rooting through long-dead weeds that lay flat from the runoff of last summer's late rains. Not ideal cover, but a man afoot wasn't a great target for even the slowest fixed-wing attack aircraft, and anyway nothing better was offered.

"What's cool?"

"Oh, the plane. It's not an A-10."

"I can *see,* Casey."

"It's just an A-7. A SLUF."

" 'SLUF'?" Sam echoed over the communicator. His chin had been bruised by the ready launcher, and one kidney was sore from being slugged by the other. He was flat on the ground with his nose and mouth full of the sour wet smell of the thin limestone soil, trying to look in all directions at once.

"Short Little Ugly, uh—" Casey began.

"Fucker," McKay finished. Casey hardly ever used bad language. McKay figured he had to keep the slack held up.

"It's just an obsolete National Guard crate," Casey said. "Years out of date."

"So that means we're okay?" Sam asked.

"Oh, no, man. Without air cover it can pound us flat." He sounded as casual as if he were describing a not particularly handsome bird he'd seen sitting on a fence.

"Casey, I should make you morale officer," McKay said. He was scanning his gaze around the horizon, hoping to catch sight of the attack jet. Why, he wasn't sure; powerful as they were, the two turret guns had as much chance of knocking down the SLUF as he had of walking to Venus, and not even Casey Wilson at the wheel had a hope of outmaneuvering the aircraft.

"Thanks, Billy. Uh, bogey approaching, eight o'clock."

McKay cranked his head left. The stubby plane was streaking right up the highway, low and fast. It passed into the south and climbed, turning right.

"Damn, damn," Sloan moaned. "I can't get a tone on him; the missile won't track."

"He'll be back," Casey said.

He had cut Callahan out of the Guardians' commo circuit, but was monitoring him on headphones as he ordered his people out of their vehicles. Against an enemy like this their only defense was to spread out and try to become one with the planet.

"Why didn't he shoot?" Sam asked.

"Making observation passes, see what we are and where we are. Third time's the charm, man."

"Do we stay with the car, Billy?" Rogers asked. He sounded no more worked up than Casey. McKay supposed it was a good thing, having two totally cool heads aboard, but irrationally it was pissing him off. *He* was scared shitless. What right did they have not to be?

"Roger that. When he makes his firing pass cut it at right angles."

"Sure that's a good idea, McKay?" Sloan asked.

"No." The Guardians were not a democratic outfit, but they were a team of experts, and any one could offer his opinion if he thought a mistake was coming down. "But if Tom and Case the Ace don't argue, it's what we're gonna do."

They were all out of time for debate. The A-7 had circled and was coming from the south again. Somehow McKay could tell it meant business this time.

Sam Sloan meant business too. He'd been a gunnery officer on the missile cruiser *Winston-Salem* in the Sidra Bay fight during the Israeli-Egyptian invasion of Libya. He was expert in using exotic weapons systems, a skilled professional who had brought accurate fire raining down on fast, over-the-horizon targets. He was damned if he were going to let a silly throwaway rocket that came with instructions in the form of a comic book even conscripts could understand get the better of him.

He was up on one knee with the launcher on his shoulder peering through the clear blast plate, holding down on the approaching plane. The little red light that indicated that the missile's seeker head was seeing its target flickered like a firefly with a spastic colon. He needed a steady light and buzz to shoot, and he wasn't getting either. The Stinger II supposedly had an all-aspect head, which meant it didn't need to be fired from behind its target. Sloan had always taken advertising claims like that with a grain of salt, and now it looked as if he'd been right.

Always gratifying to be right, he thought. Then: *Gosh, that plane's getting big.*

And then: *Jesus jumping Roosevelt Christ, it's headed right at me!*

His guts turned to cold jelly inside him. He sucked in his belly and kept fingers that felt like cold, dead fish clamped hard on the grips of the launcher. The SLUF filled the clear blast plate, fat and black and evil, roaring like the open mouth of Hell. Sam's legs quivered with the need to jump up and run, somewhere, anywhere, away from the demon rushing upon him. . . .

He held his ground. The A-7 flashed overhead, so low the exhaust buffeted him and filled his head with hot petroleum reek. He pivoted, aiming the launcher for the red, glowing anus of the craft.

A steady red, a pure fine buzz. Sam's finger tightened on the button.

A black, streamlined shape like a finless fish tumbled from the belly of the plane. The Stinger's engine ignited. The missile howled away from the launcher, swathing Sloan in acrid smoke.

A hellish orange glow lit the swirl of smoke. It parted to show a curtain of napalm flame spread across the road. The heat was hideous, even at a hundred meters. Sloan threw up a hand to shield his face.

The Stinger's booster had burned out within a fraction of a second of leaving the launcher. It was a clear shot, a textbook shot, right up the A-7's pipe.

Then the glass IR eye of the missile saw an immensity of napalm heat unfold right beneath it. The missile thought *Jesus shit howdy,* twitched its control surfaces, and dove to flaming doom in the midst of the inferno.

McKay pounded his hand on the top of the turret. "Damn, damn, *damn!*"

"Seeker head's supposed to filter out fake returns on that new Stinger," Casey said mildly. "Too much heat must have, like, overloaded it."

"Get Callahan."

"He's off the air, Billy."

McKay stared at the orange wall of fire.

Sloan was trying to remember what that goddamn comic book had said. He's prepped Stingers and a dozen other kinds of shoulder-fired missiles a hundred times during Guardians training. He'd made sure of the connections back in the car. But it took time to get the tube uncapped and into position.

He was concentrating extra hard to keep his mind from replaying the image of a human figure dancing in frenzy just inside that firecloud. It had to be a quick way to die, but still, *God, spare me that.*

He heard a rushing, glanced up as a shadow swept across him. The earth erupted around him in a dozen fountains.

"McKay, did he nail you, or are you just too mean to die?"

"I'm too mean," McKay lied. Mobile One was bucketing across the prairie, giving McKay all too good a feel for just how flat this country wasn't. "Why the hell did you go off the air, Callahan?"

"CB died. Forgot about the communicator you lent me—heat of the moment."

"Take any casualties?"

"Napalm can caught a deuce-and-a-half truck. Most of my people were clear. Not sure what the rockets did. Can Casey patch me through onto my platoon freek?"

"This baby'll do anything you want, Dreadlock," Casey said. "Sam, are you all right? Some of those hit pretty close to you."

McKay looked back toward the road. "Sam—"

"Right here, McKay. This gang can't shoot straight." He coughed. "The dust might finish me off, though."

"Here he comes again, Billy," Casey reported.

• • •

Sloan was still knocking divots of cold earth held together by tough prairie-grass roots when he heard the whistling roar as the A-7 came in on another pass. He grabbed the launcher, hauled it to his shoulder.

The jet was passing south of him, near enough that he could make out the mottled green and black of its camouflage paint. It slowed visibly, and thin smoke streamed back as its twenty-millimeter Vulcan cut loose. A ball of flame blossomed from the cold land in reply as a truck's gas tank blew.

Sam gritted his teeth—literally; he felt dust crunch. His launcher was telling him it was locked on. He pressed the firing stud as the A-7 finished its run and curved away with a grace belying its ugly form.

The unknown enemy pilot wasn't looking out for missiles. He probably had never seen the first missile ignominiously immolate itself. He gave the Stinger a clean shot at his tail for the second time. This go-round the missile refused to be distracted. It flew straight up his tailpipe.

Lots of nothing happened.

Sloan let held breath whistle free in disappointment. "But I hit him!"

"I guess that's another bug they didn't work out," Casey commented. "A shoulder-fired rocket can't carry a very big warhead. Takes a lot of luck to knock down a jet with one."

Tom had come off the accelerator. Mobile One was slowing. The SLUF had made a serious run at the armored car this last go-round. Taking off at right angles to its path had worked fine so far.

"So much for the miracle of modern science," McKay said. The flash of fear he'd felt at getting caught in the open by the stubby attack plane had vanished. Now he was seriously pissed.

"If that sonofabitch comes back," he said, "I'm gonna get out and take him on with my fucking .45."

At that moment a ball of flame farted out the tail of the A-7, and its engine went out. Its nose dropped and it dove for the planet. The canopy blew away; at the instant of impact the ejection seat shot free, arced gracefully high into the sky.

The SLUF scraped along on its belly for half a kilometer, until the watchers thought it was going to come to a halt intact. Then the port wing came off. The airplane turned slowly broadside to its line of travel, began to roll, disintegrating in a breaker of gray dust. A shout of flame lit the prairie.

The chute never deployed. The pilot had been much too low when he punched out.

"Whoo-*ee*," Dreadlock Callahan remarked. "Gon' have to pick that mother up with a pooper scooper."

McKay let out a long breath. "Yeah. Well, that ain't our problem. Let's dust off the wounded and haul ass before somebody else decides to play a little napalm tag with us."

CHAPTER
SEVEN ——————————————

"Welcome to the Repubiic of Texas, gentlemen," the large old party with the long white hair said. "Have yourselves a drink."

"Sorry, Mr. President," Sam Sloan said with a James Garner grin and a shake of his head. "We're on duty."

"What are we, cops?" McKay said. "We'd love a drink, sir. Your Excellency. Mr. President."

" 'Lamar' was good enough for my momma," said the president of the Republic of Texas, "so I suppose it should be good enough for you. Though I can't say that name speaks volumes for my dear mother's taste. Or perhaps it does; she married my pappy, after all. Find yourselves some chairs and take the load off."

The Guardians looked at one another. Four leather covered chairs on casters had been set on an expanse of maroon-tiled floor that stretched from the glass face of a floor-to-ceiling bookcase loaded with heavy old books with cracked covers to an oak-paneled wall covered by photographs and watercolor paintings, both running largely to Western landscapes.

"Don't mind if we do," McKay said, and sat. The others followed suit.

President Lamar Louis Napoleon LaRousse stood up from

behind a desk slightly smaller than the King Ranch. And up. And up.

He stood at least six and a half feet tall, and straight despite his years. He had a gigantic head with hair the shade of glass wool swept back from a tall, wide forehead; brows like ledges clad in snow-covered brush jutting over eyes as blue as a mid-winter lake; a broken nose and an immaculate handlebar mustache hanging past either corner of a traplike mouth. If his gut was stretching the front of his bright red, pearl-buttoned shirt, the pure white buckskin of his fringed jacket was taut around his shoulders, too. He had a bolo tie fastened around his neck with a silver starburst clasp inlaid with a robin's-egg chunk of blue-green turquoise. The buckle of his belt was silver, large enough to eat off and shiny enough to shave in, with a design of longhorn horns, a single star, and crossed rifles worked on it in gold.

He was either one of the most impressive sights or the silliest old son of a bitch McKay had ever seen.

As it had been the home of Fort Sam Houston and a passel of other military facilities, San Antonio, Texas had collected its own pair of megaton-range airbursts during the One-Day War, with the usual effects. Escorted by Callahan and his command, which had suffered blessedly few casualties in the previous day's attack, the Guardians could see that the tract homes in the rocky hills on the north side of town showed disproportionate fire and blast damage, thanks to focusing by meteorological conditions at the time of the blasts.

The San Antonio Valley had been a pleasant, fairly well-watered area in the old days, though like most of the West it had been hit hard by the drought of the early Nineties. The War had brought rains such as the region hadn't known for a geological epoch or two. Now, once well-mannered shrubs and lawns had damn near taken over, cracking foundations, softening the outlines of collapsed frame-stucco walls and fallen roofs.

Like most arteries leading into or out of most cities of any size across the country, Interstate 10 had been jammed with thousands of cars fleeing the warning siren when the warheads flashed off. But from the L-1604 ring road inward the blistered, sun-faded, rusted-out hulks had been pushed onto the shoulder, clearing the lanes of traffic.

"They've been working hard around here to put things back together," Callahan called up from his motorcycle, riding alongside Mobile One. He grinned and gave a thumbs-up to a work gang breaking down hulks beside the burned-out shell of a semiconductor plant. They waved back and hooted greeting. One, optimistically barechested in the morning sunlight, swung his shirt around over his straw cowboy hat and shouted. His breath was visible.

McKay was back on turret duty, riding out in the air. "Yeah. So were the folks in Kansas City. You remember them, don't you?"

Callahan laughed, his teeth very light against his tanned face. "I remember."

"Yeah. Sure." The mayor of K.C., the allegedly Honorable Dexter White, had sold out the Guardians, India Twenty-Three and President MacGregor to the Effsee occupiers. Only the timely—if not exactly accidental—intervention of Callahan and his motorcycle gang had enabled them to get away with all their parts.

Downtown had been outside the primary effects zones of both blasts, though the one that took out Fort Sam hadn't gone off that far away. Thanks to the blast-shadowing effects of city center buildings, damage was sporadic, freakish. Areas of total devastation were interspersed with blocks where the glass wasn't even broken.

"The usual," McKay said as they picked their way through the streets west of the river. There were a few people out and around, some on bikes, a few in cars. A girl with a blond ponytail and a sheepskin jacket, riding on a humongous palomino that looked as if it had a beer wagon somewhere in its past, smiled and waved.

"Funny how quickly we got used to bombed-out streets, accepting them as normal," Sloan said.

McKay shrugged. "They are, these days."

Enough of the city had survived for the Guardians to get a feel for what it had been like—and maybe still was. Just as trashed-out blocks alternated with relatively untouched areas, little twisty treelined streets with funny Spanish-looking houses alternated with clumps of the glass box and pre-stressed concrete Bauhaus crap that disfigured most cities of the entire Western world. It was a far cry from the grimy rowhouses and tenements

of McKay's Pittsburgh childhood, but it gave him the feel of
a place where people actually used to live, instead of just
commuted to.

And maybe still did live. Down one side street he saw a
flock of kids scrambling around a stripped city bus under the
supervision of a stocky young woman with straight black Indian
hair and a pistol belt. They laughed and pointed at the convoy.
They showed no fear of armed men or the armored vehicle.

The nerve center of the Republic of Texas was housed in
the black glass tower the city fathers had stuck on the site of
the old city hall in the middle of Military Plaza during the great
boom of federally-funded urban restructuring not long before
the War. It was restricted to the lower half of the building,
because another freak of dynamic overpressure had sheared off
the top of the building at a funny angle, leaving it looking like
a hound's tooth. A few twisted red-rust girders still stuck up
into the morning sky.

Callahan grandly led Mobile One down Camaron Street and
stopped with the truncated black tower on one side and the
whitewashed adobe walls of the Spanish Governor's Palace on
the other Lt. Sherri gave her CO the finger by way of salute
and took the rest of the unit off somewhere to rest and refit.

Callahan parked his bike and gestured for the Guardians to
dismount. "This is the Republic," he explained. "You could
leave that sucker unlocked with the keys inside."

Leaving the car unattended in unfamiliar territory was not
McKay's favorite idea in the world, but it would look real silly
to leave one or another Guardian parked out front with it like
a chauffeur. Besides, much as he hated to admit it, he trusted
Callahan not to lead them into traps, and he trusted the dreadlocked biker's judgment. Even if he wasn't willing to swallow
that last statement whole.

The Guardians deassed the car, made it secure and trooped
up broad cement steps past another of the ubiquitous work
parties. This one was noisily busy with sledgehammers and
oxyacetylene torches, dismantling a red metal statue that looked
like a Cubist portrayal of a Caterpillar carryall crippled by
anxiety. Callahan held the glass doors open.

"Don't expect a tip," McKay growled as they passed.

Callahan led them up three flights of stairs—the elevator
housing had gone to Jesus with the upper half of the building—

and left them among the potted ferns in the foyer of the president's office.

"What's the matter, Dreadlock, don't you rate an interview with His Nibs?" Sloan asked. "Thought you and he were on a first-name basis."

"I've seen a president," Callahan said. "More than one, as a matter of fact. I'll be down in the cafeteria; catch you later." He waggled them a hang-loose sign, loose fist with thumb and little finger extended, and strolled away.

President LaRousse poured the drinks from the sideboard himself. McKay was the only one who asked for anything alcoholic—Jack Daniels straight up—and he mentally damned his buddies as pussies for choosing fruit juice.

LaRousse settled himself behind the desk with his own man-sized jolt of Evil Jack and crossed a handtooled boot over his knee. "I've heard a great deal about you gentlemen," he said, in a voice that argued long acquaintance with the Daniels clan, as well as enough cigars and cigarettes to make a surgeon general pop an aneurysm, "and if even half of what I've heard is true, I'm impressed."

He sipped his whiskey. "Of course I've heard a lot of it from your friend Major Callahan, and he's damned near as big a liar as I am myself."

"We deny everything," Sloan said with a grin.

"How about Forrie Smith?" McKay said. "He's had a thing or two to say about us."

LaRousse regarded him with a gaze as level and hard as sheet steel. "Lieutenant McKay, as you may be aware, I am an artist." He waved a hand at the paintings on the walls. "I even enjoyed a certain renown, though I never attained much critical success; never could get the hang of following the latest fashions. Be that as it may, for an artist to work, he must have a sense of proportion.

"Now, Major Callahan and myself are the artist breed of liars. The only way to distort the truth artistically is to know the truth. The young Mr. Smith, on the other hand, is a pathological case; he lies as naturally as he breathes, and wouldn't know a truth if one bit him on the fanny."

McKay eyed him across his drink and wondered what the hell to make of him.

"So now that we know all about each other," LaRousse said, "to what do I owe the honor of your presence?"

McKay looked to Sloan. "You tell the man, Sam. You tell it prettier than I do."

Sam cocked an eyebrow. "*The whole thing,*" McKay subvocalized. "*He's the law west of the Pecos.*"

"*We're east of the Pecos, McKay.*"

"*Nobody likes a smartass.*"

President LaRousse heard the story in silence. When it was finished he stood up and poured himself another. Sloan accepted a refill on his orange juice; the others stood pat.

"Water's been less of a problem, the last year or so," he said, seating himself. "But it's still a problem, especially when summer rolls around. And there's no way of knowing how long the wet weather will last. Is it just a transient effect left over from the War, or a long-term trend?"

Sam shrugged. "We can't answer that, Mr. President."

"Lamar, son. Nobody can answer that, and there aren't enough data points for an informed guess. But I think a guaranteed source of fresh water from your desal plant would do a mess of good for a whole lot of folks, and not just here in the Republic. I can promise you full cooperation."

"Great," McKay said. "For a start, how about telling us who the hell strafed us yesterday? They blistered the paint on Sloan, over there, and it's hard to get replacement Guardians."

LaRousse frowned. "Didn't Major Callahan tell you? That was the United States Air Force. Or so Governor Hedison tells it. He runs Federal Texas. The half of the state that never seceded."

CHAPTER
EIGHT ————————————————

After a while the silence started to build up to the point where it threatened to blow out the polarized-glass window overlooking the Palace across the street.

"Did I say something wrong?" LaRousse asked.

"Uh, well, no, your Hon—ah, Lamar," Sam Sloan said. "It's just that we don't know all the ins and outs of Texas politics these days."

"Speaks well for you, son. I could never make hide nor hair of Texas politics myself."

"What the hell is this about seceding?" McKay grated.

LaRousse looked at him with mildness that was as surprising as it was deceptive. "It's how things are, Lieutenant. The War brought it on. Oh, we didn't make it official until Wild Bill Lowell turned up with his FSE trash and tried to turn the whole country back into a colony of Europe. But all declaring our independence did was recognize a condition that already existed. The United States are defunct, gentlemen."

McKay stood up, went to the window and stared down, as a purple flush worked its way up his thick neck. A small rental trailer rolled along the street below, drawn by a pair of horses, one brown, one blotched black and white. He was sure there were fancy-ass names for horse colors, but he didn't have a clue as to what they might be.

He raised a fist. It took all his effort to keep from smashing it against the glass. It was probably bulletproof anyway.

Eventually he turned back around. Sloan and Casey were looking at him, trying not to show concern. Tom Rogers just sat and looked at nothing and saw everything, as usual.

"Bullshit," McKay said.

Sloan sucked his breath in. LaRousse's face never flickered.

"What is, Lieutenant?"

"What you just said. America's down. But it ain't out."

"I think we have a difference of opinion here. Be that as it may, the Republic of Texas is a nation, sovereign and independent, determined to seek her own destiny. If the United States pulls itself together, we shall welcome its friendship and offer our own. But we're prepared to go it alone. As we've gone it up until now."

For a moment McKay stood there breathing through distended nostrils. What he'd heard sickened him straight down to the core. But he didn't know what he could say, what he could do. And somehow his usual solution to any dilemma, which was to start hitting people, didn't seem too appropriate.

"Why did the Federal Texans, as you call them, attack us, sir?" Sloan asked.

"Our relations with our sibling aren't exactly friendly. Not that a state of war exists between us. But Governor Hedison has notions of reuniting the state by force. Incidents like this aren't exactly unusual."

Sloan glanced at McKay. McKay didn't look as if he trusted himself to speak. That was fine. Sloan didn't trust him to speak, either.

"This puts us in a kind of unusual position, President LaRousse," Sam said.

"I understand, Commander."

"On the other hand, Governor Hedison hasn't seen fit to confide his plans to the government of the United States. So I'm unclear as to the legality of his actions." Sam ran a hand through his hair. "This beats hell out of me, Mr. President."

LaRousse laughed softly. "That's fair enough. My offer of assistance still stands."

Sam flipped another look sideways at McKay. The Guardians' fealess leader was still doing a slow and obvious burn.

Now, in spite of the traditional naval opinion of members of their sister service, and in spite of the way they ragged on each other, Sloan knew Billy McKay was no dummy. He was one of the more intelligent men he'd ever met, and despite the fact that Sloan had a college degree and a rank equivalent to major when he was picked to be a Guardian, he had concurred with the choice of McKay, then as now a lieutenant with a high school education, for leader.

But there were times when the engine simply overloaded. McKay was as hot under the collar as Sloan had ever seen him. McKay's brain was like a computer: If it got too hot, it just sort of shut down.

About then Tom Rogers caught Sloan's eye. Like McKay, Sloan had come to rely on the ex–Green Beret's judgment the way he relied on the sun coming up in the east. *Uh-oh,* he thought.

"Mr. President—Lamar. If you'd excuse us a moment?"

LaRousse nodded. "Certainly."

The Guardians got McKay into the waiting room as the president's receptionist, an attractive middle-aged Hispanic woman with gray streaking her heavy black hair and green eyes as startling as any Sloan had ever seen, put down the phone, smiled at them politely, and left, obviously having received The Word to make herself scarce.

"Sit down, McKay," Sloan said. McKay glared at him.

"Billy," Tom said softly. McKay sat down in the receptionist's chair with his arms folded across his chest, looking like an enormous sulky child.

"That fist-fucking old son of a bitch," McKay said. He slammed a fist down on the arm of the chair and stood up. "That treasonous old bastard. I got half a mind to go in there—"

"Half a mind is just about right," Tom said.

McKay had his head lowered as if he planned to butt his way through the massive carven oak door into the president's office like a bull. He raised his head and blinked at Tom. Rogers hardly ever said a harsh word to anybody.

McKay sat.

Casey was glancing in all directions from behind his yellow Zeiss shooting glasses. "What if the room's bugged, man?" he whispered.

"If it is, they can hear you whether you speak up or not,"

Sam pointed out. "But I don't think it is."

He took a deep breath. "All right, McKay. I know what's eating you. But we've got a mission to accomplish. And it hasn't got one damned thing to do with reconquering half the state of Texas."

"But it's treason, goddamn it. He's talking about seceding!"

"No, he's not. He's *already* seceded."

McKay was turning purple again.

"Look, McKay, I know America's sacred to you. That's fine; we all feel the same way." *Funny how strange it seems to say so, though.* "But that's why our mission is so important. The quicker Project Blueprint comes on line, the quicker America can be made strong again—whole again."

"But working with traitors—"

"Who the hell is always telling me we can't save the world? That the mission is everything? We need to work with these people if we're going to have a hope in hell of reclaiming that facility. Listen, Marine, the time has come to shut up and marine!"

For a moment Sloan thought McKay was going to come up out of that chair and maul him. His fingers clutched the chair arms so tight the knuckles threatened to pop through the skin, and his trapezius muscles were bunched so far his neck sort of disappeared between them.

"Billy," Tom said, "he's right. We got a job to do, and we got to play the hand we're dealt."

McKay sat there, knotted so tight that Sloan was afraid in another minute he'd collapse in on himself like a star turning into a black hole. Then he shook himself all over, blew out his breath like a horse coming off the track.

"Yeah. You're right. But I sure as hell don't have to like it."

Sloan fixed his eyes on McKay's. "That's right. You sure as hell don't have to like it."

At Sloan's knock LaRousse called for them to come right in. He gestured for them to sit as if nothing had happened.

"We've decided to take you up on your offer, Mr. President," Sloan said. "When can we set out?"

LaRousse was sitting back in his chair with his legs crossed and his fingers steepled before his crag of a chin. "There's just one small problem."

McKay hissed in a breath. It sounded just like a fuse burning, which it was.

"What's that, Mr. President?" Sloan asked quickly, hoping to hell LaRousse hadn't decided to jack them around.

"The cristeros."

"Sir?"

"It's Spanish, son. Means 'Christers,' literally. In this case, soldiers of Christ. The Cristero Rebellion was a messianic revolutionary movement in Mexico, back in the Twenties and Thirties."

"Something like liberation theology?"

"A little bit. More traditional, more—how the hell would I put it? More charismatic." He sampled his whiskey, let it roll around inside his mouth for a few heartbeats. "A real popular movement, a peasant movement. Not a game for middle-class intellectuals like liberation theology. From the soil and from the heart."

"What's that got to do with us?" growled McKay.

Sloan had the impression that LaRousse's eyes narrowed ever so slightly. He wondered how much the president had heard of the conversation outside his door. Even if the anteroom really wasn't bugged, the soundproofing hadn't been born that could stifle the bellow of Billy McKay in full voice.

LaRousse let his gaze drift out the window. "No day to be cooped up inside," he said, half to himself. "Just look at that light—glorious."

He sighed mountainously. "You're familiar with the name Enrique Córdoba O'Malley?"

"The president of Mexico?" Sam asked.

"That's the one. He held the country together after the War, pretty much on force of personality alone. Before the War, too; things got pretty shaggy down there when the PRI fell off its perch after ruling the roost for three-quarters of a century. But he kept the army on a short lead and started getting the government off the backs of the people, which staved off a popular revolution. And then not two months after the bombs fell the Cubans and Nicaraguans did him the favor of invading."

"And he kicked their asses," McKay said, almost cheerfully. There was nothing that could lighten him up like thinking about commies getting their asses kicked.

"And grabbed off most of Guatemala in the process. Not

something he really wanted to do, but it got the army off his back, let him keep his reforms going." LaRousse gave a gravel-pit laugh. "And isn't that just the old story? 'I didn't want to be an imperialist, but I had to do it.' But Ric was an honest man, as politicians go, a decent man. Used to go hunting javelinas with him, down on the Nueces. Jesus, that man could drink.

"One thing Córdoba was big on, and that was not taking advantage of the little embarrassment suffered by Mexico's neighbor to the north. There was a lot of talk about paying off old scores with the gringos, and some pretty frank discussion of all the loot left lying around north of the Rio Grande. But Ric'd have none of it. It wasn't the Christian thing to do, he said. Of course, that wasn't his real reason. He ready history, Ric did, and he knew that no matter how soft the *nor-teamericanos* look, no matter how ripe for the plucking, they make very bad enemies, very bad indeed."

"We heard a rumor President Córdoba was assassinated," Tom Rogers said.

LaRousse nodded. "About six weeks ago. Since then the country's gone to hell. Revolts breaking out everywhere, everyone from the communists to the ultranationalists. The army and the national police forces—they have dozens of them—too busy battling each other to be much use.

"Now, back last fall, a lot of people started flocking to hear a new prophet, down in San Luis Potosí, called herself Hermana Luz—Sister Light. Sixteen-year-old virgin, promising the immediate return of the Messiah and the kingdom of heaven. Nothing out of the ordinary, for Mexico. But after Ric bought it—" He shook his head. "This Sister Light called it the judg-ment of Heaven and whistled up the faithful to form the army of Christ the King and scourge the unrighteous."

"Which means you been invaded," Billy McKay said.

"That's right. One of the first points on her agenda was to bring retribution to the faithless gringo. Now, as it happens, the unrighteous included most of the populace of northern Mexico, which lay between the cristeros and us, and the nor-teños really are unrighteous. Mean as hell and proud of it. That gave us some breathing space.

"But eight days ago the cristeros crossed the river near Piedras Negras, about a hundred twenty-five miles from here. We stopped that thrust at Carrizo Springs, but since then we have reports they've been swarming across clear down to Brownsville.''

"How organized are they?" Tom Rogers asked.

"Like I said, son, it's a popular movement. Which means not very. Still . . ." He frowned. "They've pulled some slick maneuvers on us in a few places. Usually they rely on the good old human wave, and they got the numbers to make it work more than we'd like; ammunition doesn't grow in the ground down here—soil's too thin. But once or twice, they've foxed us good. Best we reckon is, they've got a few former military types advising them.''

"So you want us to pull your chestnuts out of the fire," McKay said.

This time LaRousse gave him an unmistakably hard look. "Son, we can shoot our own sidewinders. But if the cristeros really bust loose, we can't guarantee how secure this Houston plant of yours is going to be. So it's in both our interests to work together.''

McKay rubbed his chin. Much as he hated to admit it, this long-haired old windbag made sense. "Maybe we better check it out.''

"When do you reckon heading out? You're welcome to stay here and enjoy our hospitality as long as you like, of course. . . .''

McKay cocked an eyebrow and glanced around. "I don't have any pressing engagements," Sam Sloan said, setting both feet on the tiles.

"Yeah. How about we leave right now?"

LaRousse nodded. "I'll let our commander in Carrizo Springs know to expect you." He rapped his knuckles against his right shin. They made a loud, hollow *clonk*.

McKay jerked his head back, stared. "No need to burn your eyes, son," LaRousse said gently. "It's plastic. Left my hind leg from the knee down at Frozen Chosin. Frostbite and a Chicom bullet.''

"Chosin Reservoir? North Korea?"

"You got it. Lovely place in the winter. I was a Marine before you were born, McKay. And you might remember that next time you get the hankering to go slinging words like *traitor* around.''

CHAPTER
NINE ─────────────────────

"Incoming!" McKay yelled, and threw himself face down in the dirt next to Mobile One. A millisecond later Sam flopped down beside him as the whistling whine crescendoed.

Black earth fountained against white sky several hundred meters away. Corporal Rita Montañez looked down at the prostrate pair of Guardians with curious dark eyes. "It's all right," she said. "They're just shooting wild. They never get any closer than that. They don't know anything about artillery spotting."

"Great," McKay said, picking himself up and brushing crumbs of sticky black earth from his face and uniform. He was pissed at himself for diving for dirt like a newbie at the sound of the mortar round. Not that diving was a bad idea, as a general thing—but he should have been able to tell it wasn't coming anywhere close. *You're losing your edge, McKay.*

"Don't you know how dangerous artillery is?" Sam Sloan asked, spitting out dirt and puffs of condensation. He was clearly as torqued at being shown up by a teenaged girl as McKay was. Only he'd die rather than admit it; that wouldn't be liberated.

Montañez shrugged. "If your name's on it, that's it for you. Why hassle it?"

She tightened the strap of her coalscuttle helmet. It was outsized and made her look even smaller and younger than she was. She had a foxy narrow face, with freckles dusted liberally across a straight nose, that made an odd but not unpleasant contrast with the deep olive of her complexion. She was a Mexican national, though she'd been raised in nearby Crystal City, and spoke with a Tex-Mex drawl. She hailed from Zacatecas, "the Lair of Wild Women," as she'd earnestly informed them on the ride from San Antone. None of the Guardians had had the nerve to ask her what the hell that meant. She was their guide.

A gangly black kid in cammies was sort of hopping from one foot to the other and glancing nervously around the former onion field as if expecting the Living Dead to start popping up out of it. "CP's in a old architect's office, over on Valverde," he said, "or was last I heard. City Hall's burning—that's all that smoke you see. Been pressin' us mighty hard today."

"They got any antitank?"

"Now, how the hell would I know that, Rita?"

"Corporal Montañez to you."

"Awright, Corporal. They sure enough got Molotov cocktails, that much I do know."

The arrhythmic *pop-pop-pop* of a firefight in progress was coming out of the town. Montañez stuck her thumb in her web gear and cocked her head at McKay. "Well? Up to going on?"

"That's what we came for, Corporal," Sloan answered for him.

She turned and scrambled up the side of Mobile One, taking a seat just in front of the turret. "Let's go."

"What the hell do you think you're doing up there?" McKay demanded.

"What, *vato*, you think I'm crazy?" *Vato* was an uncomplimentary word that roughly meant *blondie*, he gathered. She'd already used it a couple of times on the drive out from San Antonio. "I don't want to get burned up if they do have any LAWs."

"What about stray chunks of lead?"

She shrugged. "Come on. *Andale*."

"*I don't know if she needs a spanking or a medal worse*," McKay subvocalized. He ducked into the car, came out with his lightweight Maremont M-603E machinegun in one hand and a stiff folded item in the other.

"Here. Put this on."

"What is it?" she asked suspiciously.

"Kevlar vest. Body armor. Give you a little protection, at least."

She jutted her sharp little chin and shook her head. "No way, man. Not when my buddies got no armor."

"Put it on, you little bitch, or I'm gonna whip your ass."

Her response was to swing up her M-16 so that the muzzle brake was about ten centimeters from the most prominent break in his nose. There was about to be serious mayhem when Tom Rogers stuck his head out the topside turret hatch and spoke to the girl in low, rapid Spanish. After a moment she dropped her head, set the rifle down on the sloped frontal armor, and held out a hand for the vest.

She took off her helmet. Her hair was short, curly, and red. She eeled into the vest. McKay started to say something. Tom caught his eye and fractionally shook his head. He vanished back inside the turret and shut the lid.

McKay shrugged, slipped the 60's sling over his head, and climbed up beside the girl. "All right, Rambette, lead the way. And keep in mind, we're gonna have to ditch this thing if Tom has to open fire. Muzzle blast alone of these guns'll tear the clothes right off you."

"Don't you wish."

He couldn't help a sidelong glance at her. Bulky as her OD fatigues were they showed enough to make him realize he wouldn't mind seeing more. She wasn't *that* young.

Carrizo Springs was a mean, hard-edged little town that somehow had a feel of the temporary about it. Like most of the country, it had been hit hard by the economic troubles of the years before the War. Of course, compared to how things were now, those were boom years.

The air was thick with smoke. They passed little knots of Texicans peering out of tract-house windows and huddling between hulks of used-car lots. Maybe half of them wore uniforms of any type, and that was if you wanted to count stuff like cammie blouses from K-Mart. The one thing they had in common was they all looked shit-scared.

Firing had lulled out ahead. Now it started to pick up again, a crack, a pause, another crack, then two more, then many, gathering volume and speed like popcorn in a popper, punctuated by the thud of grenades. McKay cracked the feed tray of his M-60, made sure the fifty-round belt coiled inside the plastic half-moon box hung on the weapon's side wasn't twisted.

This was one of those Texan towns where the main drag went through straight as a shot. Casey nosed the car out from behind an Exxon station, and McKay climbed down the glacis and craned around, holding the chopped M-60 at the ready, just as if the backblast wouldn't knock him off onto his ass if he had to fire it. He was beginning to think this wasn't such a good idea, trying to out-macho some teenybopper who came from somewhere she claimed was called the Lair of Wild Women.

Visibility dwindled until it was chopped off for good at about a click by the smoke from burning buildings and upset cars. McKay made out movement through the smoke that hugged the street like a dirty fogbank. In a moment he saw what appeared to be a parade come marching through the swirling crud, holding up banners and generally carrying on.

"Well, here comes either the Shriners or the bad guys," McKay reported.

"Shall I pull up so Sam can fire them up?" Casey asked.

"We can't open fire until we're sure, McKay" Sloan said.

"What, you think the town fathers are holding a parade in honor of our comin' to rescue 'em?"

"Cristeros." Corporal Rita spat the word like a bobcat. The olive in her face had washed out from under the freckles.

"If that's true, why aren't the Republicans dropping artillery on them?" Sloan had trouble with the word *Texican*; he seemed to think it was an insult, like *spic* or *nigger*.

It was a good question. "Some fuckup," McKay said. "These fucking Johnny Rebs run a pretty Third World operation, if you ask me."

That got him a hot look from their guide. Before she could speak up, a shift of wind brought a new sound wafting over the crackle of the firefight going on somewhere out of sight.

"What the fuck, over?" McKay asked.

"They're singing," Rita said grimly. "*Viva la Virgen de Guadalupe*. It's like an anthem for Mexican people." This time she literally spat. "Pigs."

About that time some keen lad up front of the procession spotted the wedge-shaped snout of the armored car, and the enormous man and tiny teenager perched on it like turtles on a half-sunken log. A scatter of muzzle-flashes winked through the smoke-haze.

"That settles that," McKay said. "Case, pull up enough so Sloan can fire 'em up. You, come with me."

The kid hung back. "They can't hit us at this range!"

"Never heard of getting lucky? Besides, it's our own guns you should be worrying about." He grabbed her by the wrist and hauled her bodily down, half expecting to get a knife across the back of his hand for his pains.

Casey pulled the car forward while McKay dragged Rita behind a trio of dusty, faded gas pumps standing like decommissioned robots with their fingers in their ears. Nothing happened.

"Sloan, rock and roll. What is the hangup here?"

"I—I can't. They're civilians."

"So what do you think the road gypsies are, regulars? Shoot goddamn it."

Still Sloan hesitated. McKay wondered what he would do if Sloan refused a direct order.

Then the whole universe reverberated to a terrible noise. Rita let her M-16 fall on its sling, clapped hands to her ears and went to her knees. McKay pulled his head down between his shoulders, and wished he'd had sense to go around behind the car, where he'd have been farther out of the tremendous muzzle blast of the turret guns.

He saw cristeros bowled back up the street like tumbleweeds by the thumb-thick .50-caliber slugs. Then forty-millimeter grenades were cracking off, standard Guardians party mix, two HEDP to one white phosphorus, tough on armored vehicles up to light tanks, hard death on unprotected folks on foot. Burning banners toppled to the street.

Three short bursts and the street was clear but for smoke and bodies.

"That wasn't so tough," McKay said, tearing the plastic wrap on an Indonesian cigar with his teeth. He could barely hear himself. "Let's drive on."

Rita led them down a couple of side streets, past trashy cinderblock apartments with paint peeling from them like sunburned skin, a laundry next to a video store that still had CLOSED BY ORDER OF THE DEPARTMENT OF ENERGY plastered on its front door over a poster of Merith Tobias in skintight

clothes, standing in front of a spaceship and a lot of stars with
a fancy si-fi rifle in the patrol position, advertising the cassette
release of *Rissa Kerguelen*. McKay was sorry he's missed that
one.

"This one," Rita said, gesturing. *"Derecha."*

Mobile One turned the corner.

A bullet spanged off the front of the turret between them
with a bright gong sound, leaving a smear of copper jacket on
the armor plate and tumbling away past Rita's ear with a sick
banshee whine.

"Off," McKay bellowed. He rolled left off the car without
waiting to see if his advice was followed. His old-fashioned
male-chauvinist chivalry went only so far. If girls like Rita
thought it was their God-given right to put their attractive asses
on the firing line, it was likewise their right to get them shot off.

A two-story apartment complex rose on the left side of a
tree-lined street that would have been pleasant had the trees
along both sides been green and a few less buldings been on
fire. Across from it sat a two-story Victorian gingerbread house
with a pitched roof and old-timey gables and an ornate wooden
sign that read ROYCE & WIDEMAN, ARCHITECTS swinging from
an L-shaped frame in front of it. The sign had bullet holes in
it, and the stucco on the facade was starred and split from high-
velocity impacts. As McKay glanced at the house past the rear
of Mobile One's traversing turret a muzzle flash flamed inside
a darkened, shot-out window, spraying the apartments.

That was enough for McKay. He swiveled left, bringing the
big M-60 up at the waist as he turned. He was mostly playing
Arnold Schwarzenegger, not really expecting to see anything,
figuring the defenders in the Texican CP were just busting caps
to keep the guys' heads down.

What he saw was a stocky man aiming some kind of longarm
at him from the wrought iron railing of the second floor.

"Jesus." He triggered a four-round burst. And missed. It
was about what you could expect, hip-firing like that.

While it wasn't any earth-shaking fifty-caliber boomer, the
M-60 had quite a blast to it. The dude at the rail flinched away
from the sound and fury. McKay decided he'd rather have
sound procedure go to hell than him, and he just held the trigger
down, hosing a dangerously long burst all over the cheap motel
front of the apartment building. The man went splaying back
against a door so violently it caved in. He left big bright patches

of red on the cheap stucco to either side.

Mobile One rocked back on its suspension to the recoil of its .50. Sloan was playing conservative. The WP grenades would certainly send the cheap apartment up like a Roman candle, and they were too close to the Texican HQ for a major conflagration to be a real good idea.

McKay saw Corporal Rita gesturing to him across the car's rear deck. He raised plaster dust with a last five-round burst on GPs, then ducked and ran around the rear of the V-450 to follow the little redhead up onto the porch.

A cowboy was lying behind sandbags, half under a porch swing that was swaying lazily in the random afternoon breeze. He goggled up at McKay from behind his M-16. McKay nodded. Montañez went in without knocking. He followed.

The reception room was empty except for a desk with an unlit kerosene lamp and a pile of ration packs on it, and several big pots with dry, withered sticks jutting up out of them, placed at strategic locations around the room. Montañez pushed back into an office from which voices rattled urgently.

A map of the town was spread out on a drafting table. A party McKay took for the CO of this crazy outfit was standing over it with his head down, yelling into a radio handset which he held in one hand, holding what after a moment's astonishment McKay realized with approval as a Thompson M-1A1—a genuine tommy gun, vintage WWII—in the other, while aides ran around doing things.

''—more ammo for the mortars we got left,'' he was saying, in a voice surprisingly high for a six-footer in cammies and OD baseball cap. ''We need some fire support real quick, y'all. Do it now. Out.''

The commander slammed down the mircrophone, shaking his head. Then he looked up into McKay's eyes with big gray ones.

In half a second he was around the table, with his arms flung around McKay's bull neck, Thompson and all, planting a wet kiss spang on his mouth.

CHAPTER
TEN ──────────────────

"Jesus Christ!" McKay roared. He jerked his head back as if the Texican officer's lips were red-hot.

The Texican scowled under the brim of the baseball cap. "Is that any way to greet an old comrade-in-arms?"

"I ain't no comrade-in-arms with no fuckin' fruitba— Marla?" McKay pushed the officer back to arm's length and blinked. "Marla? Marla Eklund?"

"Thought of getting your eyes checked, Yankee?"

He wondered if maybe she had a point. Even her tentlike battledress and the poor yellow light of a lone kerosene lamp weren't enough to disguise the fact she was female. And how many beautiful, six-foot, blond lady bodybuilders were there running around loose?

"So I'm under a lotta stress," he grumbled. "What the hell are you doin' here?"

She grimaced. "Runnin' a fighting retreat, looks like."

McKay tried to step back. The sling snapped tight behind his neck; their weapons were locked.

"The perils of modern romance," Marla remarked. She reeled him in and kissed him again. He didn't put up anywhere near as much of a fight this time.

The rising crackle of small arms fire outside didn't leave

them much time for it. They broke the clinch almost at once and disentangled their pieces.

"Colonel?"

McKay glanced back over his shoulder at the door. A stocky little dark guy stood there, with droopy-lidded black eyes and a sparse black fringe of beard at the bottom of his round face. He had on a pinstriped brown shirt over gray work pants and carried a battered side by side shotgun.

McKay whirled, brought the M-60 to bear on the center of the man's paunch. The man jumped back, not looking so sleepy anymore.

"What's he doing here?" McKay demanded.

"Defendin' his home," one of Marla's staff drawled, "just like the rest of us."

McKay let the '60's muzzle droop toward the floor. The newcomer spat something in Spanish and edged past to murmur something in Eklund's ear. She had to stoop to catch it. McKay stood gazing up at the sooty gloom of the ceiling, uncomfortable with the Texicans' eyes on him. He'd just made a major jerkoff of himself. Again.

An explosion rained plaster dust in his eyes and jarred him almost off his feet. The Hispanic fell into the map table and knocked it over. Rita Montañez barely fielded the kerosene lamp before it hit the scarred hardwood floor.

"Tom! Case! Are you all right?" McKay subvocalized.

"Fine, Billy," Tom came back.

"What the fuck was that?"

"Dynamite bomb. Cristeros're working their way through the houses along this side of the street."

Another blast rocketed the house. "Here they come!" a high-pitched cowboy voice rang out.

Eklund frowned. "All right, everybody move on out. Rally on the edge of town. They come on too strong, push on to the Castillo farmhouse." She was slapping shoulders as her crew policed up their weaons and hustled out.

McKay elbowed past, dashed onto the porch. The street was full of smoke and noise. Mobile One had pulled into the center of the street to rake both sides with fire. Tom had bailed out and was trying to make the opposition keep its distance, firing across One's rear deck with a futuristic-looking Franchi SPAS-12 shotgun liberated from the Effsees in California.

McKay went to one knee, slamming the M-60 down on the

splintered rail on the south side of the porch. The wall of the next converted house was only five meters away.

A skinny Texican with a shock of graying brown hair and civilian clothes was hunkered over his M-16 next to McKay. He shook his head. "Them puppies're at eye-gouging distance, and that's the truth."

His eyes went wide, and he rocked back onto his haunches. A stream of blood as big around as his finger hosed out of his neck in huge spurts, spraying the right side of McKay's face and body when he reached up to staunch it with a grease black-ened thumb. "S-sorry," he gagged, and then keeled over onto the gray-painted floorboards.

McKay snugged the MG's steel buttplate against his shoulder with his left hand and fired a long burst. A horizontal blizzard of brick dust exploded from the side of the other building, stinging his cheek with high-velocity grit. A Mexican flew back from the nearest window with a scream as the jacketed 7.62 slugs clawed at him.

A bullet cracked past McKay's head. He ducked, snapped his head left. Cristeros were running across the streets from the apartment complex, ducked down beneath a stream of bullets from Mobile One's turret .50, which was tearing black chunks out of asphalt forty meters down Valverde as Sloan tried futilely to force the MG's barrel lower. They fired as they came.

Fortunately they hadn't mastered the art of firing on the run—which wasn't surprising, since hardly anyone ever does. Bullets peppered the porch as randomly as hail while McKay tried to make himself as narrow as the corner upright. A cristero went down with his guts unraveling from a charge of double-ought from Tom's 12-guage, and then they were on the withered lawn, howling like wolves.

One of the problems with playing Chuck Norris with M-60s, even one that came in at a "lightweight" eight and a half kilos, even if you were as strong as Billy McKay, was that you couldn't hurry the sons of bitches. They had *mass*. No matter how much you wanted one to be a submachine gun, it was a huge, honking, full-dress MG and wouldn't let you forget it. The muscles in his sides and shoulers cracking, McKay tried to swing the thing around in time, knowing he couldn't, wondering if he should just blow it off and draw his .45.

A cristero with a handkerchief tied around his neck jumped

up on the porch and aimed a chrome-shiny revolver as long as
his arm at McKay. Marla Eklund loomed up in the door and
gave him three of the best from her tommy gun. The .45-caliber
bullets spun him off the porch like a ballerina on speed.

She chopped down two more with quick bursts, firing with
the piece tucked under her arm, just like the manual said. A
third hit dirt and rolled up against the porch. A Texican ran
past Eklund onto the walk, turned and jittered as if running in
place, excitedly pumping single rounds into the cristero.

A bullet thunked the porch railing. McKay sprayed the house
next door to keep the occupants honest. There were Texicans
retreating up Valverde toward them, some pausing to fire, some
running flat-out. Not even Billy McKay could blame the ones
who choose to boogie; the cristeros were washing up the street
like a tide, and not even Mobile One's turret guns were making
much impression.

A cristero screamed *"Santiago,"* and cocked back his arm
to throw a Molotov at Mobile One. Rita Montañez popped up
next to Eklund and shot him as he threw. The gasoline bomb
fell short and splashed the street right in front of Royce &
Wideman. The firespill caught a fleeing Texican; he came out
with hair and uniform blazing, hit the street, rolling over and
over to extinguish the flames. One of his buddies threw a coat
over him to damp the fire, and another helped him up and into
a staggering run down the block.

"Everybody out?" McKay shouted at Eklund.

"Affirmative."

"Time to go," McKay said. He wasn't going to risk Mobile
One—or any hard-to-replace Guardians—any longer in somebody else's fight. He stood up, blazed off the rest of his half-
moon box at the charging crowd and took off for the car.
Montañez and Eklund pelted at his heels.

At the curb Montañez stumbled, half turned, almost fell.
Eklund got an arm around the little redhead's waist, hauled her
back to her feet. McKay grabbed her wrist and practically threw
her into Mobile One.

He faced Eklund. "What the hell are you waiting for?"

She was feeding a fresh magazine into her Thompson, ignoring the bullets ringing off hull-metal centimeters away from
her. "I'll fight my way out with my men."

"Bullshit! If it's a bugout, then bug out right—"

An invisible Godzilla hand whupped them upside Mobile

One. Royce & Wideman's porch collapsed, its supports knocked loose by a dynamite bomb. Eklund swallowed hard and dove into the car.

McKay hopped up after her, then spun in the door, letting the Maremont hang on its sling as he whipped his Colt from its holster. There was a cristero sprinting for the open side door of the car not ten meters behind him. McKay's shot knocked off the right side off his head, and Casey peeled out, pausing as he took the corner to let four or five Texican troopies clamber aboard.

"Christ, what a fuckup," McKay said from the open door as Molotov flame splashed the intersection behind them. "Eklund, I thought you'd handle something like this a shitload better."

Eklund glanced up at him, looked hurriedly away. "We held them as long as we needed to," Montañez said idignantly from where she was stacked against the hull. She coughed into a freckled fist.

"And what's this 'Colonel' shit? Last time I noticed, it was Staff Sergeant."

"Lieutenant Colonel," she said, glowering at him through the semidarkness inside the car.

At a gas station on the edge of town Casey halted the car so Sloan could give fire support to the retreating Texicans. "My God," Sloan gasped, "the only way to stop them is to blow them to pieces!"

"Fanaticism's a wonderful thing." McKay kicked open the side hatch, braced his back against the turret root, and fired the M-60 from beneath his arm at the black surge of humanity a hundred yards away. Spent casings clattered everywhere, ricocheting around the car's interior like hot pinballs. Casey yipped like a kicked dog as one went down the back of his neck.

"What the hell you think you're doing, McKay?" Eklund demanded, batting at the bounding casing as if they were horse-flies.

"Beats me. I'm making a fuck-all of an impression of these guys." A bullet kissed the edge of the open door, caromed off the hull. "Case, get us the hell out of Dodge. Jesus, now I'm talking like a Texan too."

They went booming off across the ancient black furrows of another onion field, the troopies on top clinging for dear life. Behind them it was as if a dam had gone. Cristeros just poured out of town, waving their banners and singing their songs.

"What the heck is that?" Casey said suddenly, ducking his head to squint harder through the vision block.

McKay looked over Casey's shoulder. A squat, tracked shape was parked on a hillside several hundred meters dead ahead of them. "Holy shit. *Break right!*"

Mobile One heeled way over. Sloan tracked the turret around to see what was causing all the commotion. "What on earth? It looks like a horizontal pipe organ."

"It's an Ontos," Rogers said.

"Say what?"

"All the trouble in the world," McKay said, "if it ain't the good guys."

"Sounds as if the reinforcements have arrived," Eklund said.

About that time the Ontos's commander judged Mobile One was clear of his firing fan and triggered the eight 106-mm recoilless rifles mounted on his ungainly AFV. Thousands of steel ball bearings from eight beehive antipersonnel charges swept down on the cristeros like a glowing volcanic cloud. There was a whirlwind of dust and torn cloth and human parts.

When it settled the front ranks of the mob—a hundred people, two hundred, God knew how many—had simply vanished. The others broke like a wave hitting a rock, eddied back into the town in a panic even their fanatic zeal couldn't overcome.

"Oh, wow," Casey said.

CHAPTER
ELEVEN

"Lucky they were there," McKay grunted. As Casey swerved and continued up the slope he craned to watch the squatty little Ontos. It had reversed its treads and was creeping backwards, away from the town, toward a stand of trees on top of the hill, churning up moist-looking black earth. "You can slow down, now, Case; the riot's over for now, and we don't want to roll this mother."

He turned his head from the port. "Eklund, I'm ashamed of you. First you fail to provide decent artillery ssupport for your people. And then you go running off like a scared rabbit." He shook his head. "Never thought I'd see you play Yellow Rose of Texas like that."

Eklund sat in a fold-down seat across from him. With her head lowered her cap hid her face. But he could see the way her hands were bunched into fists, feel the tension grinding inside her. But what the fuck? He was in no goddamn mood to soften any blows.

"The cristeros overran . . . couple of mortar squads," Rita Montañez said. She had her head down too; her speech came slow and rough and slightly slurred. Well, she was just a kid; all this excitement was getting to her. "Rest . . . ran out of ammo."

"How do you know that?" McKay demanded. "You just got here, along with the rest of us."

"Friend of mine told me while you were . . . kissing the colonel." She shifted position slightly, made a small sound. "And we *weren't* running scared—"

"I don't know about you, sweetheart, but *I* sure was," McKay said.

"We were falling back because . . . reinforcements here. Had to hold 'em in town till our backup got here. But they can get too close . . . in town. Be all over you—*caray,* it's cold." Her chin slumped a couple of centimeters to her chest.

"Billy," Tom said, "she got a point. Republicans' firepower is a bunch more effective, out here in open country. Like we just saw."

"The, ah, colonel did say something about reinforcements, McKay," Sloan reminded him from the turret.

About then Casey, who was sulking because McKay had cast aspersions on his driving ability, and had slowed to a crawl, brought Mobile One creeping up over the crest and through the trees. On the backslopes stood a farmhouse, a whitewashed two-story with roofs peaked like a witch's hat that must have dated back to the 1880s. In the yard beside the house was parked the inevitable Giant Yellow Farm Machine— McKay had no idea what it was, and cared less—that was parked next to every farmhouse in the USA, bought on credit at the government's encouragement, only to become a humongous anvil hung around its owner's neck when times got tight.

There was also a whole trainload of cammie-painted military transport—deuce-and-a-halfs, hummers, pickups—a lot of squaddies in the usual Texican paramilitary mix of outfits digging in, and three 105-mm howitzers getting set up next to a grove of pecan trees a hundred meters away.

McKay flipped up the steel shutter over a side vision block. Mobile One was rolling within six or eight meters of an M-60 pit. Texicans with dead twigs stuck in the bands of their cowboy hats watched the V-450 warily as it went by.

"Oh," McKay said. "Yeah. Reinforcements. Well, kid, that's a lick on me; guess I came down on your colonel when I shouldn't have." He leaned over and chucked Montañez under the chin.

Her head lolled to the side. A line of blood was drying from the side of her mouth down her chin and slender throat. Her eyes were half open. She was very pale.

"Rita. Oh, Jesus motherfucking Christ—*Rita!*" He lowered her to the rubber mat that covered the steel decking. "Tom, for God's sake, get back here!"

He tore futilely at the Kevlar vest. He wasn't near strong enough to make any impression. Eklund knelt beside him, elbowed him none too gently away and with Tom's help worked the vest up over the teenaged corporal's head. Beneath, her camouflage blouse was a sodden red-brown mess.

She was already past help. It was pure bad luck: On the run to the car a cristero bullet must have passed under her left arm, just where the Kevlar wasn't.

"But why didn't she fucking say something!" McKay yelled.

"Wouldn't have done any good, Billy," Tom said. "Near as I can reckon, the round must've collapsed a lung and nicked a pulmonary artery. She bled to death, and I couldn't have done nothing to stop it."

Eklund's arms were abruptly locked around McKay's neck. Not for the first time, he marveled at the strength in them. It was easier than thinking about other things. . . . He stroked the back of her neck as she sobbed.

In less than sixty seconds she released her drowner's grip and pulled away. Her eyes were dry. "Sorry. I've lost a mess of friends today. Rita was just . . . the last straw, I guess."

"Yeah." His voice rasped his throat like raw alcohol. "Don't worry about it."

And he turned his head so she couldn't see the moisture at the corner of his eyes. *Must be reaction to the smoke*, he thought. *I'm a Marine, for Chrissake. I seen people die before.*

But she was just a kid. Just a goddamned kid.

It was a familiar whistling roar, slashing the starry sky above their heads. McKay didn't even feel the reflexive tug of muscles in his thick neck urging him to duck; this was *outgoing* mail, one of the most comforting sounds in a combat grunt's world.

"Not as romantic as a nightingale," Eklund said, looking at him with her head tipped to one side. "Or even one of our ol' meadowlarks. Wonder if they're shootin' at anybody in particular?"

She sounded casual, but she and McKay both glanced automatically at the tree against which their longarms—his a Galil from Mobile One, hers her trusty tommy gun—were propped.

Out in the barren fields, fire and earth gouted skyward.

"Naw. H and I is all." *H&I* meant *harassment and interdiction*, which in turn meant the Texican artillerists were just dropping a few subtle reminders to the cristeros about the hazards involved in crossing the no-man's-land which separated their lines. It was an expensive way to go about things, and in various places it had been tried before—Vietnam, Libya, Iraq, Salvador—it had met with uneven success at best. Still, artillery fire was the most unnerving phenomenon encountered in a battlefield environment, guaranteed to fray the nerves of the toughest veteran—or the wildest-eyed fanatic. For what it was worth, the soldiers of *Cristo Rey* hadn't felt like trying their luck since they met up with the weird critter called Ontos that afternoon.

The bulk of Eklund's command—a regiment, whatever that meant to these crazy Texans—was already here at the farmhouse. Characteristically, Eklund and her command team had been among the last to pull out; while the Guardians had been driving into town the Texicans had been pulling out by other routes.

McKay gazed off toward the town a kilometer away. A dozen columns of smoke undulated up into the clear sky, luridly underlit with yellow and orange. The wind backed; he could hear singing, nasal and strident, a cicada-buzz of guitars and fiddles and the occasional blat of some kind of horn.

He turned around, and finally asked Marla straight out what had been bugging him. "What are you doing here? I mean, with these people?"

Hands on hips, she faced him. Even with her parka bulking out she was a hell of an attractive woman. "So that's what's been on your mind, Yankee. I was wondering." She looked McKay straight in the eyes. "Only thing I know how to do. Leastways, the only thing I feel like *doing*—ain't quite up to peddling my ass for cans of salvaged beans, if you know what Ah mean. Remember when we split, I said I might go off and be a mercenary?" She shrugged. "That's how this all started out."

"You took an oath, Eklund. To defend your country."

"And I did, Yankee—have you forgotten that already? Besides, this is my country now. Always was, in a way—place I was born's in the Republic now."

"Your country's America. You're wearin' its uniform."

"McKay, there *is* no America. Not now. No, don't turn away from me. What we're doin' here is what America was all about anyway. About people bein' free, able to make their lives without having to ask permission, or be afraid of others tryin' to take it all away from them."

"You saying America was like that?"

"Well, wasn't it, McKay? Wasn't it illegal to keep a gun to defend yourself with? Didn't the tax man take half your income, and every evening on the news somebody sayin' how selfish the American taxpayer was, how he ought to cough up even more? Didn't you have to get permission from the Department of Labor to move to a differ'nt *town?*"

She turned, walked several steps away from him. Winter dry grass crackled beneath her bootsoles. "But that don't matter anymore. I did swear an oath, to uphold the country and its ideals. Country's gone now—but can't you see, I *am* upholding her ideals?"

He just shook his head.

He stood watching the town, here and there catching movement, somebody silhouetted against a fire. *Maybe I should get Case up here, he might be able to nail a couple of the bastards—*

He realized how foolish that thought was. He could make out potential targets as near as a mile, and Casey with his astonishing eye and fancy rifle could almost certainly score a hit at that range, if not a stone-guaranteed kill. But so what? Sniping those loonies would be like trying to empty the ocean a drop at a time.

He realized Marla was standing beside him, hip to his. She let her head droop over onto his shoulder. It occurred to him how quickly he got unused to snuggling up to a woman damn near as tall as he was. His arm just naturally sort of slipped around her waist. It was a good waist, narrow and firm.

After a while she turned her head and tipped her face toward his. Her lips were parted.

He dropped his mouth to hers. Their tongues met. Her fingers dug like hooks into his back. She ground her crotch against his.

She stepped back, leaving him with his head down and nostrils flared, panting like a bull. She took off her cap and threw it aside, then reached behind her head. Her hair fell down around her shoulders. It was a far cry from the boot-camp plush she'd had when he first met her.

He was horny enough to bust a seam, but he could still barely believe it when she undid her parka. "Wait a minute here," he choked out, "what do you think you're doing?"

"What's it look like?" Parka and blouse came open. Her bra was one of those that snapped in the front, the kind with the interlocking plastic catch he could never figure out how to work.

"But it's *cold*." As if for emphasis his words came out in a locomotive puff of condensation.

Her breasts were just the way he remembered them, full and heavy but not saggy in the least. She dropped the parka behind her, skinned trousers and panties down her hips, sat down on the parka and undid her boots.

"There," she said with satisfaction, kicking off the boots and pulling her trousers the rest of the way off. She lay back, raised her knees and spread her arms. Her pubic hair looked scarcely darker than her pale skin by the light of the waning moon.

"Stupid Yankee," she purred, "this is south Texas. Ain't never cold here."

He stood there like a dummy. She sat up and unzipped the front of his coveralls. "Been a long time for us, McKay. Or don't you like girls anymore?"

"Uh. Well."

She reached into his skivvies and unshipped his cock. She stroked her thumb and forefinger along it a couple of times. It stood right to attention. She gave him a grin and popped it into her mouth.

McKay moaned as her lips tightened behind the head of his prick. "Maybe I do still like girls, after all," he said, and reached down to dip his hand into her long, golden hair as though it were a mountain stream.

"Billy," Casey Wilson said in his ear. He jumped, looked around, then sheepishly realized the voice was emanating from the mastoid bone behind his ear.

"Billy, are you there? We just had Washington on the phone. They want us to shag ass out of here pronto and get over to Austin to make contact with the rightful government of Texas!"

CHAPTER
TWELVE

"Oh, wow," Casey said, craning around to stare out the viewports at the silent buildings of Austin, "it's like a ghost town."

To their left a hotel with every square centimeter of glass blown out of it, so that it looked like a giant rectilinear honeycomb, rose from what had once been a riverside park. To the right stood fire-scarred stone buildings that might have been warehouses. Ahead, the South Lamar Street bridge arced gracefully over the Colorado River.

"It's not *like* a ghost town," Sloan said, frowning at the red telltales flashing on the console, and the amber numbers on the CRT. "It *is* a ghost town. Nobody's too likely to be living here; radiation's still way to heck and gone above background. Face into a stiff breeze and take a good, deep breath, your alveolae'd glow in the dark."

He was exaggerating—some. Intensely radioactive isotopes don't hang around for long. It's their rapid decay that makes them so radioactive; they have what you call your short half-life. But a thermonuclear warhead that corks off low enough that its fireball makes contact with the earth—a ground burst—produces incredible quantities of your worse class of isotopes. The pall of death the two-megaton groundburst strike on nearby

Bergstrom AFB had laid over Austin wouldn't lift totally for
years to come.

"But I thought this was the state capital," Casey said.

"It is," Tom said. "Was, anyhow."

"Lively looking place," McKay remarked around an unlit
half-cigar.

"You sure you brought us to the right place, McKay?" Sloan
asked.

McKay grimaced. "The lady said take this route in to the
State House, and that ours was fucking well not to question
why."

He didn't bother hiding his resentment. None of the other
Guardians felt any better about what had happened last night.
To have Maggie Connoly peremptorily order them to break off
all dealings with the Republic of Texas and hie themselves
immediately off to contact the "rightful" government of the
state was bad enough. That she had intimated treacherous
intentions on their part for having treated the Republic at
all—as if Washington had warned them not to, or in fact told
them *anything* about what to expect in the Lone Star State—was
intolerable. And the result of their reflex call to President Mac-
Gregor—a weary order that until further notice they should
consider themselves under the orders of Marguerite Connoly
in her capacity as White House chief of staff—still had them
reeling.

Of course, what Billy McKay would *really* never forgive
Maggie Connoly for was interrupting his first blowjob in
months. He hadn't gotten around to mentioning that to the
others, for some reason.

They started up the bridge beneath a gray smear of sky. At
the top Casey hit the brakes even as Tom Rogers rapped a
warning from the turret.

"Company."

McKay rocked forward, caught himself on the back of either
seat. "Whoa. What have we here?"

There were a pair of Highway Patrol cars nose to nose across
the north end of the South Lamar bridge, blue lights whirling.
Behind them were parked several other vehicles and a lot of
motorcycles. In front of them stood a line of men in riot helmets
with polarized face-shields, wearing uniforms that might have
been dark blue and might have been very deep green but which
weren't quite black. Gauntleted hands held M-16s at the present-

arms postion across each man's chest.

"I don't like the looks of this," Sloan said half under his breath, as though the cordon forty meters beyond the thick armor plate might overhear him.

"Take a look at what's flying from those aerials, navy boy," McKay said. "*American* flags. These here are the good guys."

"If you say so."

"I do. Gimme a mike and an outside line." Wordlessly Sloan passed a microphone back over his shoulder.

"Hello there up ahead," McKay said, his words amplified by a speaker horn set in the hull. "We're the Guardians. We got an appointment."

A man stepped between the nose-to-nose cruisers. He looked to be above average height and on the narrow side. He had black shoes, black pants, black shades, and a black leather jacket. He raised a megaphone to his mouth.

"Good morning, Guardians. You're expected. We're your welcoming committee; come on ahead."

Casey glanced back at McKay. McKay nodded impatiently. Casey came off the brake and let Mobile One roll forward slowly, picking up speed on her own.

The line of uniformed men grounded their weapons smartly and saluted, then split and filed to either side of the bridge. The patrol cars cleared the way with a squeal of tires, bucking up onto the sidewalks and wailing their sirens. The chairman of the reception committee gave a half-salute with his bullhorn and backpedaled deliberately to the road's edge, a casual hand stuck in one jacket pocket.

Mobile One came to a stop in front of him. As McKay emerged from the side door the uniforms behind him snapped to attention and saluted again.

"You're McKay?" the man in the jacket said around the end of a cigarette. "I'm Bob Tyrone, Department of Public Safety. Welcome to Texas—the *real* Texas."

It was three hundred clicks from the gutted shell of Austin to Dallas, the de facto capital; make it six hours, if you obeyed the emergency speed limit decreed by Governor Hedison, as the blacklands buckled up into what they called grand prairie. Riding along in the back of Tyrone's open black Lincoln, McKay couldn't see what the hell was so grand about it. It was better than New Jersey, but that was all he'd concede.

"Sorry for the little charade, McKay," Tyrone had said, turning around in the front seat after they finally picked their way over to I-35, where a pathway had obligingly been bulldozed through the usual crust of hard-luck cars scabbed along the highway by the Bergstrom bomb. His driver, a specimen just about as broad as he was tall, with a neck wider than his flat-topped head and great big wads of muscles clumped at the corners of his jaw, kept his Ray-Bans locked on the road ahead and said lots of nothing.

"Say again?" McKay said. The words had gotten lost in the whistle of the wind.

"I say, I'm sorry you came here expecting this still to be the capital." His voice was soft, so soft it would have been tough to hear even without this goddamn wind that was freezing McKay's ears off. He had an East Texas accent, as much Louisiana as anything else. "I mean, this still is the capital, of course, but only in a symbolic way. Russians didn't leave us a lot to work with."

He gestured around at the dead city. Remembering what Sloan had said, McKay hunkered down a tad in his seat and tried not to breathe too much.

A half-dozen motorcycles and a machinegun jeep preceded them, with more cyclists outriding to both sides when conditions permitted. Behind the Lincoln came Mobile One. Aft of the V-450 a squad of soldiers in those odd dark uniforms, these with matching baseball caps, rode under canvas in a deuce-and-a-half.

"Who are these guys, anyway?" McKay asked, jerking a thumb back over his shoulder.

"Texas Rangers."

McKay's almost invisible eyebrows rose. "No shit? I kinda thought they'd wear big white ten-gallon hats and Dirty Harry sixguns and ride around on palomino horses."

Tyrone displayed a reasonably good set of teeth. "Times change, McKay. Texas is a mighty progressive state."

Up close Tyrone looked as if he might have had notions about being James Dean, with his jacket and shades, and his dark hair sweeping back in a well-oiled wave. His face looked as if it had started out kind of round, then got jacked out of true; had a look to it as if it were under constant tension, with up and down lines drawn deep. From the wrinkles at the side of his mouth and the slight parchment quality to his skin he was a few years older than McKay's thirty-three, but probably not enough to've had conscious memories of Dean's heyday.

Tyrone had served with the Rangers in Salvador, it turned out. They spent most of the trip swapping war stories. It would have been an enjoyable experience if it hadn't been for the open car.

The run took them a full six hours, though they had no need to bother themselves about speed limits, and what little traffic they encountered, the occasional rubber-tired two to four horse-power post-Holocaust wagon and the even more occasional truck, hauled prompt ass to the side of the road and let them pass when they hove into view. It was the semipermanent traffic jam they ran into at virtually every little tank town that held them up.

Other than the scarce civilian vehicles they saw no sign of life until they reached the outskirts of the Dallas/Fort Worth metroplex. Once they hit Arlington they started to see people moving around some. The people gave the convoy plenty of sea room and hurried about their affairs with their heads tucked down between their shoulders.

''—down in the fever plains near La Unión,'' Tyrone was saying, as they picked their way along surface streets that ran through sparsely populated suburban neighborhoods. ''Bad country, Indian country, just across the Golfo de Fonseca from Nicaragua. We caught this woman, suspected terr, real fox—not much Indian blood, y'know? So we strip-searched her. Made a real thorough job of it—you some how some of these terrorist-type broads hide razor blades up their—''

''Billy,'' Tom said over the communicator. ''*Something going on, up ahead.*''

McKay blinked. He'd been spacing out, not paying enough attention to the terrain. Easy enough to do, surrounded by heavily armed troopies. No excuse.

A couple of blocks ahead the road was blocked by city police cars. An assorted bunch of soldiers and cops were surrounding a stucco-box tract house, hunkering down behind skeletal shrubs and cinderblock walls and cars that looked as if they were permanent street fixtures, as opposed to parked. The leading riders slowed to a stop just shy of the barricade. The rest of the convoy telescoped behind them.

McKay jerked his head. "What's going on here?"

"Stop her right here, Brock," Tyrone said to the driver. He turned around, fiddled with his shades. "Looks like a shoot-out." He grinned.

"Yeah, I can see that much—"

McKay heard the unmistakable pop of a grenade launcher. His hand moved to the Pachmayr grips of his .45. The picture window collapsed inward. A moment later white smoke began to pour out. There were more pops, and more windows fell before tear-gas grenades.

The front door opened. A barefoot man in undershirt and jeans came boiling out, a little snub-nosed revolver in his hand. He took three spraddle-legged steps down the walk, and the surrounding forces cut loose with shotguns and pistols and full-auto rifles and Christ knew what. Red splotches popped out all over his undershirt and face and arms. He seemed to dither there on his lawn, making false starts this way and that way, and finally just went down in a sprawl and rolled in among the dry stalks of a flower bed hard against the pink wall of the house.

The fusillade didn't slacken. Instead the attackers shifted fire, blew out the windows the CS grenades had left, sprayed bullets into open windows vomiting white tear gas—and flames, now, where the canisters had ignited furniture and curtains.

Tyrone was lipping a cigarette out of a plain brown pack. "Happens from time to time. Real bitch. But hey, we get these criminals. . . . Usually black-market types. Hoarding gold, possessing firearms, trafficking in unlicensed salvage or ration stamps. Even these. They're illegal too."

He stuck the pack toward McKay. "Care for one?" McKay shook his head. The driver flicked a lighter and lit Tyrone's cigarette. "Randy Jim doesn't approve of them, but rank hath its privileges, you know."

The gunfire had finally stopped. Several men, alien-looking in flak jackets and gas masks, rushed the house, shotguns at the ready. Two paused on the porch with their backs to the wall while the rest barged in the open door.

Tyrone's teeth worried his underlip. "Say, McKay, a favor, how about it?"

"Shoot."

"Don't say the words *Randy Jim* where the governor can

hear you. And if by some accident you do, just forget where you heard them, okay?''

The assult team was emerging into what passed for late-afternoon daylight, herding the weeping woman and a couple of hysterical kids before them.

"McKay, what's going on?" Sloan's voice demanded.

"Law and order."

Tyrone licked his thin lips. "She's not bad looking, you know. Hey, I bet you got lots back when you were with the traitors. Fuck like rabbits all the time, over on the other side. Women do it in all kind of ways, you can't imagine, in the mouth, up the ass, two at a time. We don't cotton to that sort of thing around here." Despite the fact that it was getting cold, beads of sweat showed around the verges of his slicked-back hair.

He bobbed his head toward the house. "Bitch. These black-market types are all alike. I bet they were in there doing it in front of the kids. . . . We know how to take care of cunts like her, I promise you that."

McKay tried to speak. It felt as if the inside of his throat were rusty. "What, uh, what happens to the kids?"

"They go to a foster home somewhere. Parents're unfit. Anybody can see that; I mean, hey." A little laugh. "But they'll be looked after. This is a real progressive state, Lieutenant McKay."

CHAPTER
THIRTEEN ────────────

The Honorable Randall James Hedison, governor of the state of Texas, stood and faced the smoky floor-to-ceiling window that formed two walls of his office, looking out on the urban megasprawl from a great enough height that the effects of the odd airburst here and there were completely invisible.

"The issue, gentlemen, is *freedom*," he said.

Seated on white post-modern plastic furniture way at the far end of Hedison's corner office, up here on the ultimate floor of the giant Sauron building smack in the center of Dallas, the Guardians looked at each other.

"I beg your pardon, Governor?" Sloan said.

Hedison pressed his fingertips briefly against the window, as if in that way he could come briefly to personal contact with the vast domain spread out half a kilometer below. Then he turned to face his guests, silhouetted against a dusky, mauve and amber sky. He was a small neat man with a large, neat head, immaculate in a three-piece suit the gray of a pigeon's breast. His hair was full, blow-dried, that vaguely silver color that dark-blond hair gets when it goes gray. His features were regular and scrubbed shiny, so that he had a bit of mannequin appearance about him, an injection-molded sort of look, except for hints of bags below his hazel eyes. Those, you understand, went with the office.

"Freedom," he repeated. "The birthright of all Americans. That's why I'm so very pleased to see you gentlemen."

The Guardians traded off another look. McKay scratched the side of his neck where he'd missed a few bristles shaving that morning, and tried not to scowl. Hizzoner had definately lost him at the last exit.

"I'm afraid I don't quite follow you, Governor Hedison," Sloan said. As usual he was serving as spokesman for the group when diplomacy seemed called for. Being diplomatic was not McKay's strong suit.

Hedison came around his desk, which was placed at an angle, so that the juncture of the window-walls would be right behind him when he sat at it.

"Since shortly after the War, gentlemen," he said, "an intolerable situation has existed. Almost half of the state of Texas has been held hostage by a band of psychopaths who imagine that they can secede from the United States of America. With your help, I anticipate the day will soon come when the unfortunate citizens of that region may be rescued from tyranny and anarchy, and once again enjoy the protections extended by the American government."

This time McKay couldn't help but frown. "Now, I'm not a political scientist, Governor," he said, hoping Sloan would be proud of him for not saying *ain't,* "but how can they have anarchy and tyranny at the same time? Ain—uh, aren't the two, uh, mutually exclusive?"

"What could be more tyrannical than anarchy, Lieutenant McKay, a state in which every man's hand is turned against every other man—and woman, it's hardly necessary to add? And is it not anarchy when a region as large as some substantial European nations is ruled by the whim of a single aging madman—a political amateur at that, utterly unfit for higher office?"

"Uh, right." Somehow, McKay's mind felt as if it had been trying to grab hold of a gerbil dipped in Pennzoil.

Hedison crossed a hectare or so of carpet whose color, if you could even say it had one, McKay for one was unable to name. Something like a pastel, but blander, kind of thing designed by committees of psychiatrists, ergonomists, and other buzzword-slingers on Federal grants—like the furniture. Hedison took a place facing the Guardians on what McKay guessed you could call a sofa, though to him *sofa* meant something soft, like the battered, threadbare item of indeterminate color that bled copious amounts of stuffing and dominted the living room of the tiny tenement apartment where he'd grown up. This thing was unyielding as a mortgage underwriter.

"So," the governor said, "let's just talk for a moment about how we can make America whole again."

Sloan edged a glance toward McKay. His leader had a certain glazed look with which Sloan was not totally unfamiliar. "Governor, I beg your pardon, but we have a specific assignment here in Texas."

That jolted McKay back to reality; *duty* was one of his major buttons. "Uh, yeah, that's right."

Hedison sat with his legs primly crossed and listened as the Guardians explained about the seawater desalinization plant near Houston. He started to fidget near the end.

"Yes, yes. I'm sure that's all very vital. But what we're talking about here is the national security."

"You mean the cristeros?" Casey asked.

Hedison looked at him as if he'd farted loudly. "No, no, of course not. I'm talking about this intolerable secession."

He stood up, paced the neutral-colored carpet. "You have to understand, gentlemen, how deeply those of us in the state of Texas feel this issue. We keenly feel—all of us, men, women, children, ethnic minorities—the shame, if you will, of Texas's past. Yes, the shame."

He halted by one of the two walls that weren't enormous windows. This one was paneled in dark oak and covered with photographs and certificates. "Texas was born in revolt against duly constituted authority, led by a conspiracy of outcasts and outlaws from the young United States, whose major desire was to possess slaves—which the enlightened government of Mexico would not permit. And let me remind you, gentlemen—does not this self-proclaimed 'republic' have its headquarters within a few hundred meters of the Alamo, the very symbol of Texan truculence and machismo?"

"Uh, I guess so," McKay said. "I don't know exactly where the Alamo is in San Antone. I'm new to this neighborhood."

"I'm kind of surprised it's not *in* the Alamo," Sloan murmured.

Hedison beamed at him. "Exactly. *Exactly*. Later, of course,

Texas seceded from the Union to take part in the fight to preserve slavery—do you see a pattern here, my friends? Ever since, Texas has maintained a reputation of the most unsavory sort, for arrogance, boorishness, and bigotry.''

He shook his head mournfully. ''Over the last few years, certain leaders of business and opinion have been working hard to erase this stigma, with the full support of the people. So I believe you can understand, my friends, why it's especially urgent for us to destroy this throwback to a particularly vicious past.''

When he finished his fists were clenched. He looked down at them, uncurled them, a trifle sheepishly. ''I mean, of course, welcome our erring brethren back to the fold.''

''Mr. Governor,'' McKay said, ''I think it's a hel—a fine idea to reunite Texas. But that's not our job. We came to Texas to reclaim a facility for the Blueprint for Renewal.''

Hedison looked surprised. ''But didn't Dr. Connoly send you here?''

''Well . . . yes,'' Sam Sloan said.

Hedison reached up and tapped an exactingly manicured finger on a photo above his right shoulder. It showed half a dozen people seated behind a long table set on a dais. They were looking to Dr. Maggie Connoly her own self, who stood behind the podium. Immediately to her right sat Hedison.

''We're old friends, doctor and I. Comrades in arms in the good fight. The picture here—'' *Rap.* ''—was taken shortly after President Iacocca formed the National Emergency Energy Review Board, on which Dr. Connoly and I were privileged to serve. It was a time of rebuilding, of repairing the damage done the country by rampant individualism and *laissez-faire*— the same evils that abound in the so-called republic. The result was the formation of the semi-public corporation called the Southern American Union for Resource Oversight and Normalization, of which I was chairman, which handled energy-resource allocation for this part of the country. A pilot program we would eventually have extended to include the entire U.S.''

He sighed. ''We were making such great progress toward reviving the country. But the War intervened.'' He sounded as if they'd held it just to spite him.

McKay scratched an ear; his impression of the country before the One-Day War was that it was going to hell on a bullet train. Maybe he just didn't hang with the right people.

"That's all good and well, Mr. Governor. But as far as I can see, it isn't our concern."

Hedison pursed his lips. "I'm afraid you have a touch of the sickness that afflicted America before the War, that contributed so much to her ills. Being unwilling to make things our concern, to reach out, to take steps."

McKay suppressed an urge to reach out for Hedison's neck and take steps in the direction of those humongous windows, do a little experimenting into just how unbreakable they really were. *Hey*, he reminded himself, *he's one of the good guys*.

"What about the cristero incursion, Your Honor?" Tom Rogers asked.

"Until the secessionists see the error of their ways and petition for readmission, that's a purely local problem, is it not? We can hardly force our protection on them. That's the very sort of 'governmental interference' they so resented, after all."

"We got a job to do, Governor," McKay said. "What we need to do right now is secure this Blueprint place. Then we can talk about this other stuff."

"I'm disappointed by your inability to see beyond your self-ish concerns, Lieutenant McKay. Very well. I hoped it wouldn't go this way." He took a deep breath. "It is my understanding that Dr. Connoly instructed you to cooperate fully with the duly constituted authorities of the state of Texas. Which is to say, me. Therefore, as of this moment I am taking you under my command in accordance with the wishes of the president and his chief of staff."

"Errand boys," McKay said. "Fucking *errand boys*."

His voice rattled down the corridor like the A train coming into a station. Inside an open door to their right, secretaries raised beehive-hairdoed heads from their word processors, gazed at him with shocked disapproval compressing pastel lips.

The seal-sleek aide serving as their guide gave McKay a nervous smile over his shoulder. "Cool it, McKay," Sloan hissed. "You're making a scene."

"We have a *job* to do, dammit!"

"I thought you were the one outraged over the fact half of Texas had seceded."

"Don't confuse me with facts, navy boy. Anyway, it ain't our job to go rounding up people's little lost sheep."

" 'Mavericks,' McKay. Calling a party a sheepman used to be grounds for a shooting, hereabouts.''

"What're we going to do, Billy?'' Casey asked. He was twisiting his Spirit tour cap uncertainly in his hands.

"Call Washington and find out what the hell is going on.''

"It's never gonna work,'' Casey said.

"He's right, Billy,'' Tom said. "We got our marching orders.'' His eyebrows were pinched together, which was as much sign of being pissed off as he ever showed.

They stopped at a widening of the corridor. "You gentlemen shouldn't get the impression Governor Hedison doesn't appreciate what you're doing,'' the aide said, in a voice from which most of the Texans had been scrubbed. "He's given permission for you to ride the elevators.''

He punched the button. McKay glanced at the elevator doors. STATE LAW: USE BY UNAUTHORIZED PERSONNEL STRICTLY FORBIDDEN read the sign taped to both. ENERGY CONSERVATION IS EVERYBODY'S BUSINESS.

"That's big of him,'' McKay said. He rooted in a pocket of his silver-gray uniform coveralls.

A door slid open. "We can find our own way to the car, Junior,'' McKay said, as the other Guardians filed inside. "Here's something for your trouble.'' He pressed something into the aide's hand and stepped back into the car.

The man stared down at the pre-1965 silver dime glistening in his moist, soap-smelling palm. His eyes flicked left and right to take in the dark-uniformed guard standing to either side of the elevators. He pushed quickly forward into the elevator.

"But it's illegal for private citizens to hold—'' he started in a whisper.

"We won't tell if you don't,'' McKay said.

He put his hand in the center of the aide's chest and gently pushed. The man stumbled back a step. He hesitated, then tucked the dime into an inside pocket of his suit coat as the door shut in his face.

"Hey, you! Get the fuck away from there!''

Casey looked up from the long limousine, gleaming black in a jittery fluorescent shimmer, as a straw-haired man in mechanic's coveralls came running toward him with his beer belly jouncing over his belt.

"What's the matter, man? I'm not hurting anything.''

"You got your hands on the president's personal—oh." His eyes latched onto the gigantic Dirty Harry magnum tucked in Casey's shoulder holster and got real wide. "You're packin'," he said.

Casey blinked at him, taking a moment to get his drift. "So?"

"You must be one of them Guardians. You go with the heavy wheels." He jerked a greasy thumb back at Mobile One, mostly visible beyone a support pillar fifteen meters away.

"That's right. I didn't mean to hurt anything, man. I was just, like, admiring the car."

The mechanic pulled a rag from his hip pocket and wiped his hands with them. It had the effect of redistributing the grease. "Yeah, a beauty, ain't she? You wouldn't know it to look at her, but she's armored like a tank. Oh, nothin' like y'all's car, but—you know."

Casey nodded and made noncommittal throat sounds.

The mechanic patted a fender like a favorite mare's flank. "Yessir, every square inch of her body's lined on the inside with Kevlar. Put that together with the metal of the body and it'll stop any bullet up to fifty caliber. An' the windows, they're some kind of glass and plastic sheets sandwiched together, they call it laminectomy or something like that."

"Laminate. Same as our vision blocks."

"Liniment, yeah, like I said. The beauty of it is, she don't hardly weigh no more than one of these old Lincolns usually does. And pickup—whooee." He shook his head. "Old Randy Jim's got a fleet of these dogies. We call her his American Express: He don't leave home without it."

"Yo, Casey." It was Sloan, waving from Mobile One.

"Been nice talking to you, man," Casey told the mechanic. "Stay cool." He wandered back to the V-450.

"How'd it go, Sam?"

"You were right. It didn't work."

Sloan, something of a communications wizard himself, had run a lead from Mobile One to the SAURON building's wiring, creating an antenna amply large enough to allow them to transmit and receive from the underground parking garage buried in the structure's roots. McKay had been on the horn to Washington.

Casey heard a muffled rhythmic thumping from inside the car. "What's that?"

"McKay pounding on the hull."

"Oh. He talked to Dr. Connoly in person, then."

"That's right."

"And she backed up the governor."

Sloan tipped his head toward the car. Casey could vaguely hear the word *fuck* being repeated over and over, with feeling.

He scratched under an edge of his tour cap. "How could she do that, man? We're supposed to be working on the Blueprint. Not this other stuff."

"Yes. But the President's put us under Connoly's orders." He shook his head. "McKay's going to try calling Dr. Jake, but you know he won't be able to do anything but let us cry on his shoulder."

"Bummer."

"I couldn't agree with you more."

CHAPTER
FOURTEEN ─────────────

"So Randy Jim's using you boys as messengers," President LaRousse said. He tested the cleaver's edge with his thumb. "Y'all are staying for dinner, aren't you?"

McKay's reflex scowl turned to a look of puzzlement. "Why certainly, Mr. President," Sloan interjected smoothly. "We're much obliged."

The President held up a peeled onion between scarred thumb and forefinger, squinted at it through lantern light. "Elena! Git on in here a minute, will you, honey?" He nodded and set the onion on the block.

A woman stepped under the heavy, ancient wooden lintel over the door that led to the dining room of the Spanish Governor's Palace. She looked to be in her forties, but she had that quiet, sculpted Hispanic beauty that ages as splendidly as fine wood. Her hair was heavy and black, dusted with gray. A green velveteen blouse and blue jeans set off a fine, firm figure and bright green eyes.

"Elena, set four more places for dinner, will you?" the president asked, dicing the onion with precise, strong strokes. "We got us some company."

"Certainly, Lamar," she said. She stood in the doorway with an expectant half smile.

"Oh. I'm forgetting my manners. Elena, these here are the Guardians—" She shook their hands as he ticked off their names. Her grip was dry and surprisingly strong. "Boys, this here's my wife, Elena."

"We're enchanted to meet you, ma'am," Sloan said.

We're enchanted to meet you, ma'am, McKay mimicked noiselessly from outside Mrs. LaRousse's field of vision.

"It's very thoughtful of you gentlemen to stay for dinner," she said. "Lamar does love to show off his cooking."

The president slapped her on the fanny. "Now scat! A woman's place is outside my kitchen."

McKay watched the play of her buttocks beneath the taut denim, and decided that she either spent a lot of time on horseback or this joint had a Nautilus setup in the basement.

Sloan nudged him, trying to indicate that a fit of jealousy by the six-and-a-half-foot-tall president of the Republic of Texas would not simplify their lives.

But LaRousse was stumping here and there, assembling dinner, his plastic foot clocking softly on the tiles, and apparently hadn't noticed McKay's interest. He picked up a clove of garlic and beamed. "You boys got no silly prejudice against garlic, do you?"

"I got to tell you," Billy McKay said, stifling a belch, "looks to me like you Texicans're fiddling while Rome burns. At least, up here in San Antonio. When we rolled in here this afternoon I saw jack shit in the way of military preparations going on."

He ignored a warning look from Sloan. If President Lamar had been in the Marines—McKay didn't think the man was shitting, not with that foot, to say nothing of those shoulders, even if he grew his hair past them in these days—then he's heard worse in his time. Nor did the president of the Republic of Texas strike McKay as the sort to've picked up a case of tender ears in later life.

"We got 'em stalled at Carrizo Springs," said a stocky guy in a denim workshirt and jeans. He had a wide face and wider jaw and innocent looking blue eyes. Curly blond sideburns trailed down his cheeks from beneath the brim of a white straw Stetson with an eagle feather in the band. He looked twenty, might've been more.

A dude in the semi-inevitable cammies, with black hair brush-cut up top and long in back and tied with an OD rag, hung his lean, brown face in the lampglow welling up from the long table in the dining room of the Palace. SANDOVAL, read the name stenciled on his chest.

"Maybe you been too long with the Federals," he said. Between his mustache and his skin, his teeth seemed to glow white. "Over there they live on permanent fuckin' war footing anyway."

"Reckon we can look after ourselves," said the sideburned blond kid in an easygoing, oil-on-the-water sort of way. McKay knew it well; Sloan used it all the time on him. "We got three thousand men between us 'n' them."

"Plus a whole bunch salvaged support weapons, like that there Ontos you boys you ran into," said another sideburned blond kid past his shoulder.

McKay blinked, shook his head, looked again. *This shuttle diplomacy shit's too much for me,* he decided. *I'm starting to see double.*

The clones looked at each other and said something. In Russian. Both grinned at McKay.

A familiar laugh brought McKay's head around. "Don't burn your eyes, McKay," Dreadlock Callahan said, stepping in to join the dozen or so Texican officers gathered at the president's official residence to brief the Guardians of the cristero situation. "Permit me to introduce the Cherenkov twins, Boris Yosefovich and Gleb Yosefovich."

"*Dos vdanye,* y'all," grinned Boris, tipping his hat. His accent was pure West Texas—except for the greeting. "Y'all can call me Joe Bob."

"And I'm Billy Joe to my friends," added Gleb. "Right pleased to meet you."

"Are you, uh, immigrants?" McKay asked.

"Nope," said Joe Bob. "Folks were, though."

"But shoot," said his brother, "there been lotsa Russkies around Odessa since the turn of the century. Ma and Pa had a mess of kinfolk living there when they moved. Said it was just like the old country."

"Right," McKay said dubiously.

"Where did that Ontos come from, anyway?" Tom Rogers asked. "Thought they scrapped the last of those in the Seventies."

"They did—mostly," said a man in civilian clothes, with

a trucker's build down to the beer gut and a bright red face. "But a whole load of stuff everybody thought was decommissioned wound up gathering dust on the lots of National Guard armories. You'd be surprised what we got to work with."

He shook his head. "Cristeros ain't got a chance against us in open country. Now we got that worked out, reckon we got 'em stopped."

"I hope you're right," Sloan said in a level voice. "We saw them up close and personal in Carrizo Springs." He hesitated, shrugged. It said all that needed to be said.

"Listen, dude," Sandoval said, "we stopped 'em, okay? That's our problem, anyway. All you got to worry about is trying to talk us into kissing Hedison's gringo ass."

McKay turned red. "Listen, you—"

"Gentlemen." LaRousse held up a hand. Everybody shut up—even McKay, much to his own surprise. "The Guardians have delivered proposals from Governor Hedison, in accordance with their own orders. They have been informed these proposals were not satisfactory to the people of free Texas. The proposals themselves weren't their responsibility; they're just doing their duty."

"Just following orders," Sandoval sneered.

"Anytime, punk," McKay said, "and any place."

LaRousse's Rushmore brow lowered into a frown. "At ease, Bob. If you gentlemen see a serious need to kill each other, please do it outside. In my home you're both guests, and I'd appreciate it if you didn't get blood on my Navajo rugs."

"Can we expect Lieutenant Colonel Eklund to join us?" Sloan asked brightly, while McKay and Sandoval glowered at each other across the table.

"She's still holding the line outside the Springs," the president said. "She sends her regards. She especially regrets that you had to leave without properly saying good-bye, Lieutenant."

McKay stared in the general direction of his combat boots. His ears burned red, and it had nothing to do with his temper this time.

The president rolled up the U.S. Geologic Survey map of the Carrizo Springs area. "I believe that's all the business we had to transact, boys," he said. "Who's willing to join me in a drink?"

The Guardians spent the next ten days shuttling back and forth between San Antonio and Dallas, carrying sealed proposals and counterproposals from the president of secessionist Texas to the governor and back.

Though Mobile One ate up kilometers by the thousands, the Guardians went nowhere. At least the governments of state and republic were supplying the gas.

"Slavery," Maggie Connoly said from the speaker.

"Say *what?*" McKay asked, screwing his unlit cigar butt around to the side of his mouth. They were parked in the lot of a Stuckey's shut down by the Department of Energy before the War, on their way into Dallas for yet another round of playing Henry Kissinger.

"Certainly even someone so desultorily educated as yourself is sufficiently conversant with American history to be familiar with the Civil War?"

"They mentioned something about it in parochial school. Then I went off to public high school, and they didn't bother us with shit like history anymore."

They could have heard her catch her breath a few klicks away. "Thank you for confirming my belief that public education provides pupils insufficient socialization. There'll be a greatly reduced role for them in our rebuilt America, I can assure you."

"You were saying something about 'slavery,' Doctor?" Connoly even strained the hinges of Sloan's well-oiled politeness.

"Thank you, Commander; I had not forgotten." Sloan grimaced at the speaker. "I was in the process of explaining to your leader the reason that it is impossible even to contemplate compromise with the secessionists. I frankly confess myself surprised he even confronted the notion, to say nothing of advancing it."

As a matter of fact McKay was kind of surprised by it too. Outside the hull distant coyotes complained about the half moon. "What they said," he grunted, neglecting to punch the SEND button.

Then he did. "I don't like it any better than you do. But the only way we're gonna get back to work is if Randy—uh, Hedison agrees to just let the Texicans alone for now."

"That's *Governor* Hedison. And you are working now."

"No, ma'am. This ain't what we do. We have a Blueprint

facility to reclaim. *That's* our job.'' Knowing there was a
Blueprint facility lying just *waiting* to be trolled in worked at
him like a bit of glass wool stuck under the skin.

''Guardian McKay, your job is rebuilding America. At this
time the most important service you can perform to that end
is to help eradicate this rupture in the fabric of our nation.''

''Negative, Doctor. Our job is to put the Blueprint back
together. Hell, there isn't even anything we can *do* to the
damned Texicans. We ain't the army.''

''McKay, you are under *my* orders. Don't you dare forget
that. And I'm telling you that we cannot and will not consider
coming to terms with this—this antebellum dictatorship!''

''So.'' Randy Jim Hedison rubbed his palms together.
''We've tried, gentlemen. Haven't we?''

McKay and Sloan looked at each other. Sunset and a com-
pulsory blackout had drawn ebony curtains around the glass
walls of the penthouse office. Tom and Casey were with Mobile
One down in the subterranean parking garage. Just in case.

In case of what? was a question McKay wasn't even permit-
ting himself to ask.

''I beg your pardon, sir?'' Sloan said.

''We have made every effort to reach an accommodation
with that renegade LaRousse. And you have to admit that even
treating with self-proclaimed secessionists—I might as well say
it, with traitors—was an all but intolerable concession for duly
constituted authorities. But they remain adamant, and now—''
A helpless gesture with well-manicured hands. ''Now the time
has come to act.''

''That's great, Governor,'' McKay said, ''but you can count
us out.''

Hedison's outsized head snapped up. ''What are you talking
about?''

''Suppressin' sectional rebellion ain't in our job description.
We have a facility to reclaim, and other ones after that.''

''This—'' Hedison shook his head. He seemed about to burst
into tears. ''This is insane! The sheer *materialism*—''

''We call it duty, Governor,'' Sloan said softly.

Hedison's jaw firmed. ''Out of the question. Dr. Connoly
has placed you completely at my disposal. So, now that we've
got that nonsense out of the way, I've called a meeting to
discuss our plan of campaign against—''

"Billy," Casey's voice whispered in McKay's skull, *"you'd better get down here. Right now, man."*

McKay and Sloan stared at each other, then turned and raced out of the office. They passed Bob Tyrone of the Department of Public Safety, sitting on the corner of the receptionist's vacant desk in his leather jacket, reading an outdated copy of *Texas Monthly*. He looked up as they raced down the corridor without slowing.

The goons at the elevators looked hard at the Guardians beneath the rims of their caps. McKay punched the call button. One of the guards put a hand on his chest.

"Hey! Where do you think you're going?"

McKay reached up with his left hand and caught the guard's head in an *aikido* grip. He twisted. The guard grunted in pain and dropped to one knee. The other stepped forward. Sloan swung into his path to block him.

The elevator doors slid open. "You wanna watch where you put this thing, son," McKay said, giving the hand an extra twist. "You might lose it."

They stepped backwards. The doors closed as if on cue.

"Cristeros," the dry voice said. It belonged to none other than Dr. Jacob Morgenstern. "We don't know how they got so far undetected, but they're well beyond Republican lines in the southern part of the state, and in considerable force."

"As best we can determine, they're headed directly for Houston."

CHAPTER
FIFTEEN ─────────────────────────

The sound like small-caliber bullets ricocheting off the hull was Bob Tyrone pounding on Mobile One's carapace with a heavy gold ring on his right hand.

McKay poked his head out the door. "Just the man we wanted to see. You can get 'em to open the doors for us."

"Don't you think you were a little hard on Steve back there? He's just trying to do his jo—What?"

McKay jerked his head toward the bulletproof metal doors of the underground garage. "Tell them to open up. Save wear and tear on your doors."

Tyrone blinked several times rapidly. "What are you talking about, McKay?" He stepped back, pulled a comb from his back pocket and ministered to his duck's ass. He seemed to draw strength from the act.

"Are you deaf or just dumb, Tyrone? We're out of here, son. Duty calls."

"Your duty is here."

"Right. Hit it, Case."

With a growl and a squeal of tormented rubber the big car lunged away from Tyrone. "You're making a mistake, McKay! You can't run out like this."

McKay slammed the door.

The V-450 bucked onto the main aisle of the garage and slewed to a stop. Thirty meters away the doors were still shut. It was made of overlapped metal strips to save weight and looked like a giant Venetian blind.

"Billy?" Casey asked. The tapping of his gloved fingers on the wheel were the closest thing he'd make to a concession to nerves when he was in combat mode.

Servos whined. Rogers was cranking the turret around so that the guns were trained astern, out of harm's way. The door stayed shut.

McKay gripped a strap and braced himself on a fold-down seat. "You're not going anywhere, McKay," came Tyrone's voice, caught by pickups in the hull.

"Do it to it," McKay said.

Casey put the hammer down. Mobile One's snout pitched up momentarily as the huge cleated tires dug at the oily floor.

Ten metric tons hit the shuttered door. There was the screaming of metal as it gave up the ghost, and then Mobile One was running free through the dank, oil-flavored Dallas night.

"We're on our way, McKay."

They were doing the old backroad shuttle, yet again. For the ten thousandth time McKay squinted out the vision block. Outside, another derelict little town was creeping by, showing no light, no life. There was a feeling of desolation, as if no one had ever lived here, not before the War, not ever, as if the place had been built to house nothing more than shadows. He wondered if anybody lived in Federal Texas, except for a few black marketeers and a lot of guys in uniforms that were almost black.

Being up here by himself in the turret made him worse. He scratched his chin and gathered himself. He didn't want to sound anywhere near as lonely as he felt.

Especially not to Marla Eklund, former staff sergeant in the United States Army, current lieutenant colonel in the Army of the Republic of Texas.

"What's your ETA?" he rasped, pleased by the rough George-Scott-as-Patton edge to his voice.

"Noon, and I think that's wildly optimistic. It don't account for breakdowns, nor running into any of our friends from across the border. What about y'all?"

McKay checked the timepiece strapped to his massive wrist.

He checked it again, restrained the urge to slam it against the turret wall. He knew it wasn't slow; it just seemed that way.

"Sloan says we're halfway there, and if there's one thing the navy boy can do, it's navigate."

"Thanks, McKay," Sloan said over the bone phone.

"Anyway, that puts our best arrival time at 0800 and change. It's these damn roads, all clogged to shit. We can't average any better than forty klicks an hour—can't Hedison get the damn stalled cars pushed off the highway, if his state's so fucking organized?"

"Ah'm sure Randy Jim'd make the trains run on time," Eklund said sweetly, "if the Federals had any trains that ran. How do you like bein' forced to work cheek by jowl with us bad rebels?"

"Hard to imagine you havin' jowls, Eklund."

"Well, now, aren't you sweet, McKay. Imagine that, a yankee actin' like a gentleman! My grandma'd be *sooo* surprised—"

"Give it a rest, Eklund."

She laughed. The sound gave him a twinge in the crotch. *Great. Just what I need: a case of lover's balls up here in the turret in the middle of nowhere.*

"How soon do you figure on cristeros showing up in the vicinity of our objective?"

"Can't say. It was a patrol out of Corpus Christi that spotted a mess of 'em. Our communications aren't all that good; EMP didn't leave us that much t' work with. We don't know where their spearhead has got to, nor how many of them there are."

"Wait a minute, McKay," Sloan said. "Aren't we assuming a little much here? I thought we were going to Houston on a just-in-case basis. What makes you think the cristeros are actually heading for the desalinization facility?"

"Sheer paranoia, all right? With everything that's gone down since the War I've decided there ain't no such thing as coincidence. At least not where the Blueprint's concerned."

"If we get hung up I'll send Dreadlock ahead. He's got some of his old crew together with a bunch of bikes."

"How many?"

She laughed again. "Maybe twenty. Shoot, McKay, I don't even have a hundred. Eighty, more like."

"Yeah, but we're going to get some relief here soon? Lamar promised us rapid reinforcements."

"That's the plan."

"How many cristeros could there be?" He didn't even want to imagine how many cristeros there could be. "It's a long way from the border to Houston. McKay out."

Eklund dropped her voice a husky octave. "Now, don't get *too* lonely, riding up there in that ol' cold turret all by yourself—"

"Knock it off, Eklund."

" 'Bye."

"I wonder if we're doing the right thing."

McKay squeezed his eyes shut, then opened them again almost at once. He had the wheel, after all. And with false dawn tickling the eastern sky the most treacherous visibility of the day was coming on quickly to the coastal plain southwest of devastated Houston.

"Whaddaya mean, Sloan?" he growled.

"You know perfectly well what I mean, McKay."

Yeah, he did. That was why he'd winced. Sloan had voiced the thought that had been pounding on the inside of McKay's skull as if it were trying to bust its way out, even since they'd split from Dallas.

"We got a mission," he said. His tongue felt and tasted like an old tennis shoe.

"But we have orders, McKay. We've been told to disregard that mission."

McKay felt his upper lip bend toward one corner. Dr. Connoly had been on the horn, even before they'd talked to Eklund and the Texican relief column.

"This is treason, McKay!" she squawked.

"No, ma'am," he'd replied. *"It's mutiny."*

"But the president—"

McKay had reached over Sloan's shoulder to punch up another channel, breaking the connection.

"I was brought up to follow orders," McKay said. "But I was also brought up to do what's right."

"Wasn't that, like, what the Nuremberg trials were all about?" Casey Wilson asked from aft, where he was ostensibly taking his break. "Didn't they decide that you had to do what was right, no matter what your orders said?"

"Not exactly," Sloan said from the turret. "Or, rather, that was what they decided, but that principle hasn't been upheld much since then. President MacGregor delegated authority over us to Dr. Connoly. That makes it legal—and what we're doing is mutiny."

"But is it?" Rogers asked. He was pulling ESO duty next to McKay.

"What do you mean, Tom?" Sloan asked.

"We're not in the usual chain of command. We were recruited to carry out a particular mission: to put the Blueprint back together. Nothing's supposed to interfere with that."

"But that's been superseded."

"I don't reckon it has."

"What are you talking about? Connoly speaks for the president, when all is said and done."

McKay steered around the ancient wreck of a stakebed farm truck. "So what?" he said.

There was crackling silence. "What are you saying, McKay—"

"So what if Connoly speaks for President Jeff?"

"Have you forgotten he's the commander in chief? Has that little detail slipped your feeble mind, McKay?"

"He's commander in chief of the military," McKay said. "We ain't military."

Sloan sputtered like a cold engine. "Are you crazy? We're not *military?*"

"Army–Navy–Air Force–Marines," McKay chanted the cadence of an old recruiting jingle. "Which one are *we?*"

"Well, we're—that is . . ."

"We're part of Project Blueprint," Rogers said. "We used to answer to Major Crenna. Now . . . I dunno. Maybe we answer to Dr. Morgenstern. And we answer to our duty."

"I still answer to Crenna," McKay said. The words came out hoarser than he'd expected.

Sloan said nothing. Not even he was willing to argue with the ghost of the one-eyed Special Forces major who had made them what they were, and who had died to help them get clear of Heartland with the president and a few dozen Blueprint specialists.

"Well, Sloan?" McKay demanded harshly. "What's it

gonna be? If you want, I can drop you off by the side of the
road somewhere. I'm sure you can hitch a ride with some of
Randy Jim's ee-lite Texas Rangers.''

A wet, clammy midwinter coastal cold had settled into
Mobile One, one that had nothing to do with the temperature
outside, nor even the humidity, which was rising steadily.

''I'm a Guardian, McKay,'' Sloan said at last, in a voice
like a rag being torn in two. ''I've lived as one and I'm ready
to die as one. You're not the only one who takes this duty
thing seriously, McKay.''

They drove in uncomfortable silence while the world gathered
itself around them for another run at daytime. Eventually Casey
broke the deadlock.

''So, like, what's going to happen to us, Billy?'' he wanted
to know. ''I mean with, like, Dr. Connoly on our cases and all.''

McKay shrugged. ''She's been on our cases before. Shit, it
seems like we get called traitors all over the airwaves by our
own side at least twice a year. I guess we just get used to it,
and take our lumps in Houston.''

''Answer me one question, McKay,'' Sloan said.

McKay knotted up inside. His face clenched like a fist. There
were four Guardians or none at all, the way he saw it, but if
Sloan pushed him one millimeter more—

''*What?*''

''You're the one who hated the idea of secession so badly
you almost took a swing at President LaRousse. Now you're
all fired up to go into battle right alongside the Republicans.
What gives?''

The tension came out of McKay in a rush that left him weak.
''Because at least the Republicans are willing to fight the cristeros for a piece of property America needs. That makes 'em
good guys in my book.''

''They're going to have terms,'' Rogers reminded gently.

''Yeah. So they are. But four of us can't hold off a million
fucking religious nuts, even if we are a bunch of hardcore
heroes. And I got a feelin' we'll have a lot more luck bargaining
with the Texicans than with the Soldiers of Christ the King.''

''I just had a thought, Billy,'' Casey said.

''Must be lonely. Spit it out.''

''Uh, shouldn't we, like, call Dr. Jake and find out what he
thinks of this whole thing? That is, if you think we should
answer to him, and all.''

"Details, Case. I mean, we can't bother the man for every little thing; he's got a busy schedule, and anyway it's still the middle of the night back in California—"

"Billy." Rogers had hunched forward and was straining to see through his forward block. "There's something in the road. I thing we'd best slow down."

CHAPTER
SIXTEEN

McKay snapped back to reality, thankful he hadn't blundered into a wreck while he was preoccupied. Or run the damned car into the drink; off to the right a stream glinted black and evil as something from a cheap sci-fi flick in the half-hearted light, paralleling the highway maybe forty meters away.

Up ahead around a bend a battered pickup truck lay on its side on the gravel shoulder in the magenta glow of a circle of flares. Next to it an old woman sat sobbing on a crate, while a younger one knelt at the side of a prostrate child. The child's clothes and face seemed to be spattered with blood.

Another young woman had stepped into the road and was waving the armored car down. Despite the dazzle of headlights her eyes were wide and frightened as a deer's.

"Accident," Sloan said. "Maybe we should stop."

McKay frowned. He was braking, mainly because he was afraid of running into something, whatever had spilled the pickup, maybe. The road here had two lanes, and there was an old wreck halfway in the oncoming lane just short of the upset truck. A two-meter grassy bank shouldered to within a few meters of the road on that side.

"I don't know . . ." he said.

"It looks like that kid's hurt, Billy," Casey said.

"Damn." McKay hated to slow down for anything, but he guessed they couldn't just cruise on by. Anyway, the woman in the road was too foxy to run over . . . and that summer-weight dress was *mighty* thin, and clung to her in some real interesting ways, and he wasn't any too sure she had anything on under it. . . .

He slowed to a stop. The young woman brushed her black hair from her face and smiled gratefully. Tom Rogers turned away from his panel to fetch his medical kit.

The world turned yellow and shocking bright.

Molotov! rang in McKay's brain, even before the crash of glass on the front armor registered. Through a dancing curtain of hot light he saw more gasoline bombs arc down from the bank, comets blazing against a mauve and black sky. The players in the touching family scene by the roadside got up and boogied for cover through flameshot half-light. The young woman in her thin dress just stood their smiling, with the wind molding fabric to her firm breasts.

McKay kicked down the gas. Mobile One surged ahead like a charging triceratops. The angle of its snout caught the young woman in the thighs. She slammed forward, splayed and martyred on the hard glacis, and for a micro-moment her wide, brown eyes stared into McKay's. Then blood came from her mouth and her momentum spun her high up into the air like a gored bullfighter.

A score of hands were pushing the pickup over onto its back, in Mobile One's path. The V-450 struck it a glancing blow, spun it away, grinding men and women to pulp against the weed-cracked blacktop. The guns birthed thunder overhead as bullets rang off the hull like hail.

A giant kicked Mobile One in the ass. The car rotated three times quickly around to its center of gravity, tires shrieking. Casey went all everywhere; McKay's head slammed into the dash. He was unaware of any sound attending the blow, but where his hearing had been remained only roaring emptiness.

It was getting hot. Through his hand still clutching the wheel McKay could *feel* the vibrations as gasoline-filled bottles shattered themselves on the hull. Mobile One sat parked crosswise on the road at the center of a lake of burning gasoline.

The vehicle was NBC-sealed, which meant that gas was un-

likely to seep in. But the roaring inferno outside could melt
even the tough honeycomb tires, could raise the temperature
within until their blood boiled and their ammunition cooked
off. And that wouldn't take long—

Another massive impact raised the car off its portside wheels.
McKay barely stopped himself from cracking his head on the
hull as it rocked back down.

Dynamite bomb, Rogers mouthed at him. He had his Galil.
He slid open the shutter of a firing port, stuck the SAR through
the rubber gasket out among the flames, fired a burst—though
all McKay could see through the vision block above was im-
penetrable flame.

McKay rammed home the ignition pedal again. The Super
Commando seemed sluggish off the mark. Maybe the tires were
melting into the pavement. McKay drove straight ahead, mostly
on instinct, while figures loomed up before him, turned into
specters by a filter of flame. He could just hear their cries as
the car butted them from its path.

The V-450 carried a man into a barbed wire fence. The three
wire strands sectioned him like a cheese slicer; then they parted,
creating a faint musical chord. McKay's hearing was definitely
coming back; he could make out the hammering of bullets on
their rear armor, and the roar of fire, and even—at least he
imagined—the rush of ankle-high grass beneath the tires.

Then Mobile One shot out over the bank of the stream. For
a moment it hung there in the air, then bellyflopped into the
water. Water exploded up around the car, and the steel-and-
titanium belly thumped hard against the stream bed. McKay
feared that the tires had been driven so deep they'd stick there,
but then bouyancy and water rushing back plucked them up
off the bottom.

For several seasick heartbeats the car lurched up and down
like an enormous metal fishing bobber. Then it settled down
with the cleats just kissing the bottom weeds, enough to give
a touch of traction so the car didn't have to swim—it could,
theoretically, but McKay had long ago learned to be skeptical
of military specifications and manufacturers' claims.

Another Molotov cocktail crashed against the rear of the
turret.

"These fuckers don't give up," McKay said, his voice
sounding as if it belonged to someone else—somebody on his
last legs. "Do something about them, Sloan. They bother me."

The former naval officer needed no encouragement. The limit to how far he could depress the turret guns' barrels had spared the ambush from retribution—they'd been too close to get at. Now, however, they were right up there on the bank, lined up like bottles on a fence.

His scruples didn't even twinge as he knocked them down with a long, soul-satisfying blast of .50-cal.

McKay turned the car to follow the stream. Rogers popped the hatch about the ESO seat and climbed half out with a fire extinguisher to deal with the patches of flaming gas the car's swan dive hadn't doused. Several hardy souls gouged bright streaks in the char-marks around him, blazing away from cover beyond the streambank. Sloan dropped a curtain of forty mike-mike between them and Mobile One, spoiling their aim and most likely splattering them with starfishes of white phosphorus.

After a hundred meters or so McKay turned Mobile One toward the bank. Her front tires tore at soft black soil bound with the roots of tall, tan weeds, hauling the car dripping from the water like a dinosaur emerging from a swamp.

McKay paused on the road while Rogers got out to spray a few stubborn flames clinging to life aft of the turret, keeping the V-450's bulk between him and the ambush party. Sloan hosed 40-mm death onto anything that resembled motion in the eerie gray dawnlight.

"Ease up, there, navy boy," McKay said. "We need to save some for the house-warming."

"We have plenty, McKay," Sloan said. "We darned near cleared out that cache." He was referring to the cases of ammunition and other fungibles, bungeed into almost every free cubic centimeter of space the vehicle offered. They'd taken them from one of the countless supply dumps which had been dotted around the country before the One-Day War in secret preparation for Project Blueprint.

"How long do you think that'll last when the Christers start coming over the wire?"

Sloan ceased fire. Tom clambered back into the car, secured the hatch and extinguisher. His face was blackened with soot.

"That was a set ambush, Billy," he said. "It was no spur-of-the-moment thing.

McKay didn't reply. He just turned the wheel and let her roll.

●   ●   ●

The sun squeezed itself up from the horizon, an enormous ball of self-luminous pus caught in miraculous super-slow-mo as it spurted up into a yellowish sort of sky.

"McKay."

"Now what?" McKay hadn't been driving all that long, but his eyeballs felt sunburned. Maybe he should think about retirement. He applied the brakes.

They had just crested a hill. How many encounters of theirs, in this wonderful Day-After world they lived in, had started out like that? Well, this was another.

It was one of the billboards—long banned—still standing in the state of Texas, half a klick away. Not even a billboard, really, just a make-shift wooden sign, two meters by three perhaps, and long erased by rain and sun. There was a man tied spread-eagled in front of it. There was a lot of flammable-looking debris, smashed furniture and driftwood and old tires from a trashed out trailer court not far away across a grassy field, piled up beneath him. There were maybe twenty or thirty people gathered around, and in case anybody had any doubts as to who they might be they were waving around a banner with the miraculous image of the Virgin of Gaudalupe.

They seemed too preoccupied with their morning entertainment to've heard the grunting approach of Mobile One. No doubt they'd been singing.

"They're going to burn him," Sloan gasped.

"No shit, Sherlock," McKay said.

"Funny," Tom Rogers mused. "The cristeros haven't been going in for the usual atrocities much."

"Just killing everybody in their path."

"Uh-*huh*. Well, we are gonna rain on their parade. Just on general principles."

"Could it be another trap?" Casey asked.

McKay looked at Rogers. The former Green Beret shook his head. "Isn't likely."

"How are we going to rescue him?" Sloan asked.

"We make a lot of loud noises and cause parts of people to go flying off in various directions," McKay said.

"I think they have gas cans down there. They've probably doused him."

"Um—yeah." That let out the grenade launcher. The Browning, too, come to think of it—every fifth round was a tracer.

It wasn't that McKay cared all that much about setting the

poor fuck off, though he didn't generally hold by setting fire
to people he didn't actually have a grudge against. It was mainly
that he was determined to spoil the cristeros' fun.

"Tear gas?" he suggested.

"Cans burn hot, Billy," Rogers said.

"So they do. Well, fuck."

"Give me a shot, Billy," Casey said. He already had his
rifle unshipped.

"Go for it."

He let Casey slip out the side, then ran the car back down
until Sloan could barely see the show going on even by opening
the hatch and sitting up out of it like a prairie dog. He turned
the wheel over to Rogers and bailed out himself with the Maremont. He wasn't going to miss the fun, and he knew Tom
didn't care.

This bunch of cristeros seemed interested in talking, both to
each other, and to their apparent intended victim. That gave
Casey time to slip forty or so meters away from the car and
get himself set up. McKay mirrored him in the other directon.

Just about the time McKay had the bipod down and the
buttplate tucked against his shoulder, a guy in white pajama-
looking clothes held up one arm and began strutting around
while the crowd *oohed* and *aahed* approval. McKay couldn't
make out details at this range, but he would've bet his left nut
the dude had a lighter.

"Ready, Case?"

"Sure."

"Hit him."

He heard the thump of the rifle. Part of a second later the
man with the lighter dropped to his knees and fell on his face.
People shied away from him as if afraid he was possessed by
devils. Others were staring around; they'd heard the *crack* of
the supersonic round's passage, but had no idea which way it
had come from.

The banner bearer was next to go. The Virgin on her crescent
moon fluttered into the dirt. Onlookers cried out in horror. One
rushed forward to seize the sacred flag.

McKay could actually see the cloud of blood mist out of his
head where Casey drilled him.

After that Casey started plunking them at random. They had
edged away from the guest of honor at this point, perhaps

fearing he had something to do with all these people suddenly coming down with death.

McKay sighted in one clump, let off two five-round bursts, letting muzzle-jump disperse the rounds for him. It was perfect. Six wound up thrashing on the ground, as many more ran desperately away from the thunder booming down from the hilltop.

He swung the MG this way and that, dispensing death in judicious doses. Fanaticism or no, the survivors were shortly lined out and headed in the right direction. There was just something about sudden, hard-hitting death you couldn't even *do* anything about that spoiled the best of intentions.

Aside from a few short bursts, nipping heels to keep the cristeros moving rather than firing for effect, that was it. Regretfully McKay watched the fleeing mob. They had a good two hundred meters between them and decent cover; he might have bagged every damn one of them. But he remembered his own advice to Sloan—they had to save up for the main event.

"That's it," he said, pointing the M-60 skyward and slapping the bipod down against the hot barrel. "Let's go see what we got."

CHAPTER
SEVENTEEN

What they had was a minister, Methodist, middle-aged.

He was the Reverend Foster, and he was looking for his lost faith.

"Did you mislay it somewhere around here?" McKay asked. Since all the hatches were open he put a cigar in his face, intending to light it. Then he remembered *why* the hatches were open. Though they'd dunked the liberated captive in another handy tributary of the Brazos, he still exuded a powerful reek of gasoline, and might even be flammable. Regretfully McKay tucked the cigar back in his breast pocket.

Sloan was giving him pained looks from the driver's seat, but Foster only smiled. He had reddish hair that had retreated well back from a high forehead, giving him a slightly bullet-headed look, and blue eyes that were permanently squinted with laugh-lines and the bright sun of a year and a half on the road.

"It wasn't exactly around here that I lost it, Lieutenant. That would be Utica, New York. Not long after the air-raid sirens started telling me that the war we'd all survive if we only had enough shovels had begun."

"Griffiss Air Force Base," Sloan said. "You were lucky." The heavy bomber base had been a high-priority Russian target.

"Not necessarily. Though I confess I didn't have a shovel with me when the warhead flashed, though I believe some of the poor souls I ministered to afterward might have. Most weren't in any shape to tell me."

He rubbed his sunburned bald spot. "Since then I've been all over. I was always taught, you see, that humanity *needs* faith to survive. So I thought I'd find out what other people and places had to offer in that line."

"Why were the cristeros trying to, like, burn you?" asked Casey, who was taking his turn in the turret as they made their final approach to the alleged location of the desalinization facility.

"I started asking questions. They wanted me to take what they told me on faith. They didn't seem to understand that that was the whole point of the exercise, that if I could take anything on faith I wouldn't have been taking up their time. They seemed to take exception to that."

He shook his head. "A good many people are extremely touchy on that point, I can assure you. Oh, they'll tell you about their faith readily enough. But when you start to ask more probing questions, try to get to the root of *why* they believe, they grow quite resentful. You wouldn't believe how lucky I was to escape Oklahoma City after my interview with the Reverend Mr. Smith."

"Oh, yes we would," the Guardians chorused.

"What about these cristeros, padre?" Tom Rogers asked. "What do they believe in?"

"Desperation."

"Beg pardon?"

"They are people with literally nothing to lose but their lives, Lieutenant. Farmers displaced by the government before Córdoba's election, urban poor from the vast shantytown that surrounds Mexico City; given the way this world has treated them, even their lives seem to them a small enough loss.

"As for a specific creed, I'm not sure; nor do I think they're any too sure, strange as it may seem. These are simple, unsophisticated people, with a highly intuitive approach to religion. Mostly what motivates them would appear to be intense veneration of the Virgin Mary, in the person of the Virgin of Gaudalupe and a girl they call Sister Light. She's their prophet, as it were."

"We got that much," McKay said. "What else?"

Foster spread his hands. "Nothing else, to speak of. Just a species of hyperthyroid Mariolatry, at the risk of sounding like a typical Protestant bigot. Intuitive, as I say. Though I'm by no means criticizing; it's just that in my typical Western, overly rationalized manner I'm too far out of touch with my intuitions for their solutions to satisfy me." He chuckled. "Their solution to *that* was to set me on fire."

"You know anything about their organization?" Rogers asked.

"Very little—that applies to how much I know for sure and how much organization they appear to have. They do not seem to enjoy the support of the Mexican clergy; such leaders as they have, spiritual and otherwise, are those personally anointed by Sister Light. Though she does seem to have one main acolyte—a high priest, you might almost call him—name Manuel Tejada. A former businessman in Mexico City, I understand. A rarity in this movement."

"Does he pull her strings?" McKay asked.

Foster shrugged. It was clear that he was bored with the direction the conversation was taking.

"Tell me about yourselves, why don't you?" he suggested. "I'm curious as to what motivates men such as yourselves."

Oh boy, McKay thought.

Half an hour later when they saw the sign, the Guardians were beginning to understand why the cristeros had been getting ready to put the Reverend Mr. Foster to the torch.

It wasn't that he was unpleasant or anything. He was the soul of courteous interest. But he kept after them, probing with incessant questions like a dental hygienist working over your gums with one of those steel-hook things they love so much, until McKay was about ready to pull the pin on a Willy Peter grenade and tuck it into a pocket of Foster's gasoline-impregnated blazer.

The sign was official U.S. government white-on-green paper. It read BERNARDO GALVES EXPERIMENTAL SALTWATER RECLAMATION FACILITY.

"Right up here by the highway," Sloan commented admiringly, as he turned the car into the graded dirt road indicated by the sign. "God, why can't they all be like that?"

The plant seemed to rise up and out of an expanse of white

sand dotted with clumps of high weeds and brush, just beginning to show hints of early green. Beyond a line of dunes the sun glinted at random off the Gulf of Mexico.

McKay's heart sank as he panned his binoculars across the scene from the vantage point of a low bluff.

"They sure don't believe in making the place easy to defend," he commented bitterly. "Their perimeter's better than a kilometer long, just along this side."

"It sure is Texas-sized, man," Casey remarked. He seemed obscurely pleased by the fact.

"They didn't make it particularly inconspicuous, either," Sloan commented. Like McKay he'd opened the hatch above his head and was sitting up in the sunshine, squinting off toward the plant. "The place was designed with research in mind, not security."

"That Wolf Bayou joint was designed with plenty security in mind."

"Fusion power's a lot more controversial than turning saltwater into fresh. It has a lot more immediate strategic implications too, not to mention one or two tactical ones."

"Besides, it's hard to *hide* a desalinization plant from the air," Casey pointed out. "Shoot, I bet you could, like, see this place from *orbit*."

"What about the reactor? Lots of nut groups would love to picket a place with a reactor. Or maybe blow it up."

"The reactor wasn't common knowledge," Sloan said. "With all the controls on the press that came in before the One-Day War, the government had a way of keeping items like that from coming out, if it really wanted to."

"A good thing, too," McKay said. "Keep commies from homing in on the place with satchel charges."

Sloan glanced at his commander, wisely decided to let it slide. Tempers were still too frayed from last night for any kind of debate.

The area secured by the perimeter wire, McKay was noting with something less than ecstasy, was pretty well built up. To the right of the access road running straight through the middle of the place were all kinds of towers and pipes and tanks, all of which had been made of a rustproof alloy, so that they still gleamed pristinely as if somebody'd been polishing them every single day; to the left, barracks and prefabs for admin and onsite personnel. The northern corner, at the extreme left, was a parking lot dotted with cars that looked like lumps of raw silver in the Gulf sunlight.

A skeleton crew had been supposed to stay on at the plant when the balloon went up, keeping an eye on the reactor and various valuable hunks of equipment, maybe carrying out a little research. As predicted, the Soviets didn't drop any fallout-producing groundbursts on Houston—which wasn't all that nearby anyway, perhaps fifty klicks; Galveston was marginally closer. As part of the little game they played with themselves, pretending their gimped economy could sustain a prolonged war even after the strategic nuclear exchange stage was reached, the Soviets had dedicated a lot of firepower to making sure the port complex couldn't be used to sustain an effort against them—but all in the form of airbursts, more cost-effective destruction than groundbursts, but which would have done little harm to people down here unless they were cleverly gazing at the warheads when they flashed off.

In spite of this, there had never been any communication logged from the facility after the One-Day War, and attempts over the last few weeks to contact it from Washington and California had met silence. The consensus was disease. Whether the Russians had used plague-bombs on America was still unsettled—their attempt at battlefield deployment of the vaunted NBC-warfare capability in Europe had been a hideous flop—but God knew any number of wholly natural, organic, no-preservatives-added pathogens had partied down in the wake of the bombing.

"Good news is we got three to eight hundred meters of more or less open country before the bandicoots hit the wire," he said, reflexively applying the old South-West Asia Command slang for Arab guerrillas to the cristeros, "though they got more dunes and bushes to hide behind than I'm happy about. The bad news is, once they get inside the wire they got all kinds of places to hide."

"And we can't go dropping ordnance at random in the middle of a Blueprint plant," Sloan said.

McKay nodded grimly. Destroying something in order to save it had never made a shitload of military sense to him anyway. There was always denying resources to the enemy.—*never leave nothin' for Charlie!*—but that was something completely different, like Monty Python used to say, something last-ditch and desperate. Besides, wrecking this place would be denying it to *America*.

Had this been the Project Starshine skunk works, a few hundred klicks away around the coastal curve in Louisiana, he would have considered blowing the place rather than letting it fall into enemy hands; the Apollo generator was too damned dangerous. But *fresh water*—

It wasn't that McKay was too soft-hearted for scorched earth. But that would be ceding these fucking Christers too much, implying they had come to stay. No, he'd fight the battle he was faced with, and if they lost—well, shit, it'd save Maggie Connoly the trouble of cashiering them.

"Let's get a move on," he ordered.

"Billy," Casey said from the turret, "there's people at the gate."

"Shit," McKay said, thinking cristeros. "Take us in slowly, Sloan. Case, be ready to shoot."

The wire-mesh gates, with loops of razor tape spiraled along the tops, stood wide open. There was windblown trash piled up against the fence, making it hard to see past. McKay could see the outline of a human head and shoulders through the polarized glass of the security booth. It didn't tell him a lot.

He unclipped the single-shot M-79 grenade launcher from the dash, broke it, stuck a multiple-projectile round into it, turning it into an outsized shotgun. He wasn't going to sit on his butt in the ESO seat while cristeros lobbed bottles of napalm cola at Mobile One.

He glanced out the forward port, glanced back down as he snicked the grenade launcher shut—did an incredulous take at the gate forty meters away.

"What the fuck, over?"

"Horsemen, McKay," Sloan said. "You wouldn't know that, being a city boy and all."

McKay snarled wordlessly at him. It wasn't easy to assimilate: a dozen men on horseback, each and every one of them wearing cowboy hats and ankle-length duster coats, each carrying a longarm—everything from AKs to Winchesters. They crowded into the open gates and halted facing the oncoming armored car, the horses tossing their heads and sidestepping.

"O-*kay,*" McKay said. He laid the M-79 down on the console, opened his overhead hatch and stood up.

"Good morning, gentlemen," he said as Sloan slowed to a halt.

A big dude with an impressive sweep of black mustache nudged his horse a little ahead of the others. The horse was an impressive sonofabitch, large, shining like a DI's boots, dark all over but not black, except at mane and tail. McKay knew there was a word for horses that looked like that, but he didn't have a clue as to what it was.

"I'm Jesse Carr," the big dude said. "Are you the Guardians?"

"Yeah. So?"

Carr turned the horse sideways. The other riders backed their mounts to the sides. Carr gestured at the cleared gate with a gloved hand.

"Then it's my honor and pleasure to welcome you, in the name of the South Texas Protective Association."

CHAPTER
EIGHTEEN —————————

The STPA permitted Mobil One to roll through the gates and between their ranks, making McKay feel as if he were getting married; he halfway expected them to bring sabers swooping down behind the car as it passed. Then the riders broke rank and went racing for the cinderblock admin buildings a couple of hundred meters away, waving their hats and yipping shrill—what else?—rebel yells.

McKay rode in state at a more sedate pace, with a salt-sticky sea breeze ruffling his short hair. Jesse Carr and several of his cohorts dismounted and went into a white-painted building. Sloan stopped in front of it. McKay boosted himself out the hatch and dropped to the sand. Sloan turned the wheel over to Rogers and came out the side door to join him.

Inside the admin building it was gloomy, hot and close. It was hard to believe that not two weeks ago they'd been freezing their asses off in Montana—or that scarcely more than a week ago it had felt like winter in San Antone, which was usually not much more arctic than the coast zone.

"Going to be a long, hot summer," Sloan subvocalized. *"This plant could save a lot of lives."*

"Yeah."

Jesse Carr sat with his boots propped on a receptionist's

desk. "Good to see you, gentlemen. We expected you earlier; feared you might be delayed."

"We were. No big deal. I'm Billy McKay, and this is Sam Sloan."

"Pleased to meet you. This is Amon, and Buddy, and my little brother Jamie, and that's Raschid."

The boys in the Wild Bunch suits nodded and shook hands in order as the elder Carr named them.

"Raschid?" both McKay and Sloan blurted before they could help themselves. The man in question, slim-built but round-faced, grinned and bobbed his head.

"His family's in oil," Carr said, by way of explanation. "Runs a few cattle. Pretty much like the rest of us." He rolled a cigarette one-handed and lit up with a match.

"How did you happen to be here this morning, Mr. Carr?" Sloan asked. "You hail from these parts?"

"Nope. We're from around San Antone, mostly. Though lately we been up to the Colorado River line, eyeball-to-eyeball with the Federals."

"What are you doing here?" McKay asked bluntly. He wasn't in the mood for surprises this morning.

Carr raised a brow. He had a weathered, beaky face, with a long jaw and prominent incisors. "You might say we're civilian militia. Picked up word of this little expedition over the radio and came down to lend a hand."

"We're helpin' defend sacred Texan soil against the brown-skinned invader," said Jamie Carr, a fresh-faced if slightly-dopey looking blond kid of maybe twenty. He shouldn't have tried the mustache. The twenty or thirty hairs were virtually transparent.

McKay looked at him hard, trying to figure out whether he meant that or not. If he did, he was in for a surprise or two. *So much for radio security,* he thought. He wondered if the cristeros had been listening in to all that Texican chatter too; that might account for the dawn ambush they'd hit. But no, it didn't feel right.

"You rode all the way here on horseback?" Sloan asked.

The Protective Associate introduced as Buddy laughed deep in his throat, a sound that reminded McKay of a man trying to swallow a hard-boiled egg whole. Buddy was your authentic Redneck Mother, by the looks of him. Maybe six-four, with a tanned, red, full-cheeked face set on a thick neck and lineman's shoulders, a sandy mustache and eyes as filled with expression as a couple of chips of blue glass.

"Nope," he said. "Brought the horses here on trailers."

Sloan raised an eyebrow at McKay, who shrugged. "And just what is it that you gentlemen protect, by the way?" Sloan asked.

"South Texas, of course," said Jesse Carr's brother, Jamie.

Noon came and went. The day got hotter. Carr's fifteen-man militia patrolled the perimeter while McKay poked around and fretted. There was no word from Eklund's flying column. San Antonio hadn't heard from her either.

Shortly after 1330 a motorcycle rolled through the cut where the access road passed through a long, low ridge. McKay was in the main admin building drinking Kool-Aid and going over Rogers's estimates of their supply situation when the call came back from the gate by walkie-talkie. He tossed the clipboard down on a desk and raced out.

Even at this range there was no mistaking Dreadlock Callahan, with his Little Orphan Annie hair bouncing around his shoulders. As McKay watched, more motorcycles cruised into view, followed by a convoy of canvas-covered trucks.

Reinforcements had arrived.

McKay gave Eklund and Callahan a grand tour of the facility, riding in an open Toyota four-wheeler that had come down with the Texican reinforcements. Over half of the plant was as McKay had seen from the outside—but there had been a surprise.

"Now we're coming to the real meat of the operation," he said, driving out onto a three-hundred-meter causeway raised out of a tidal swamp on a bed of crushed white seashells. Ahead of them rose an island, several hundred meters in extent, dotted with strands of palmetto. From the middle of it rose a blocky building that resembled a miniature Vehicle Assembly Building at Cape Canaveral. It was surrounded by more modest structures and more pipe-tangles like the ones in the main compound behind them.

"What the heck's that?" Eklund asked. She had on cammie trousers and a red tank top. With her grown-out hair—which McKay still hadn't gotten used to—piled up on top of her head, and a set of shades, and a plastic cup from the commissary through which she was drinking grape Kool-Aid through a straw, she looked like a coed hitting Fort Lauderdale for spring break. A very large coed, granted, and not many coeds tended to tote issue Beretta sidearms on web belts cinched around their narrow little waists.

"Masking for the cooling tower. Got big vents in it to let the air circulate. Just camouflage; wanted to avoid as much controversy as they could when they were building this place."

"Reactor running?" Callahan asked from the back, where he was sitting crosswise. He sounded a tad nervous, which was unusual for him.

"Nope. Pulled the rods at Condition Yellow, as the war in Europe started heating up, stored everything fissionable in special subterranean vaults. But as far as we can tell it's all ready to put back together and fire up, as soon as we get somebody who knows what he's doing. We're transmitting data to Washington—" He ignored the peculiar look she passed him. "Case and Sloan have a computer up and running off solar-accumulator power, and are rooting around in the database."

He gestured off to the left, where a bunch of half-cylinder structures lay almost buried by drifts of sand and debris. More exposed to the Gulf weather systems than the rest of the complex, the island showed more signs of the hurricanes that had punished this coast since the One-Day War, including the monster storm that had finally written off the FSE attempt to grab Project Starshine late last summer.

"They got living quarters and food storage to last a hundred people a year out here. We won't starve, anyway."

A hundred meters on, the island shelved rapidly away to the water. Surf played among a checkerboard of pens where saltwater was collected for processing.

"Looks like the pens for the dolphins at SeaWorld," Marla remarked.

"So how does it all work?" Callahan asked.

"Well, they take the water, and they get all the salt out of it, and pump it through a big pipe that runs under the causeway to be stored or distributed or whatever the hell it is they do with it."

"Thanks, McKay. I feel like I could write a doctoral dissertation on the subject now."

"Got to ask questions, Dreadlock my man. That's how you learn things."

"*Billy,*" came Rogers's voice over the communicator, "*we*

have a little problem up front. You'd better come.''

McKay sighed. "And how often have I heard *that* over the last couple years? I'm on my way."

Eklund's relief column consisted of volunteers who, like their equipment, were what the Republic, still dealing with the cristero incursion south of Crystal City, reckoned it could spare on a moment's notice. At the moment, about half her eighty-odd assorted bods were split into fire teams and dispersed along the two kilometers of perimeter wire looped out from the swamp that backed up the mainland complex. That added up to a combat front of about fifty meters per man—or woman; the Republicans didn't seem to have a lot of scruples about sending their fair womenfolk into action, which fit strangely with McKay's preconceptions of Texan chivalry. That, in turn, meant that if the cristeros reached the wire they were in.

To compensate, the Texican force had fourteen machine guns, ten 5.56 M-249s and four big M-60s, as well as twenty grenade launchers and two 82-mm mortars, dug into sand pits two hundred meters apart on either side of the access road. Pretty awesome firepower—while the bullets lasted.

The bulk of Eklund's contingent was playing mobile reserve, which for the moment meant hanging around the admin area, which was fairly central to the mainland part of the place. Just now, most of them were gathered in a big semicircle, looking mean at Jesse Carr's Wild Bunch out in the middle of the admin parking lot.

The boys in the coats—McKay couldn't figure out how they stood them in this heat—were holding back big Buddy, whose face was even redder than usual. "I ain't takin' orders from no niggers!'' he was bellowing.

The troopies were hanging onto a skinny black guy with an enormous Afro and lieutenant's bars on his arm—Velcro ripa-ways, to keep him from playing Team Target to snipers when things hit the fan. *"Nigger?* Is that what you called me, you two-bit peckerwood?"

McKay was out of the Toy four-by the second it stopped. Tom Rogers sauntered over. "Kept 'em from killing each other," he said, nodding at the opposing factions, not just the two screaming endearments at each other.

McKay grimaced. This was Rogers's department, really; *he* was the hardened Green Beanie A-team leader, used to keeping the indiges from slitting each others' throats. Had he been in charge, this mess would have been settled already, and with no—or few, anyway—bodies to enrich the sandflies. But McKay was The Man here and now.

Command's a wonderful thing.

He hooked his thumbs in his pistol belt and swaggered over, hoping he looked a lot like John Wayne. "Well, gentlemen, what seems to be the problem?"

Everybody answered. He could still hear the two main antagonists; Buddy was sticking foursquare with "nigger," while his opposite number had escalated to "motherfucker."

"Shut the FUCK up!"

Silence landed like an Airborne Ranger with a non-deploying chute. McKay smiled. It was good to be a former Parris Island drill instructor.

"Now—" He pivoted to face the black officer. He was tall and skinny, with big, sleepy eyes and wide lips. He had a red headband tied around his temples. "Chi, I am ashamed of you. You used to be the definition of cool, my man, back when you were a corporal with India Three. Or did turning into a shavetail take it out of you?"

Chi—McKay said it *shy,* as in Chi-town, the dude's hometown—hung his head. "I'm sorry, man. He refused an order. I just lost it when he called me nigger."

"You can't afford to lose it no more, son. That's part of wearing those bars." He turned to face Buddy, "What's your excuse?"

"I ain't lettin' no nigger boss me around."

McKay stepped up close, crowding the larger man. "Show me some rank, cowboy."

"I-I'm a member of the South Texas Protective Association." Some of the sauce had leaked out of him.

"That's militia, right? Well, since you decided to want to come play soldier, you're now under military discipline."

"I ain't takin' orders from no *nigger!"* His voice rose to a hog squeal, and he sprayed spittle over McKay's face.

McKay smiled. "You will follow orders from any superior officer, whether that officer is a nigger, a greaseball, a chink, a dink, a kike, a honky motherfucker, or any other ethnic persuasion, soldier—and I use the term loosely—or it will be my very great pleasure to put a bullet through your fucking head."

He turned to address the mob at large. "Listen up, everybody. We are the Guardians, and we are in charge here. Next in line is Marla Eklund—*Lieutenant Colonel* Eklund."

There was some rumbling from the Texican troops at that. Marla stepped up beside McKay. "That's the way we agreed," she said, projecting her voice just like a drill sergeant—which she'd been, too, back before the War.

The combatants had cooled down enough that their buddies let their arms go. Now Buddy puffed himself up with fresh outrage. "I ain't takin' orders from no uppity bitch, neither!"

Eklund turned and faced him. Big as she was, she was four inches shorter and forty pounds lighter. But her straighthanded right to Buddy's jaw rocked him back on the high heels of his Tony Lamas, and her knee to his nuts dropped him to the sizzling asphalt like a wet bag of flour.

He spent a few moments huddled around himself, then looked up to see the muzzle of Eklund's Beretta two centimeters from the break in his nose.

"C'mon," Eklund said, grinning. "Make my day."

"Y-you . . . wouldn't."

She clicked off the safety.

Jesse Carr pushed his way forward. Eklund never took her eyes off the prostrate Buddy. Nobody else was actually aiming a piece, but a whole lot of guns were generally focused on the center of the circle.

Jesse Carr looked hard at Eklund. "Ma'am, I for one am honored to serve under your command. I take off my hat to you."

He reached up and swept off his Stetson. His riders followed suit. A couple hoisted Buddy to his feet—he was still sort of crimped in the middle, and had to be held up—and stuffed his hat into his hand. Moving with arthritic slowness he held the hat briefly to his head, lowered it, and put it back on, glaring hatred at Eklund the while.

"I'm prepared to recognize you as holding the rank of, ah, captain, Carr," McKay said. "Pick yourself a couple of lieutenants. I'd suggest one of them not be Buddy boy, here."

"I reckon President LaRousse will confirm that," Eklund said. "I'll recommend it in my report tonight."

She put the Beretta away and stuck out her hand. Carr took it, shook it, and everybody cheered.

Except McKay. *And I'm in charge of this looney bin,* he thought. *We are gonna die.*

• • •

The cristeros showed as the sun was swelling and getting heavier and heavier, fast approaching the moment the sky wouldn't hold it anymore and it would drop behind the dunes with an almost audible splat. Or rather, one cristero showed walking slowly down the access road from the cut.

Lying on his belly behind sandbags laid behind the gate, McKay focused binoculars on the figure. It was a teenaged girl, pretty in a full-faced, sad-eyed way. She wore a long white shift with Juan Diego's image of the Virgin painted on it, and held a white flag fluttering on a pole in the sea breeze.

"Is that Sister Light?" McKay asked Reverend Foster, who was belly down beside him in case negotiations broke out.

Foster shook his head. "I don't believe so. As near as I can tell, she's still in Mexico—there's a lot of fighting going on in the northern states. They always send out a young virgin when they want to parley. Symbolic, you see."

"Practical," Tom Rogers remarked. "People're less likely to fire her up."

"Blasphemers," Hector Rodriguez said from a sandbag nest next to the road. A small, intense man in white pajamalike peasant garb, with an eye that looked off at nothing in particular and the inevitable Zapata mustache, he was head of a contingent of a half-dozen actual Mexican volunteers, norteño farmers dispossessed by the cristeros. He looked as if he'd been carved out of dark hardwood. McKay guessed he was forty, though he had an ageless quality. Tom said it was common among those with a lot of *indio* blood. "They defile the image of our Brown Mother."

When the girl was two hundred meters away McKay stood up, leaving his Maremont lying with its bipod down, ready to rock and roll. When she was fifty meters off he raised a bullhorn to his lips.

"You don't have to come any farther. I'm Billy McKay of the Guardians. We've taken possession of this facility in the name of the United States of America and the, uh, Republic of Texas."

She stopped. McKay was ready to get Rogers, who spoke excellent Spanish, to translate, but she raised the white flag high, and answered him in English. "I call upon you in the name of la Virgen de Guadalupe and Hermana Luz to throw down your arms and accept conversion into the true Catholic faith."

"We got Catholics here," said McKay, who'd been baptized one himself, though he had no more religion in him than an armadillo.

"They are heretics. Only in the arms of the Virgin can they find salvation." Her accent was heavy, but the words were clear. They came on strong in the face of the wind off the sea.

"That's up to them as individuals. Now I got to ask you and your friends to withdraw. This entire area is under security. Your people are trespassing, and will be fired upon if they come any further."

"So be it," she said, and cast her banner down.

On the ridge behind her to either side of the road cut appeared a solid line of people a kilometer long. They stood a moment, black against the gaudy sunset sky. Then they rolled forward like an ocean wave.

CHAPTER
NINETEEN —————

As they came on they began to sing: *"Yo soy un cristiano
y soy un mejicano—"*

"Hold your fire," McKay said, keying his communicator
to the command channel. "I mean it. Anybody shoots without
the order is meat."

"Que viva mi Cristo, que viva mi Rey."

They started at a slow, nerve-winding walk, gradually gathering speed. Around him McKay could feel men and women
drawing taut as violin strings. Across six hundred meters of
sand the horde rolled, line upon line, waving banners and rifles,
their voices filled with inexpressible joy.

"Que viva mi Cristo—" Four hundred meters.

"Wait for it!" Three hundred. *God, there's a bunch of them!*

The woman in the painted shift stood her ground fifty meters
from the fence. She was singing too.

"Que viva Cristo Rey!" Two hundred.

"Oh, dear God, I can't take it anymore!" a voice shrilled on
the firing line.

"Almighty, Almighty, this is PBR Street Gang, over!"

A high, edged whistling passed over McKay's head. He
grinned. "I've always wanted to say that."

Four hundred meters away two mortar rounds exploded in air, scattering fragments in lethal circles—two hundred fifty meters behind the front ranks of the cristeros, who were now running flat-out for the wire.

McKay became one with the Maremont. The young woman who'd carried the truce flag filled his front sight. He found he couldn't tighten his finger on the trigger. She was so lovely, so innocent—

Yeah. And that's the plan. He thought of Rita Montañez, stoically bleeding to death in the back of Mobile One. She'd been a pretty Mexican girl too.

"Rock and roll!" he yelled. He pressed the trigger. All three bullets of his first burst hit the flag-bearer in the body. She hurtled backward to the sand, blood washing out the image carefully painted on her dress.

There was a beat, a horrified moment. The cristeros kept coming, a hundred meters away now.

The fenceline exploded in fire.

The defenders had expected a pure frontal assault along the road to start things out; faith was the cristeros' strong suit, not finesse. Nine machine guns and sixty assault rifles were ready along the front fence, with overlapping fields of fire.

The front rank fell. To a man, to a woman—to a child. McKay saw his bullets strike a boy no more than ten, tear an arm from his body as if he were a cheap doll. His lips drew back from his teeth in a feral snarl.

The cristeros came on over the bodies of their comrades.

More mortar rounds were dropping on the cristeros' rear ranks. Forty mike-mike grenades popped off among the mob. Their voices beat against the defenders like explosions.

But they were running into a solid wall of fire. Jacketed metal matched itself against flesh. Metal won.

The front ranks were staggering, stumbling over the bodies of their predecessors, wading through sand that clung in cakes to their blood-reddened shins. Then they weren't coming any more.

The idea had been to let the cristeros close, then hit them hard while dropping mortars behind them, an anvil to the firing-line hammer, to massacre them on the retreat—cold-blooded, yeah, but they weren't handing out second-place trophies this time around. It was a good idea.

But it didn't work as expected, because hardly any of the

attackers retreated through the rain of splinters. They died in their tracks, with a song on their lips.

McKay clambered shakily to his feet. He'd gone through a hundred-round belt of ammo as quick as he could, with no time to reload; he felt the heat beating off the barrel, distinct from the day-heat radiating from the sand. Reverend Foster prayed at his side. He could hear Marla Eklund sobbing brokenly over his communicator. Others were crying nearby. He saw Jamie Carr with tears flowing freely down his broad cheeks, but he wasn't the only member of the hard-bitten STPA to weep.

"Sweet Jesus," somebody yelled, "they're twenty-five meters away!"

Jesse Carr stood up, dusting sand off the fronts of his jeans. His face was frozen and deeply lined. "Must be a thousand of them out there."

"Six hundred," McKay said. "Close enough. How many casualties we take?"

He frowned as the reports came in. A strange sound was rising into the gathering night, a weird, whistling moan.

"What's that sound?" one of Carr's men asked.

"The wounded," Tom said.

Foster got to his feet. "We must help them."

McKay dropped his hand to his shoulder. His fingers dug in. "No way."

"But they're *hurt*."

"The idea's for them to be dead."

"My God, man, have you no humanity?"

"No."

Chi came running up, his long legs going every which way, holding his coal-scuttle helmet onto his 'fro with one hand. "Radio's out, sir," he reported. "We didn't have any casualties. O-orders—?"

Then his knees fell out from under him and he threw up.

"We took no casualties," Tom Rogers said. "Not one."

The others stared at him, faces washed out by the light of the driftwood fire burning next to the admin complex. McKay and Eklund had agreed the morale-boosting effect of building a few fires outweighed the risks. The cristeros were quiet, showing no inclination to snipe at the figures by the fires, and in case they got ideas about infiltration there were watchers on the wire with starlight scopes and crews ready in the mortar pits.

"Anybody take incoming rounds?" McKay asked. "Thought not."

"But what were they *doing?*" Sloan asked. His face had a gray pallor to it, visible even in firelight. McKay was just as glad Sam and Casey had been sitting in Mobile One waiting on a call for fire support during the attack. *Though they're gonna have to get used to this shit, all too soon.*

"Testing our strength," Marla Eklund said, staring into the fire with blind eyes. Her arms were crossed under her heavy breasts. "Makin' us burn ammo."

"That was *all?*" Sloan almost screamed.

"What's the matter with you people?" thick-necked Buddy demanded in his oddly shrill voice. "We whupped their asses! Shoot, I bet there ain't nobody out there—bet there ain't a cristero inside of twenty miles!"

Rogers raised his steel-gray Weimaraner eyes to the young rider's. "You think that, son," he said softly, "why don't you take a little stroll about eight hundred meters to the northwest? Nobody's gonna stop you."

Buddy dropped his eyes.

"I never seen anything like it," Jesse Carr said.

"Nobody has," Callahan said.

McKay caught Rogers's eye across the fire. His mouth tightened into a line. For once the biker-leader-turned-mercenary was wrong. McKay and Rogers had seen something much like this: Iranian human-wave attacks in south Iraq. The memories weren't pleasant.

"Now, you dudes saw some heavy shit when you were fightin' my man Coffin and his friends up in Colorado, didn't you?" Chi asked. He was sitting cross-legged by the fire. He'd recovered most of his composure, if not his normal cockiness.

Callahan sketched a thin smile. He'd started out on the other side of that campaign from the Guardians.

"It was never this bad," McKay said. "I mean, they came near to kicking our asses. But they weren't so—so—" He shook his head, unable to find a word.

"Fanatical?" asked a Texican mortarwoman, taking a break from the pits.

"No. Those New Dispensation drones were plenty fanatical."

"Cheerful," Callahan said. "That's your word, McKay. The Crusaders were never this goddamn *cheerful.*"

McKay sighed. The San Antonio-brewed beer Eklund had lugged along had started tasting like stale piss. He tipped the bottle to pour the rest out, then changed his mind and chugged the dregs. It was going to be a long time before they had any more.

"That ain't all of it, Dreadlock, but it's close enough for government work."

He hurled the bottle as far as he could toward the wire. "One thing's for fucking sure. We are gonna need help, Eklund, and we're gonna need it fast."

People drifted off to sleep or went to take their turns on watch. Eklund said the cristeros didn't like to attack at night, and Foster concurred—*just how much does that dog-collar know?* McKay wondered. At any rate he was content to leave a skeleton crew on watch. The cristeros weren't yet feeling enough of a strain to depart from their standard approach; today's casualties were nothing special for them. Besides, the fire- and sight-lines around the perimeter were open enough that if—when—they made their move, the defenders would have plenty of warning.

As a matter of fact, the defenders had plenty of advantages: firepower, heavy-weapons support, training and discipline (to varying degrees, but more than the cristeros), the tactical defensive from prepared positions, interior lines, enough food to keep them all fat for a year.

All the cristeros had going for them were numbers and an utter indifference to death. And a limit on the number of bullets the good guys had to burn.

"Sandy quit," Chi was saying, sitting with his long legs drawn up and his arms around his knees. He was reminiscing about the old gang from India Three. "Cato bit the big one in a hassle with the Federals near Austin about six months ago. Nguyen, Rosie and Torrance are all scattered through the Texican armed forces. We keep in touch; I think one or two may hitch up with the relief column, just for old times' sake. They all got commissions, now. Jamake, I don't know what happened to that nigger."

"What about my man Tall Bear?"

Chi shrugged. "Split with us not long after we split with you dudes. Went back up north to Luxor, look in on little Gillet.

Ain't heard from him. He was pretty bitter, man."

"Yeah." He'd been Marla Eklund's right-hand man. He'd never liked the Guardians, nor trusted them, and he blamed them for causing the death of half the squad he and the then–staff sergeant had kept alive so long.

He had a point, too.

"So, tell me, Dreadlock," McKay said, taking another hit of boiled coffee. He wasn't worried about it keeping him awake. As an old grunt he could sleep any time and anywhere. Of course, the coffee wasn't up to the standards he'd gotten used to in the Med, but you had to make allowances for your siege situations. "Just how do you account for the coincidence of the first two Texican commanders we run into being our old buddies you and Marla?"

Callahan squatted on his haunches staring into the dying fire with his hair hanging around his shoulder, looking more than usual like one of the Black Lectroids from *Buckaroo Banzai*. He shook his head, blinked, looked up at McKay.

"No coincidence, man. Or not much. The Texicans are short on officer material that's seen the elephant, as they used to say in these parts. I have some, ah, modest knowledge of the methods employed by the Reverend Smith's armed forces—"

"From having served with them, back when they still belonged to Coffin."

"Well, yes. And who better to know how to fight them? Marla, now, she's got a lot of talent, and she's had some damn good on-the-job training."

"Say what? Where?"

"Bunch of guys she hung out with for a while. Call themselves the Guardians. Supposed to be a real strak outfit—almost as tough as they think they are."

"Oh."

"Besides—" he gave his bad-boy grin "—we had some warning from a man in California you were on your way. Your most likely route happened to bring you through the area I was working anyway, so that worked out. And old Lamar could've picked any one of several combat zones to pack you off to for a look at our pals the cristeros. He just thought he'd show you a little Texican hospitality, maybe rekindle an old flame or two."

"Great. Just what I need. A crusty old fart of a cowboy artist playing matchmaker for me."

"My man Lamar takes care of his people, McKay," Chi said.

"Not always. Look at you. I figure *you* should be at least a field marshal in this outfit, the way they hand out promotions hereabouts. No offense, Dreadlock, but—you, a major? And Marla a light colonel? Shit, Idi Amin barely promoted himself that fast—"

"What do you mean, 'no offense,' Yankee?" a low and deadly voice said behind him. "You reckon I ain't entitled to my maple leaf?"

He made himself get slowly to his feet and face her. He knew the smoulder in those big blue eyes, all too well.

"What I said, Eklund. It's pretty fast—Third World fast."

"Lot of opportunities for advancement in the service of the Republic," Callahan said dryly, "what with the constant skirmishing with Reverend Forrie and the Federals, raiders up from Mexico, and, up until pretty recently, guerrilla warfare against your friends and mine, the FSE Expeditionary Force."

"Who your good buddy Randy Jim was busy suckin' up to, right up to the moment they pulled out," Marla said. "Or didn't you know about that?"

"Well, at least he's legitimate. He's not the tinhorn boss of a bunch of loonies who think they've seceded from the United States!"

Lots of silence surrounded the fire.

"Hearts and minds, McKay," Callahan said quietly, after an eternity or two. "Be glad not too many people who're putting their asses on the firing line next to yours are close enough to hear what you think of them."

"Like, what's this chip you got on your shoulder about the Republic, anyway, dude?" Chi asked.

"I can't hack this whole secession trip. And hey, much as I hate to admit it, Doc Connoly's right. So is this Randy Jim. Texas don't have the most spotless reputation. They revolted against Mexico so they could keep slaves, and after that make all the Mexicans they could catch eat shit too. And they played on the slaveholders' side in the Civil War. And this ain't exactly been a hotbed of civil rights since, either."

Chi looked at his wrists. "Whoa. I don't see no chains."

"Neither do I," Callahan said, "and I'm as much a nigger as Chi here to any self-respecting bigot, even though I could pass for white, were I to suffer a catastrophic lapse of taste."

McKay waved his big hands in the air. He was floundering. "But, look, you got your capital right next door to the Alamo—"

"Across downtown, as a matter of fact," Callahan offered.

"—and that glorifies the whole damn Texas tradition of, ah, violence and racism and all that shit."

"When did you become a bleeding heart, McKay?" Callahan asked. "And since when are you down on military machismo?"

McKay chewed his lower lip for a while. As a matter of fact, he still had a soft spot in his heart—or head—for the whole Alamo trip. Even though as an adult he knew it was military idiocy to defend the place.

Just like this one.

"Listen, McKay," Eklund said. "There's two Texases, and there always have been. A lotta people back in the Revolution wanted to throw out the Mexicans so they could keep slaves. But the Mexican government was no prize—Santa Anna had been murdering peasants down there before he marched into Texas, and he walked a few thousand of his own troopies to death on the way—not to mention getting a bunch more of them dead in the fight at the mission of San Antonio de Bexar.

"Half the people who fought for the Texan Revolution were Mexicans themselves, McKay. Maybe more. And yeah, they got treated like dogs after the Revolution. They were betrayed. So were the principles of the Revolution."

She paced past him, whirled around. He couldn't stop himself admiring the way her breasts jounced around inside her cammie blouse. Fat lot of good it did him now.

"There's one Texas that stands for freedom, for people bein' what they *can* be, without others pushing them around, telling them they can or can't. And there's the other one, the one that's as bad as you say. Now, Mr. High and Mighty Billy McKay, stand there and think for a moment: You've seen 'em both—*which is which?*"

"See many nigger officers over to the State of Texas, McKay?" Chi asked. "Or Spanish ones? Or women?"

"Well, what about Jesse Carr and his Long Riders? They weren't going to serve alongside any niggers—"

"We ain't *perfect,* McKay," Eklund said. "We're trying our damn best. And we can't try to force everybody to think only the right thoughts. Unless we want to be like Randy Jim Hedison. Or his good buddy, Dexter White, the mayor of Kansas City."

McKay did a lot of looking at the sand around his boots.
His head was whirling like a tumbled gyro. Nothing anybody
said or did made secession right, to his way of thinking—but
who would he rather have fighting at his side, Dreadlock Callahan, and Chi, and Eklund, damn her gorgeous ass—or Bob
Tyrone and his Imperial Storm Troopers?

Hedison was loyal to America—so he said. Loudly and a
lot. But he didn't even acknowledge the cristeros were a threat,
even though they'd invaded what he himself called American
soil. And what Eklund said about the Effsees—

The cry almost took his head off: *"Here they come!"*

This time they came shooting. But they were firing as they
ran, firing wild, and this go-round the mortar crews weren't
trying any fancy hammer-and-anvil tricks. This wave never
made it nearer than two hundred meters before falling back,
leaving at least a hundred more bodies cooling on the sand.

But this time the defenders took casualties, two hurt and one
dead. And they burned a measurable percentage of their ammo
driving back the attack.

The next attack, at about 0200, came closer still. Three more
dead. Seven injured, though some of them were back on the
firing line while the cristeros were still retreating.

The next push didn't come until after four. This time, though,
cristeros had been infiltrating under cover of their own casualties. They were on the wire almost without warning.

Claymores peeled them off it, heaping disassociated body
parts for three hundred meters right up against the fence. The
defenders didn't take a scratch.

This time.

"McKay."

"Huh?" McKay half-snored. Then he was wide awake, his
.45 in hand and pointed at the tip of a very startled Chi's nose.

The sun was in the sky, though not very high up. He must
have dozed off behind his machine gun after the last attack.

"McKay, we're in trouble," the lieutenant said, not even
bothering to push the big autopistol aside.

McKay sat up, spat out a mouthful of sand. "What?"

"We finally got through to San Antone." The Texican capital
had been out of contact since last night. Whatever else you
could say about the Republicans, their commo sucked.

"What'd they say?"

"We ain't gettin' any reinforcements any time soon, McKay. Your pal Governor Hedison launched attacks along the entire border at midnight.

"We got to fight this out with what we got."

CHAPTER
TWENTY

"So that's it, Doc," Billy McKay said. "We hold out as long as we can. As long as the bullets last—beans ain't the problem. Then—"

He shrugged. The fact that Dr. Jacob Morgenstern was twenty-five hundred klicks away at the other end of a satellite relay in Northern California didn't make any difference; the doctor could *see* the gesture, right enough.

"That would be quite a waste," the dry voice said. "I despise waste. . . ."

"Thanks for the sentiment, Doc," McKay said with half-hearted sarcasm. The heat and humidity and that stink that came in through your very skin were getting him down. Maybe being doomed had something to do with it too.

"I will see what I can do," Morgenstern said crisply.

"Thanks, Doctor," McKay said again, meaning it this time, "'but it won't do no good. Unless you can magically arrange for an air strike all the way from California, this looks like the last roundup. Maybe it's just as well; I'm starting to talk like a Texan."

"Hold out as long as you can, McKay."

"You didn't have to say that, Doc. McKay out."

• • •

They came again at eight o'clock. This time they came cagey, spread out across the sand, halting to fire from cover. And cover wasn't in short supply. Not with all those bodies lying out there. Even Billy McKay had to wonder how they could bear taking cover amid piles of corpses already beginning to go soft around the edges.

The firefight got pretty brisk. The Texicans were far better shots that the cristeros, and the sandbagged rifle pits they'd prepared offered far better protection than hundreds of bodies and the occasional clump of tall, tough grass. And the Texans had support weapons to call on when the cristeros found cover that was too good.

As long as the mortar rounds and the forty mike-mike lasted. That was the bottom line.

At 1013 the cristeros came up en masse out of the corpses piled in front of the wire, firing and hurling dynamite bombs. A big one went off in a machinegun pit across the road from where McKay was dug in, blew the 60 man and his A-gunner to shreds, and blasted Lt. Chi like a cork from a champagne bottle. He missed impaling himself on a steel fence post by a hair, and landed practically on top of the red-hot barrel of McKay's Maremont, buck-naked and charred all over.

By this time Mobile One had pulled up into a prepared position of its own, fifty meters behind the lines. Tom Rogers was firing into the ranks of the cristeros right over the defenders' heads. White phosphorus octopi unfurled their tentacles of smoke twenty meters from the fence, so close that glowing fragments embedded themselves in the sandbags. Screaming figures ran for the wire, trailing smoke and pale flames, only to be knocked down by a fusillade of gunfire and fans of steel marbles blasted from freshly emplaced claymores.

As the attack faltered and failed McKay uncoiled from his position, flew over the sandbag parapet, hit, rolled, lay down next to Chi.

He put his head on the skinny chest. The heartbeat was strong. Chi opened his eyes and looked at McKay.

"Aw, shit," he said. "My gramma was right. I done gone to hell."

"Very fucking funny." McKay got him over his shoulders in a fireman's carry, duckwalked back and dropped back behind the shelter of the sandbags as a couple of bullets plunked into them.

Sam Sloan turned his head at the sound of a body landing in soft sand next to him. It was Eklund.

"Yo, Sam," she said, squinting out across the sand. In the noonday sun the sand looked white as a sheet of typing paper. It was blinding. "Just wanted to see how you're makin' out at this end of the line."

"As well as could be expected, given the—" His throat clogged as he said it. "—smell."

"I hear you," Eklund said with a nod. Her face had a greenish cast beneath the rim of her helmet. "It's like gas warfare. Funny how you don't get used to it."

"Yes. McKay warned us it would be like this." The heat was baking his brain through his boonie hat. The Kevlar vest he wore alternately clung to his skin like itchy Velcro and slipped and slid as if it were greased by the sweat that rolled off of him in torrents. The heat inside it was like an iron band around his ribcage.

The ripstop vest with twenty-four of their dwindling supply of 40-mm grenades tucked neatly into rows of pockets lay next to him. He'd finally been unable to take lying on the damned things any longer.

"I find myself in a strange position," he said, speaking just to keep his lips and tongue limber.

"You have a talent for understatement, Yankee."

"Now, no call to resort to personal comments. Besides, you do me injustice, ma'am; I'm a Missouri boy."

She grinned at him. Even with the fatigue smears under her eyes she would have been almost ridiculously cute, with her snub nose and big blue eyes, if she wasn't taller than he was and capable of busting him over one shapely knee.

"But here I am praying for evening to come so we get a little breath of breeze in from the sea," he went on, "and yet I know when that time comes it'll be showtime for *them*." He nodded meaningfully toward the distant frowning ridgeline.

Tom, Eklund, and Billy McKay had all pretty much agreed the cristeros had changed their tactics. Apparently there was limit even to their zeal; they were clearly going to wait until the light went bad to launch another attack.

Two hundred meters or so away something moved. Sloan's finger tightened convulsively on the trigger of his Galil. With an act of will he kept from squeezing off a shot. That was what the enemy wanted, to get him to burn another precious round of ammunition.

They're willing to spend their lives to make us burn a single round, he thought. *How can we win?*

"I know," Eklund said softly. He looked at her, suddenly alarmed, afraid he'd voiced his thought aloud. "All we can do is hold out until—"

Until they ran out of ammunition. Until the cristeros just overwhelmed them in one massive charge. Until the contagion brewing in a thousand festering bodies exploded like a bomb and wiped them out, as disease had wiped out the personnel supposed to guard the plant in the wake of thermonuclear war.

"Why?" he croaked, unable to hold himself back. "Why are you here? You, Callahan, your soldiers, even those madmen in their Wild Bunch outfits—why are you doing this?"

"For Texas. For ourselves." She looked at him. "What about y'all?"

"We have our duty." *And nowhere else to go.* The bitterness was poison in him, fetid as the death-smell that filled his head and stirred his stomach with every breath. That was the worst part about the inevitability of dying here, with tangles of machinery gleaming inscrutably at their backs: that they were merely going through the motions.

"You're not the only ones who feel a sense of duty."

A minute or two ground them a little further down. Except for the wind, and intermittent low moaning from some of the wounded out there before the wire—you never got used to that, either; or at least Sam hadn't—it was quiet. The cristeros weren't making any threatening moves, not even bothering to snipe at the defenders.

"How are the others?" he asked.

"Tom's looking after the wounded. McKay's pissing about how much he wants a beer and yelling at that creepy Reverend Foster to quit praying around him. Case is off in a world of his own, as usual. Sometimes I worry about that boy."

"I envy him," Sloan said. "How's my man Chi?"

"Still pretty shaky, and he lost an eardrum. But Tommy says he'll be fine. Lucky son of a bitch." The lanky lieutenant had come out on the long side of the freaky nature of blast dynamics.

Sloan wondered just how lucky he really was.

McKay sluiced salt-stinging sweat out of his eyes and stuck his boonie hat back on his crewcut. These damned cristeros had an evil talent for psychological warfare, playing a waiting game out there in the hills and letting sun and humidity and tension and the reek of a thousand bloating deaders do their work for them.

Or maybe this heat was too much for them too.

It was a killing heat. McKay could scarcely believe it at this time of year, even down here on the Gulf Coast. At least they had plenty of water—big underground holding tanks of the stuff, courtesy of pre-War experimenting. He'd fought in the desert; he knew the importance of water.

He wondered what the cristeros were doing for theirs. He thought of asking Foster, since the clergyman had clearly spent some time with them before their doctrinal differences got to the *auto-da-fé* stage, but he was tired of hearing the man go on about how miraculous their faith was. He'd have worried about Foster selling them out to the cristeros, the fact they'd tried to barbecue him notwithstanding, if he could figure out any way the man could make their own situation any worse than it was to begin with.

He'd ordered the mortar crews pulled back onto the island. It had probably not been a good idea to emplace them this far forward in the first place. They had plenty of range to reach clear out to the ridge that faced the wire, even from back by the cold reactor. But he was just improvising this as he went along.

Just as he was improvising a scheme for what happened when the bad guys made a push that kept on coming. He didn't delude himself they could hold this gigantic perimeter much longer, not with the cristeros being able to snoop-and-poop forward under cover of their own decomposing dead, not with the ammunition supply dwindling like the fuel supply of a fighter on afterburners.

He didn't delude himself they could hold out much longer no matter what. They were dead men, dead women. But he was going to force-feed the Christers as much shit as humanly possible before he went belly up. Just on principle.

At about 1500 Buddy the Long Rider went berserk. He

jumped up from his sandbag nest fifty meters down the line
from McKay and clambered through the wire.

"C'mon!" he screamed at the reeking mounds of corpses.
"Come on, you chickenshit greasers! Show you ain't afraid to
take on a real white man!" He was scattering shots from one
of the two big cowboy pistols he wore down low beneath his
duster. The bodies sucked in the bullets. The dead don't care.

He began scrambling over the bodies, hands and feet slipping
in decomposing flesh, coattails flapping. His hat came off. His
pistol ran dry. He jammed it back in the holster and hauled out
its mate, looking wildly around for enemies.

A hand appeared and stuck a knife in his thigh.

He fired downwards, once, twice. The watchers on the line
heard a soft sigh, like the sound that happened when the gas
pressure inside a bloating corpse got too much for sun-softened
skin and vented, but different somehow. The hand vanished,
leaving the knife hilt sticking out of a dark patch on Buddy's
jeans. He screeched a laugh.

"There! Y'see? Yellowbellies ain't near a match for us. What
are you waiting for? Come on and help clean out these sidewinders!"

Dreadlock Callahan, who was in charge of the flying reserve,
had been paying a little visit to the front. Now he shook his
head behind the gasoline-soaked scarf he was holding to his
nose. "Boy's seen too damn many cowboy pictures."

"Do something," the Reverend Foster pleaded. "For the love
of God, you've got to help him!"

"Help him yourself," McKay snarled. His fists clamped down
on the Maremont's pistol grips until the knuckles threatened
to pop through the skin.

A knife came flying and hit Buddy in the side. It was either
a lucky shot or extremely well thrown; it went in and stuck
there. He looked down at it, a hurt frown on his round, stupid
face.

They came up out of the stiffs like something from a George
Romero flick. Hands and weapons clawed at the burly young
man in the canvas coat. He fired four times and his gun was
empty. A few shots cracked from the lines, but the cristeros
were already on top of him. A machete thunked into his shoulder
and he fell.

The defenders could make out movement behind one of the

long parallel rows of bodies. There were squealing, pig-slaughtering sounds. McKay grabbed an M-79 from a troopie who'd come up with Callahan in his armed jeep and lay gaping beside him.

"What's in this?"

"Uh, white phosphorus. Willy Peter."

"Heard you the first time." He jumped to his feet, bringing the stubby launcher to his shoulder. He didn't even bother using the stand-up front sight; this range didn't read on the scale, was barely long enough for the grenade to arm. He fired. The propellant punched the blunt round through rotting flesh, and the round went off with its characteristic starfish of smoke.

Shots sought McKay from out in the corpse-field. He stood and watched as figures jumped into view, screaming and beating at the flakes of burning metal that clung to them devouring like soldier ants. A volley of shots cracked from the fence, single rounds only, under penalty of heavy retribution.

Then there was only the silence. And the dense, deadly heat.

CHAPTER
TWENTY-ONE ───────────

The came at dusk, and they came singing.

The mortars began to chug as the wave of bodies broke over the ridge. Hundreds more sprang up from hiding-places closer to the wire that they'd worked their way to through the heaped bodies of their comrades.

Machine guns chattered, sweeping the oncoming ranks with miserly bursts. Many fell, and more kept coming.

Sam Sloan triggered off a final white phosphorus grenade. He'd quit flinching every time he fired one, even when the enemy was so close he could smell flesh burning. He broke the M-203 slung under the barrel of his Galil and rammed in a multiple projectile round.

There were so many of them the singing drowned out the screams. *This is it,* he thought in panic, *they'll never stop.* As if to counterpoint his fear the last few claymores cracked off with gouts of white light. The steel marbles carved out fan-shaped gaps in the mob. They closed up at once; the mines might as well have discharged into the surf.

They were at the wire now, scrambling to climb over. Sloan could smell sweat and the clinging foulness of the bodies they'd waded through to get to him. That was how it felt—as if they were all after him, Lt. Cdr. Samuel Roberts Sloan, in person.

So thinly were the defenders spread along the fence it was just about right.

He fired the outsized shotgun charge. Pellets a third of an inch thick sprayed bodies scant meters away. One man took the brunt, fell off the fence with his ribcage torn open so comprehensively it looked as if he'd been split with a surgeon's bone-saw, his guts falling in loops around his knees. Others fell back clutching punctured faces, limbs, bodies. The rest pushed on, past them, over them. Onto the fence, scrambling like monkeys.

Sloan thumbed his Galil to full auto and fired a burst. Half a dozen slumped on the wire. Others climbed up their bodies.

They were slopping over the wire to his right. He heard a panic-fire burst from the next foxhole, then silence. To his left was only deep swamp with island and ocean behind.

Right in front of him, ten feet before his face, a plump middle-aged woman threw her arms over the razor-tape tangle at the top of the chainlink. Others scrambled up, using her as a ladder. The sharpened wire slashed her throat as their weight pulled her down. She rolled her eyes prayerfully up and smiled.

Dear God, Sloan thought. The SAR clicked empty in his hands. He dropped the magazine, pulled the last plastic banana-clip from his belt.

A brown hand grabbed the hot barrel. Sloan dropped the magazine, hauled his nickel-plated Python from its shoulder holster, punched a pumpkin-sized ball of flame at the man. He went back with the front of his white smock stained red.

They were all around him. Southern chivalry rebelling, he shot a woman point-blank in the face, blew half her head away. Someone clutched his arm. He slashed a face with the vented rib of the pistol, fired, smelled burned hair from the muzzle flash.

A rifle butt hit him in the kidneys. Fire flashed through his guts. He went to his knees, holding the Python two-handed before him like a Crusader his crucifix.

White smoke surrounded him, and his vision blurred away.

With an ugly thud McKay's M-60 gave up the ghost. The barrel glowed like a branding iron in the twilight. He'd burned out the barrel lining. There was a spare quick-detach barrel lying beside him for just this turn of events, but he lacked even the minute-and-a-half a change would take. They were *right here,* and about to come in.

The gate was the weak link, even though the defenders had welded extra lengths of chain around the juncture and ends of the gate to strengthen it, using an oxyacetylene rig from the desalinization plant's shop. Both sides knew it, and concentrated their efforts on it.

Now it was bulging inward under the sheer weight of bodies. Mortar rounds crashed amid the mob, as near as the crews dared drop them. The cristeros weren't singing any more. They were cheering.

McKay heard the rising scream of metal stressed unbearably. Chains parted. The gates sagged on broken hinges. The crowd came in.

The gatehouses were burning. A trooper stumbled from one, screaming, too far gone even to beat out the flames that enveloped her. A bullet hit her and she fell.

Across the road Eklund was firing single shots into the crowd, as precise as though she were lying on the practice range. McKay felt an urge to go to her.

Instead he picked up a Smith & Wesson 3000 riot gun, one of the spares brought by Eklund's column, began to pump rounds into the cristeros charging him.

Mobile One was parked right in the road two hundred meters behind, pouring fifty-caliber straight through the gate. McKay could feel the wind of passage of the huge slugs, could literally hear the impacts as they struck home. the horde faltered under the lead storm, but kept coming.

The twelve-gauge's eight-round magazine ran dry. McKay threw it down. A big dark man hacked at him with a machete. McKay danced back, pulling his sharpened Swiss entrenching tool from his belt. The Mexican grinned at him.

He swished the machete through a figure eight, its broad blade gleamed dully. "I saw *Radiers of the Lost Ark,* cocksucker," McKay said. He switched the E-tool to his left hand, drew his .45 and shot the machete man through his paunch.

Cristeros rushed him. He swung the E-tool, split a face to the bridge of a broad nose. *Another broad,* he thought. *Shit.* He shot a man who grabbed at him, then wrenched the E-tool free and lashed out, chopping a chunk of meat out of somebody's arm and baring a white streak of humerus.

They drew back away into a wary circle. Mobile One's gun had fallen silent—time to change ammo cans, the worst timing possible. Dynamite bombs slammed like giant doors. From the direction of Eklund's foxhole McKay heard a pop, and a sudden insistent hissing.

He grinned, felt drying blood crack on his face. "That's the ticket," he said. He stuck the .45 in its holster and snatched a grenade from his belt.

He tore the pin out with his teeth, John Wayne-style, and dropped it to the sand at his feet.

Sam Sloan couldn't see. His eyes were full of pain and tears. He could scarcely breathe, and his sinuses felt as if somebody had planted hot coals in each and every one. He was aware of heat, and screams, and flashes of red light.

So the PTL Club bunch were right after all, he thought dully. *I'm in hell.*

—More hands, clutching. He batted at them, feebly. Then something cool and damp settled on his face. He flashed on the old sci-fi horror flick *Alien,* grabbed at it frantically. Hands took his wrists and pulled them away.

Gradually his vision cleared. There was a face hanging in front of his, lit sporadically by pulses of red-orange light. It was a dark face, long, lean, sardonically mustached. It grinned.

"Mephistopheles," Sam croaked. "It's a pleasure. I've heard so much about you."

There was an old marine trick called the grenade duel. You played it when Charlie was on top of you and you were wearing a flak jacket or reasonable facsimile. You just popped the pin and let that sucker drop. Then you went down and curled into a ball and prayed.

McKay figured he didn't have near the celestial firepower to go prayer-to-prayer with these people. But then, he wasn't going the full grenade-duel route. He was following Eklund's lead and wussing out.

The can hissing at his feet was a CS grenade. The cristeros got horrified looks on their faces as their eyes blossomed into tears and their throats started to seize up. They backed away, fearful of the gringo techno-deviltry unleashed on them.

Mobile One's big Browning tuned up about then. The

sweetest cliché McKay's ears had ever heard. Weeping and staggering, the cristeros fell back.

McKay did some weeping and choking too. But he knew what to do about it. He fumbled open his canteen, sloshed water onto a handkerchief, held it against his face and backed slowly out of the white tear-gas cloud.

The cristeros were in retreat, routed by the tear gas and the timely intervention of the mobile reserve teams at the breakthrough points. McKay stood and watched them go, ignoring the occasional incoming round, mopping his face.

Eklund stumbled up to him. One sleeve of her uniform was bloody. Her face was covered in sweat and tears that gleamed gold in the light of the burning gatehouses. Her eyes were bloodshot. She grabbed McKay and kissed him hard.

"Didn't think I'd see you alive again, Yankee."

"I didn't either," McKay said in a voice that sounded like ten clicks of bad road. "Good thing you thought about popping CS on them."

"That was the plan, for when they got through the wire."

"Yeah. But thanks for reminding me. They thought that shit was killing them."

He looked past her shoulder. A mortar round went off fifty meters away, flying body parts outlined black against the flash.

"They're never going to fall for it again," he said. "Time to initiate Operation Eastern Front."

Two hours later the cristeros attacked again, waving their banners of the Virgin of Guadalupe and singing her song. They had strengthened themselves with prayer and mouthfuls of beans and rice, and knew their time had come.

The hated mortars began to go off, flinging the living and the dead in all directions with Satanic indifference. But the enemy ranks were silent. Perhaps the *norteamericanos* had run out of ammunition, as the holy men had assured them they would. Or perhaps the Virgin herself was staying their hands. It made no difference. This time they would sweep the gringos before them, to the glory of Christ the King.

A cheer floated up like a flock of seagulls as they reached the wire. They could see the gringos now, staring fixedly from their sandbag nests. Some paused to clip the metal mesh with wire cutters. Other, more exalted, swarmed over it, ignoring the deep-biting razor tape. They hurled themselves at the sandbags, lusting to be at grips with the *ateos*, the heretics who did not acknowledge Sister Light.

The first man into a rifle pit grabbed a bare arm beneath a rolled sleeve. Instantly he snatched his hand back. The woman's flesh was clammy, hard and cold and lifeless. Her head lolled back on its neck. Half-open eyes stared fixedly past him.

Others were dropping in beside him. He opened his mouth to cry a warning. And then he and a hundred or so of his brothers and sisters were propelled directly to Heaven.

Or at least in that general direction.

Back in the Second World War the Germans had a general named Heinrici. He was a genius, one of their finest field commanders. But you've never heard of him.

The reason for that is that he was a master of defeat. He was sent to command the Nazi forces of the Eastern Front at the beginning of 1945, when not even Joe Goebbels could pretend to any doubts about how things were going to come out. Heinrici's assignment was to hold off the enormous, vengeful Red Army while withdrawing as many troops as possible.

He performed miracles. He didn't beat the Soviets, not in the sense of preventing their ultimate victory over the Reich (you did know how this came out, didn't you?). Alexander the Great couldn't have pulled that off, not at those odds. But Heinrici held off the Russians far longer with his undersupplied, outgunned and outnumbered army than even the giddy Hitler could have believed possible.

History illuminates even the luckiest, dullest, least competent victor much more brightly than the most brilliant of losers. Heinrici was forgotten, while any number of lesser leaders on all sides got to be household words. But one-eyed Major Crenna was an admirer of his, and the Guardians had studied his doomed, masterful campaign during their training.

Billy McKay dropped the electrical command detonator and grinned a shit-eating grin around at Sloan, Dreadlock Callahan, and a half-dozen troopies and displaced Mexican ranchers who'd stayed behind to watch the fireworks. Old Heinrici had had a trick where the Russians launched a giant attack on German lines, only to find the defenders had snuck back a couple hundred meters and boresighted their guns on their former positions. It was great for letting the steam out of an assault and buying time—all either Heinrici or Billy McKay could hope for.

"—dynamite was a good touch." Callahan was saying when McKay's hearing came back. Even the earplugs the Guardians wore to keep from going deaf from the voices of their own guns hadn't kept the roar of about two metric tons of high explosives going off at once in their former positions, where it had been planted the night before.

A facility such as the Galves Desalinization Center, which did a lot of construction-type work, naturally had plenty of explosives on hand. McKay had put them to good use. The cristeros weren't the only ones who could play with dynamite bombs.

The *Beau Geste* bit with the dead defenders had been McKay's idea, too. A situation like this brought out the worst in him. Or maybe the best.

"You can touch me if you want, Callahan," McKay said. "Somebody had to show some class, before your head swelled up and busted over Sloan mistaking you for the devil."

It had been Callahan's own jeep that had come to Sloan's rescue, M-249 blazing. His silver-haired sleep-in second in command, Sherri Sparhawk, had dropped a forty-millimeter CS grenade right behind Sloan in the proverbial nick of time.

"Mephistopheles, please," said Callahan. He preened his handlebar with the back of a finger. "I've always thought I bore a marked resemblance to him. How do you think I'd look with a rapier, McKay?"

"Dead. With a bunch of bullet holes in your jump suit and a pitchfork in your back."

The biker looked offended.

They were holed next to one of the residential blocks, which McKay thought bore a depressing resemblance to those cinderblock no-tell motels that dotted the outskirts of every American town with a population in three figures or better. Everyone else was gone with the wind, even the South Texas Protective Association's goddamn horses, back to the island, with three hundred meters of swamp that was too deep to wade through, even at low tide, between them and the cristeros.

That was the heartmeat of the complex, as well as the only really defensible part. The rest was secondary; they weren't even going to make a show of defending it, now that the perimeter was breached. If they could hold the island, they'd won.

And if Tinker Bell the Fairy came fluttering down from the sky she could turn the cristeros into Cabbage Patch Kids, and their rifles to spun candy.

Given time (which they had) and numbers (which they had more of) the cristeros would push their way over the causeway. The good guys weren't going to win this fight. But McKay was going to fight it the best he could, just like Heinrici.

They lay on their bellies next to ugly, spindly ornamental shrubs, and watched the wire. The big bang had sent the cristeros reeling. But the glory was upon them, and they were soon back, filtering past the craters blasted in the sand, with their rifles ready and a watchful silence. All the songs had been knocked out of them for now.

McKay lowered his binoculars. "Time to go." They didn't have ammo to waste popping off attackers at this point, though it would have been fun. Besides, demo wizard Tom Rogers had scattered a few surprises around the mainland part of the facility. The booby traps should keep them busy for a few hours while the good guys got settled in on their island.

He started to get to his feet. Callahan stopped him with a hand on his arm. "What's going on?"

McKay brought the binoculars back up. A party of cristeros had almost reached the admin building a hundred meters from where the little group was lying up. As McKay watched a single stocky figure stepped out into the starlight.

"*Buenas*," the Reverand Foster called. A freak of the wind brought the word clearly to the hidden defenders.

The cristeros halted, covering the redheaded minister with their rifles. Others were coming up behind, craning curiously to see what was going on.

"I've found faith, my friends," Foster said in his clear, carrying, preaching voice. "I still don't have it. But it's all around me."

The cristeros muttered and shook their heads. Some of them probably understood him. Or the words, anyway.

"You have faith. And I salute you. But the people you're fighting also have faith. McKay—you should meet Billy McKay. He has the kind of faith that moves mountains. He believes in his country as you believe in Christ and the Brown Virgin."

McKay felt all kinds of eyes on him. The back of his thick neck burned.

"They have faith. You have faith. I have seen that faith perform miracles the past two days."

Growing impatient, the cristeros were starting to close in on him. "So I can see faith is real," Foster declaimed. "But I don't have it. All I have is—this."

And he brought up the Luigi Franchi SPAS-12 shotgun he'd lifted from Mobile One, up from behind his right leg. The first charge of double-ought hit a greyhound-lean cristero in the center of the chest and sent him flying back. The second turned the face of a stout peasant woman to bloody mulch.

The cristeros opened fire. The unseen watchers could hear bullets slapping into the Reverend's body. But he stood there matching them shot for shot.

"Bless you, my children," he gasped, blowing a skinny teen-ager practically in two. "You know happiness. And you're enabling me to share . . . that happiness—"

The Franchi went empty. Swaying fragilely, the Reverend fished out a service pistol he'd scarfed from somewhere. He never go to fire it. A fresh volley knocked him back two meters. McKay could see blood spray out where sharp-pointed rounds exited his back.

"Bless you all. Bless you. *I love—*" A bullet knocked the back out of his skull and he fell.

They closed on him. Knives glinted. "Great God, what are they *doing?*" Sam gasped.

By the time he'd finished it was already too clear what they were doing. A slim girl held something above her head as though it were a trophy.

It was the Reverend Foster's right arm, fingers still clutching the pistol.

Busily they dismembered the body. They had started to sing again. Lucky souls ran off clutching parts of the Reverend to bloodied breasts.

"What are they doing?" Sloan choked, fighting a losing battle at the sour vomit that filled his throat. "The—the *barbarians.*"

"Your liberal conscience is gonna make you suffer for that, Sloan," McKay said.

"They honor him," said one of the ranchers. Everybody stared at him. "They understood what he was doing. It was a very holy thing, to die for faith." He nodded off toward the crowd that had gathered where Foster fell. ''They may—how you say?—revere. Revere parts of him as the relics of a saint.''

''I'll be damned,'' Dreadlock Callahan said. It was the first time McKay had ever seen him taken aback.

''No shit—Mephistopheles,'' McKay said. ''C'mon. Let's blow this malt shop.''

CHAPTER
TWENTY-TWO ————————

At dawn the cristeros hit the causeway. Straight up the middle—the only way to go. Actually, some had tried their chances and their faith by plunging into the swamp separating island from mainland. None of them made it.

Neither did anybody else, with every erg of firepower the defenders had left funneled along a paved strip not twenty meters across. The cristeros hadn't even gotten halfway.

But they reckoned they'd won a big victory by taking the mainland sector. So they tried again. Three times.

None had made it within fifty meters of the island.

Dusk came. Pulses sped up, fingers tightened on triggers, eyes stared at the causeway so hard the residual heat shimmer off the blacktop practically scorched them.

The sun kamikaze'd into the tangled pipes of the mainland complex. Darkness filled up all the cracks the day had left behind, and still the cristeros didn't show.

Two hours after sunset McKay and Eklund gave the order to stand down, leaving a force of ten watching the road. If anything went down there'd be plenty of time for everybody to get back to his or her post. You couldn't wander very far on this island anyway. The Texicans lit defiant bonfires and broke out the last of the beer that had come in with the convoy.

Even as he drained off his final bottle McKay regretted the space hadn't been used to carry ammo.

The home team was down to under forty effectives, and fewer than three magazines apiece for them. The 40-mm grenades were almost exhausted, the ever-thirsty machineguns nearly dry. Tom Rogers and the medico who'd come in with Eklund could scarcely keep up with the casualties, especially since wounds were showing a gruesome tendency to fester almost instantly. They could withstand maybe two more pushes up the causeway, and those only because of two mortars—which previously hadn't really been enough to cover the huge front of the mainland complex, and had only been as effective as they had because of the clumsy mass tactics of the attackers— could concentrate their fire on the ribbon of road with amazing effect.

Maybe there wasn't anything to celebrate. Or maybe there was everything in the world. They'd already held out a shitload better than anyone had a right to expect.

He thought of Randy Jim Hedison, who'd stabbed them in the back. He thought of Maggie Connoly, who was standing by and doing nothing, and calling them criminals into the bargain.

He thought of Jeff MacGregor. He wouldn't believe— couldn't believe—the president was deliberately letting them twist slowly in the wind like this. He couldn't know what was going on. And there was no way to get word to him. Since their "mutiny" they'd been stonewalled by Washington.

Fucked again, he thought. He let the empty bottle drop into the sand and turned and stomped off out of the firelight.

"McKay?"

Arms crossed over his chest, chin on breastbone, McKay stirred. The cement shell built to camouflage the reactor was dark and quiet and lonely. Fitted his mood just fine.

"McKay?" His name chased its tail around the high walls again. "Billy? Where'd you get off to?"

"Over here, Eklund," he called grudgingly.

She came picking her way through the debris, cursing as she turned her ankle on something hidden by sand that had been blown in in small drifts by the hurricanes. "What did you want to run off and hide for?"

"Felt like shit," he said harshly.

"You gon' feel worse, Yankee. Balls'll glow blue from the radiation."

"Tommy went over this joint with his Geiger counter. It's just a shade over background in here. You'd pick up more rads driving through Kansas with the windows open. Jesus, you're fucking crude."

"It's part of mah rustic appeal," she said, exaggerating her accent. She sat down beside him with her back to the outer wall. She smelled of soap and fresh water. It was a comfortable contrast to the must and mildew in here. "Besides, I purely love to see you blush. You're such an innocent child."

He grunted.

"Still mad at me?" She reached out, took his chin and lifted his head.

"Why the fuck would I be mad at you?"

"For bein' a successionist."

"Shit." He pulled his head away. "You Texicans are here with your asses on the line. Fucking Hedison ignores an invasion of American territory, and then he fucking helps it out. I don't know what to think anymore." He glanced back at her. "Thought you were mad at me."

"Why would I be mad at you? To express myself in a more dignified manner than you saw fit to— Shit! What was *that?*" She jumped up, hitting at a fluttering shadow that had brushed her bare head.

"Bat," McKay said. "Fucking bats. Place is lousy with them. We'll probably get rabies."

"Nope. They're mutant bats. They bite us, we'll grow wings and pointy ears and great big teeth." She settled herself down again. "Why would I be mad at you?"

"I left in a hurry. And we were having a fight."

"Shoot. Lover's quarrel."

"It was a shitload more serious than that."

"You take things too seriously, McKay."

"Part of my gritty urban appeal." He kissed her. "That's what you came here for, isn't it?"

"You ain't as dumb as I thought you were." Her face went to his. Her tongue trolled his in. His hand went to her breast. The nipple was hard beneath the issue bra.

Someone cleared his throat.

They broke apart as though jerked by those rope-and-harness

rigs they use in the movies to stimulate getting hit by a gunshot. A mostly naked man stood over them.

"Good evening," he said. "I trust I'm not intruding."

His blond hair was matted to his sleek head, the decathlete's body sheened with water. He smelled of swamp.

McKay scooted his ass back, unobtrusively braced his boots to jump to his feet. "I thought you were dead."

"Close, but no cigar. I presume I've young Lieutenant Wilson to thank for my brush with the Grim Reaper? I thought as much. And speaking of cigars, feel free to smoke. I'm upwind of you, and cancer is hardly going to be a substantial risk for you, inasmuch as it's usually associated with old age."

"Ah'm afraid Ah don't know your charming friend," Eklund said, sitting up straighter and rearranging her hair with one hand. The other worked its way to the butt of her Beretta.

"Allow me to introduce Colonel Ivan Vesensky, formerly of the KGB. He speaks good English because he's a lousy Russian spy and assassin."

"I'm an FSE spy and assassin, if I may take the liberty of correcting you, Lieutenant. Incidentally, let me say how pleased I am to meet you in person, after all this time. You'll forgive me if I don't shake your hand."

"I'll write to fucking Miss Manners. I hear she's holed up in a bunker outside D.C." McKay fished in a breast pocket for cigar and lighter, moving deliberately. He knew Vesensky well enough not to assume he wasn't packing a concealed weapon, though where the hell he'd conceal it McKay had no clue. Mainly he didn't want the man to bolt just yet. He had a few things to ask him.

"So what the hell are you doing here?" he asked, lighting up.

"I came to urge you to surrender."

McKay raised his eyebrows. "To who? Chairman Max is a long way away, if Iskander Bey hasn't cut his nuts off yet."

"The Pan-Turanians have been pushed out of most of Europe, you'll be pleased to know," Vesensky said. "But I was advising you to surrender to the soldiers of Christ the King and the Virgin of Guadalupe."

"*You're* back of all this shit?"

"At a remove or two—yes."

"Bull puckey," Eklund said. "Mexicans don't take kindly to foreigners trying to push them around. They'd kill you if they thought you were messin' with this Hermana Luz."

"Very perceptive, Sgt. Eklund. But note, I said 'at a remove or two.' I have what the imperialists used to call puppets. To the masses I am just a gringo who showed the rare good judgment to realize that Sister Light is in fact an instrument of the Virgin Mary. Nonsense, of course. But a useful facade."

McKay closed his eyes and let his head fall back against the wall. The cement was still hot from the departed sun. "I was wondering why the cristeros were so goddamn eager to get their hooks on this plant."

"The will of God, as revealed through Sister Light. With, ah, a little help from her friends."

"What kind of deal are you offering?" McKay asked. He still hadn't opened his eyes.

"Safe conduct out of here for you and all your friends in exchange for the facility."

"Why? Your little fanatic friends are gonna get it on their own soon anyhow."

"I hate to see this promiscuous waste of life continue."

"Bullshit."

"Truth. Believe what you will. Also, I feel a professional regard for you Guardians."

"Yeah. I can't figure why you're not demanding we surrender ourselves too."

Vesensky shrugged. "Perhaps I hate to see the game end, my friend," he said softly.

McKay puffed his cigar. The ember glowed like a hot eye. He could almost believe that. Maybe he felt a bit of it himself.

"Good of you not to show yourself naked in front of a lady," he remarked, gesturing toward the tight, tiny racer's swimtrunks the Russian wore.

Vesensky grinned. "To be honest, I couldn't abide the thought of *things* nibbling at my private parts as I swam over. Snapping turtles and the like."

McKay kicked his legs out from under him.

Unfortunately, Eklund picked that exact second to haul out her Beretta and shoot him. The shot went perfectly where his heart had been before McKay took him down. From the floor he kicked the pistol out of her hand, then kicked McKay in the face. McKay's head cracked against the cement wall and momentarily filled with whirling light.

By the time his skull was clear and his pistol out the Russian was standing at the far end of the building. "I'm sorry it has to end like this," he called. "What are you fighting for? Don't you realize you've been set up? Betrayed at every turn?"

Then he vanished around the hip of the cooling tower a microsecond ahead of the snap-shot McKay sent his way.

At dawn McKay was lying beside the causeway, peering sleepily along the barrel of his M-603E. At the far end were the cristeros. They were gathering on the mainland, silent for once, carefully arraying themselves beneath their banners. It looked as if they were getting ready for a parade.

To either side of the causeway the defenders were spread out behind sandbags, their weapons angled toward the causeway. Few had slept well, or at all, but they had a bright-eyed energy, almost an eagerness, as they watched their enemies assemble.

When the first rays of the sun fell directly on them the cristeros all began to move, funneling onto the causeway, advancing slowly, in perfect order, without jostling or impatience. They had all the time in the world.

And now the song began: *"Yo soy un cristiano, y soy un mejicano—"*

"Here we fucking go again," somebody said. McKay realized with a start it was him.

Jamie Carr struggled to his feet and threw away his bat. The rising sun struck golden glints off his pale blond hair. He faced the cristeros and began to sing, in a high pure tenor, "Oh, say, can you see, by the dawn's early light—"

The defenders looked at each other, shifting uncomfortably in their firing positions scooped out of the sand. Even McKay thought it was unbelievably corny. But one by one they all joined in. Their voices rose in eerie counterpoint to the cristero song, then drowned it out. They didn't sing it well—hardly anybody did—but what they lacked in skill they made up for in enthusiasm.

The cristeros advanced with unbelievable slowness, almost as if they were waiting for something. Jamie finished his song and launched into "Yellow Rose of Texas." The Texicans sang lustily. McKay didn't try—he had no idea what the words were—but could hear his three fellow Guardians belting out the song with the rest. It sounded as if Sloan was even on key.

The song ended. The cristeros had just reached the center of the causeway. McKay could make out details in the front rank as if they were three meters away: the mustache on the tall, skinny man in the straw cowboy hat, the embroidery on a woman's frilly blouse, the Merith Tobias t-shirt on the kid carrying the banner.

Jamie Carr started "The Eyes of Texas Are Upon You."

A jeep came screaming along the road behind the defenders, with one of Callahan's Volunteers clinging onto the muzzle brake of the M-249 so it wouldn't whip around and clock somebody on the skull. It squealed and fishtailed to a halt right behind McKay.

The driver was Lt. Chi, his bushy Afro still defiant, though what the dynamite bomb had left looked as if the moths had been at it.

"Damn radio's out," he panted. "Tried to call."

"What's on your mind?" McKay asked. He waved a hand at the slow-marching cristeros. "We're about to have company."

"We already *got* company," Chi said. "Comin' in from the sea in about a hundred goddamn boats!"

CHAPTER
TWENTY-THREE —————

"Fucked again," McKay said.

Parked where tough grass roots had stabilized the sandy soil, up on a brow of ground that shelved rapidly down to a broad white beach, Mobile One loosed a burst of 40-millimeter. The grenades fell among the boats struggling at the verge of the gridwork of tanks Eklund had said looked like dolphin pens. An HEDP round scored a direct hit on a little cabin cruiser, and the gas tank blew with a very satisfactory ball of yellow flame, which quickly rushed skyward on the top of a stalk of black smoke and became a miniature mushroom cloud.

It meant jack shit. There were just too many of them.

If it hadn't been for the ''dolphin pens'' they'd already be all over the island. But the tanks wouldn't hold them long. Already cristeros were teetering on the rims, hauling smaller boats bodily over—rowboats, dinghies, little jobs with outboard engines McKay doubted were ever meant for the ocean, even canoes, for Christ's sake—ignoring the sprinkle of gunfire from the handful of defenders ashore. Often one would lose his balance and fall into the water, and quite frequently that was the last anybody saw of him. These were mainly inland Mexicans, and not all of them had any good idea how to swim.

It didn't matter. Nothing mattered to them. People who would run singing into a solid wall of automatic-weapons fire were not going to be daunted by a few boating mishaps.

"Vesensky," McKay said. "He's behind this shit."

Dreadlock Callahan casually lit a cigarillo. "I thought you said he was dead."

"So I was wrong again."

McKay had to admire the neatness of it. The cristeros must've scoured this section of coastline for anything that would still float after time and the hurricanes had been at it. Only people who truly believed that death would simply land them square in the bosom of the Virgin of Guadalupe would dare take to sea in such a bizarre collection of cockleshells and colanders.

But it was paying off, big time. It would take every effective on the island, walking wounded included, even to slow them up.

Except it would also take every man or woman who could fire a piece to stand off the thrust along the causeway.

And the ammo crates were as empty as a derelict's pockets the week after the welfare check got cashed.

The machinegun slung around McKay's neck weighed like an anvil. He wanted to let it just tip him forward and bury his snout in the sand. It was hardly worthwhile doing anything else.

"What do you say, McKay?" Callahan asked. He unslung a fancy H&K sniper's rifle, complete with scope and set triggers. God knew where he'd got it. "It seems to me we might as well die here as anyplace else."

That snapped him out of it. McKay liked Callahan a hell of a lot, respected him even, but he was just good and goddamned if he was going to let a raggedy-ass ex-biker show him up.

"Roger that," he said gruffly. He unflung the machinegun. "Let's get down and party."

They looked at each other, Chi and two troopies and a lone rider from the STPA, looking kind of shrunken and lost inside his hat and coat. With McKay and Callahan as well as Casey and Tom in Mobile One, they represented better than twenty percent of the island's defense. They spread themselves out into a firing line and lay down in the sand to pot at the invaders.

Half an hour later the first cristeros hit the foot of the beach, a hundred forty meters away. Tom dropped a neat three-round burst of forty mike-mike on them, eradicating a dozen or so. Their comrades behind came on, floundering in the pens, kicking and splashing and singing their goddamn songs.

"I'm down to twenty rounds of forty millimeter, Billy," Tom

reported. "Got about seventy rounds of fifty-caliber left."

McKay looked at the half-moon–shaped Aussie ammo box sitting on the sand next to his M-60. It was the last; about eight rounds were rattling in the box hung on the weapon's receiver.

"I'm almost dry, too. Sloan? How're things at your end?"

Sam Sloan lay on his belly beneath the concrete pedestal of a tall halogen light. He'd just fired off his last MP round. That left him a pair of flare grenades. *Probably won't do much good,* he reflected. *We won't be here for dark.* He winced as a bullet hit the face of the pedestal and whined away.

"We're still here, McKay," he said grimly, and spat out sand. "Some of us."

To the right he saw Jesse Carr sitting cross-legged, ignoring the bullets that cracked past his ears, holding his brother's blond head on a canvas-covered knee. There was a round, dark hole in the boy's forehead. The sky-blue eyes had a distant look.

To Sloan's right Sherri Sparhawk, the platinum-blond Volunteer lieutenant, grimly tied an OD rag around her bleeding thigh. A cristero lunged up from behind a stack of corpses at the very end of the causeway not ten meters from her, a dynamite bomb with a sputtering fuse in hand. She snaked her Beretta from the fancy combat holster one-handed, snapped two shots at him. Two red flowers blossomed on the front of his white smock. He dropped like so many wet rags, and the bomb went off.

Sloan became one with the planet. The explosion's overpressure got inside his skull and threatened to pop it like a piece of popcorn. He felt small splattering impacts as bits of cristero hit his boonie hat.

When he looked up again Sherri was calmly tourniquetting her leg again.

He started to say something, but motion caught the right corner of his eye. He looked around. A Long Rider was sitting up pointing to the north. A bullet knocked him down, but by then Sloan saw what he was excited about.

Two shapes, black against the painfully blue sky, coming in low and fast.

"*Aircraft, McKay.*" Sloan sounded a million miles away, a million years old.

"What kind, Sam?" Case wanted to know.

"How do I know?"

"I'll give you a hint," remarked Dreadlock Callahan, who still had a loaner communicator. "The good guys don't have any planes."

The defenders overlooking the beach could hear the whistling whine of jet engines as the unidentified craft swept south past the mainland side of the island. The noise curved around and then the planes came into view, out over the water beyond the dolphin pens.

They were squat, ugly craft, painted mottled green and brown, with stubby, straight wings, and engines like beer kegs hung to either side of the fuselage, well back, between tailfins mounted at the ends of the horizontal stabilizers. Thick cannon muzzles protruded from beneath their blunt snouts like insect proboscises.

Casey Wilson had the lid popped and was sitting out in the morning breeze. He whooped and pounded on Mobile One's front glacis. "A-tens, Billy! That's them!"

"I'm very happy for you, Casey," McKay said ironically.

"Federals," Callahan said, getting on his feet and dusting off his coveralls. "Guess they finally decided to put their money where their mouths are and get down to help the cristeros for true."

McKay bounced up and ran a few meters down the slope. Cristero bullets kicked up sand by his feet. He ignored them.

"You fuckers!" he screamed, as the A-10s soared away to the north. He whipped out his .45. "Come back here! I'll show you and that cocksucker Randy Jim what you can do with your goddamn airplanes. *You fuckers!"*

"Billy." Casey had a hand to his ear and was frowning quizzically. "We got a radio communication coming in, man."

All of a sudden McKay felt very silly and very exposed. He dove back unslope just ahead of a whole hailstorm of bullets as the cristeros got the range on the crazy, bellowing gringo. Fortunately they were suck-egg shots.

"Put it on the horn, Case," he ordered, trying to sound nonchalant.

"—morning, ladies and gentlemen," a voice said in a mellifluous East Texas drawl. *"This is Spectre One. I'm your host, Captain Lightfoot. To begin our in-flight entertainment, it gives me great pleasure to introduce my ace associates. Captains Delgado and Swarecky. They will be flying those ugly green*

Warthogs you see coming in from the north.''

Open-mouthed, Sam Sloan stared at the A-10 as it came gliding straight for him. Even now, staring death in the face, he had to admit the grace of those graceless machines. His grandfather had always said there was beauty in any tool doing what it was well designed to do. For what it was worth, he was absolutely right.

Cristeros crowded the whole length of the causeway, defying the last few remaining bullets the defenders sent their way. Some of them turned to point at the swooping aircraft. They cheered and clapped.

Smoke puffed out from under the chin of the Warthog, trailed aft along the fuselage. The plane slowed as if the pilot had slammed on brakes.

There was a sound like an unoiled door closing. The center of the causeway erupted in fire and smoke and chunks of asphalt and bits of shredded bodies. The A-10 swept past.

''That was 'Raindrops Keep Fallin' on My Head,' as performed by Captain Delgado on the GAU-Eight thirty-millimeter. Let's have a nice hand for Captain Delgado.

''Our next selection will be Captain Swarecky, performing that old favorite by the Doors from the Sensational Sixties—''

The second A-10 was dropping down from the sky. A fat something fell from its underbelly.

Sam Sloan felt his eyebrows crisp as a wave of orange napalm fire swallowed up the far end of the causeway.

''—'Light My Fire.' Wonderful, wonderful. Beats the ass off José Feliciano, don't he?''

The cristeros on this end of the causeway were milling around, crying out in horror. The defenders were cheering, joyfully loosing off their last precious rounds of ammunition, not knowing what the hell was going on but enjoying the hell out of it.

The eight surviving Long Riders were up and running for the rear, dusters flapping behind them. Sloan shook his head. He thought they were a pack of bigoted rednecks, but they'd fought well. Why were they chickening out *now*, when a pair of hideous green *dei ex machina* had appeared out of the heavens to stomp on their enemies?

''Sloan,'' Billy McKay said. *''What's happening, Sloan?* Sam, what the fuck's going on?''

There was all the thunder and tarnation in the whole fucking world going on on the other side of the island. There was no mistaking that fat black napalm cloud boiling up into the otherwise peaceable sky. But if the can had dropped on the defenders he should have been able to feel the heat from here.

"Talk to me, Sam," he pleaded.

"And now it's our turn, ladies and gentlemen. If you'll turn your attention to the skies above your lovely tropical island, you'll see our main event for the day—"

They heard a buzz of engines and looked up to see a four-prop Hercules flying down from the north, fat and black against the blue. It was maybe two thousand meters up.

"Changing pace to a classical mood, the Guarneri Doom Quartet will be performing Bach's immortal Toccata and Fugue. *The Quartet this morning consists of three twenty-millimeter Gatling guns, accompanied by a bass hundred-and-five-millimeter howitzer."*

The Herkie tipped to the port side. Thunder broke the sky into little tiny pieces.

It looked as if you had taken a handful of pebbles and tossed them in a pond. The surface of the sea in and beyond the dolphin pens was speckled with thousands of dancing water pimples, jittering around like snow on a TV screen. Boats flew into matchwood. Frantic cristeros floundered in the water, vanishing into red fountains as the bullet storm found them.

Then silence. Infinite silence, heavy as the hand of death.

Only the fact that the comm speaker piped the words directly into his skull enabled McKay to hear: *"Wasn't that lovely? I love classical music, don't you? I could tell our friends in the little boats enjoyed it too.*

"Uh-oh, I see we've got a little audience participation going on to the landward side of this tropical paradise. That's risky; a good thing we saw you—"

With a rebel yell Jesse Carr and his riders came boiling out from among the buildings—on horseback, waving six-shooters and sawed-off shotguns. They flew past the stunned defenders and straight into the cristero horde.

There were maybe two hundred cristeros still on their feet at this end of the causeway. More than enough to tear this impertinent handful of riders limb from limb. But the cristeros had seen the sky open up and drop death upon them; and on the far bank the banners painted with the image of the Virgin burned brightly.

They came unglued. Their songs turned to screams, and they flung themselves off the road, down the white crushed-shell bank and into the salty swamp water, thinking only of escape. Some turned in their panic and ran straight into the wall of flame that closed off the far end of the causeway. Those weren't men on animals they were fleeing, but demons.

For ten minutes the Herkie gunship and the two A-10s worked over the cristeros, in the water, in the mainland part of the complex, in the white hills beyond. Then they flew back over the island, the C-130 climbing as grandly as a dowager ascending a staircase, the Warthogs roaring so low the palm trees bowed to their passage.

"We hope you've enjoyed the morning's diversion, ladies and gentlemen," the voice said over the radio. *"And we hope that next time to travel, you'll remember to fly the Spooky skies. On behalf of Captains Delgado and Swarecky, the crew of Spectre One, and the entire Texas Air National Guard, I wish you a very good day.*

"Lightfoot out."

Casey frantically diddled the dials on Mobile One's electronics console. They hadn't monitored the airwaves very closely the last couple of days. Somehow it hadn't seemed worth the bother.

It seemed he was only down the hatch for thirty seconds before he popped up again, vibrating like a horny prairie dog. "Billy, listen to this! The Texas National Guard's revolted. They've declared a unilateral truce along the border with the Republic. They've got all the radio stations in Dallas—that's where I'm getting this; they're reading bulletins on all the channels.

"I—oh, wow! They say Governor Hedison refused a direct order from President MacGregor to cease hostilities with the Republic and join with it to repel the cristero invasion. That's when the Guard turned their guns around.

"Now they've got Randy Jim surrounded in the Sauron Building, and they're shooting it out with the Texas Rangers!"

Four hours later a Cadillac convertible with the top down

rolled out onto the far end of the causeway, gleaming white in the afternoon sun, the kind that was long and low and with fins. President Lamar Louis Napoleon LaRousse rode in the back, wearing fringed buckskins as white as the car, his long, snowy hair trailing behind like a pennon.

Behind crawled an olive-drab serpent of military vehicles. The Stars and Stripes and the Lone Star flag both fluttered above the column.

The defenders of the Bernardo Galves Experimental Saltwater Reclamation Facility had been relieved.

EPILOGUE ──────────

SPECIAL EXECUTIVE ORDER 000023 1035 AM
EFFECTIVE IMMEDIATELY

DUE TO PRESS OF DUTIES OF CHIEF OF WHITE HOUSE STAFF
DOCTOR MARGUERITE CONNOLY IS FORTHWITH RELIEVED
OF RESPONSIBILITY OVER PROJECT BLUEPRINT AND THE
GUARDIANS.
DOCTOR JACOB MORGENSTERN IS HEREBY APPOINTED TO
OVERSIGHT PROJECT BLUEPRINT AND THE GUARDIANS.

JEFFREY MACGREGOR
PRESIDENT OF THE UNITED STATES